"I know it's asking a lot, but..."

Ben regarded her with compassion, this time working hard to hide his emotions. Finally, he caught her small hand in his and brought it to his lips. "Look, you're exhausted. Why don't you go to bed? If you want me to stay, I can drag one of the exam cots onto the porch and sleep there." He gave her a lopsided grin. "But if you wake up before me in the morning, just don't mistake me for a patient...."

She managed a little smile. "Thank you, Ben. That would be perfect." They stood in silence for a few seconds. It took all of the self-control Ben had left to refrain from taking her in his arms again. Finally, he turned to leave. At the door he paused and looked back at her. Her face was red, her eyes were swollen and her hair was mussed. She had never looked more beautiful to him.

He smiled and whispered, "Good night."

Dear Reader,

In 1998, I was part of a team of nursing educators asked to travel to Kenya for two weeks to provide continuing education programs for missionary nurses. Most of these nurses were American or Canadian, and many had worked in Africa for years.

The missionary nurses were amazing and inspirational. During our time together, I learned about the problems they encountered in their practices, as well as the less-than-ideal circumstances in which they often found themselves. I witnessed firsthand the grateful responses of the local people to their tireless work and loving care as they did whatever they could to manage the challenging situations, cultural differences and pervasive health problems.

Out of the Shadows grew from stories shared by the nurses, as well as my observations of the country and the people. Several of the characters are based on people I met while there. For example, the leader and unofficial head of the group of nurses was a longtime missionary from Alabama; she became the inspiration for "Mama Joe." The Merdians–the Bible translators who play a significant role in the book–were based on a family who lived and worked in Kenya for more than twenty years. I hope I did them justice, as they deserve respect and admiration.

Enjoy the book!

Melanie Mitchell

HARLEQUIN HEARTWARMING

Melanie Mitchell

Out of the Shadows

ISBN-13: 978-0-373-36654-5

OUT OF THE SHADOWS

This is the revised text of a work first published as
PILGRIM SHADOWS by CreateSpace in 2012

This edition published by arrangement with Harlequin Books S.A.

For questions and comments about the quality of this book, please contact us at CustomerService@Harlequin.com.

Printed in U.S.A.

MELANIE MITCHELL

is a native of Texas. With her husband, Scott, Melanie has lived in Belgium, South Korea and a number of cities in the United States. She has traveled throughout the U.S., Canada, Europe, Asia, Africa and the Middle East. Melanie draws on her travels and work abroad to bring a variety of settings, experiences and an understanding of different cultures into her work.

Melanie has been a registered nurse for many years and currently teaches nursing in the Houston area. While she has written extensively–nursing textbooks and articles–she recently turned to her love of romantic suspense with *Out of the Shadows,* her debut novel.

To Scott, my support and inspiration
(also a darned good pilot).

Eldorado

Gaily bedight,
A gallant knight,
In sunshine and in shadow,
Had journeyed long,
Singing a song,
In search of Eldorado.

But he grew old,
This knight so bold,
And o'er his heart a shadow
Fell as he found
No spot of ground
That looked like Eldorado.

And, as his strength
Failed him at length,
He met a pilgrim shadow;
"Shadow," said he,
"Where can it be,
This land of Eldorado?"

"Over the Mountains
Of the Moon,
Down the Valley of the Shadow,
Ride, boldly ride,"
The shade replied,
"If you seek for Eldorado!"

–Edgar Allan Poe

PROLOGUE

Dallas, Texas

BRIAN CARPENTER GAZED at his wife's reflection in the mirror as he fumbled with the knot on his tie. She was sitting cross-legged on the bed, looking frustrated, restless and lovely.

"What would you like me to bring home for supper?"

"I don't know. I'm tired of takeout, and I'm starting to resemble a whale." Leslie frowned and shifted restlessly. "If I don't get out of this bed soon, I'll go crazy."

Brian decided the tie was neat enough and fastened the buttons on his collar. "Well, the bed rest won't last more than a week or two. Isn't that what your OB said?"

She wrinkled her nose and sighed. "That doesn't help me feel any better."

He sat beside her and gently brushed his fingers across her cheek. Despite her pregnancy, or perhaps because of it, she was beautiful.

Her complexion was a little lighter than normal, enhancing her remarkable deep blue eyes. Her glossy brown hair seemed even curlier, and her skin practically glowed. He sympathized with her frustration, though, knowing that being confined the past ten days had been hard for her—she was active by nature and loathed relinquishing the care of their two-year-old daughter to anyone else.

"Any more bleeding?"

"Not this morning." She brought her hand to her belly as if she could feel the baby growing. "Maybe everything is all right now. Maybe I can…"

"Not so fast." Brian placed his hand over hers. "The doctor said you could slowly resume normal activities—not start running a marathon—after the bleeding has stopped for at least twenty-four hours."

She slumped back on the pillows and frowned again. "I know."

"Honey," he said, forcibly upbeat, "you're only ten weeks along. Give the baby a chance to get stronger. Then there will be less chance of a miscarriage."

"Thank you, *Dr.* Carpenter." Although her tone was mildly sarcastic, she smiled at him.

"You're right, of course. It's worth it." Leslie adjusted the lightweight quilt to cover her legs. "I just hate being useless."

Sensing that the worst of the current mini-crisis had passed, Brian changed the subject. "You're sure your mom can pick Emma up from day care?"

"Yes, positive. The only reason you have to take her this morning is because Mom has a dental appointment."

"Good. I won't worry about leaving early to come home." He squeezed her hand. "Can I get you something to eat?"

Leslie shook her head. "No. Thanks." Her smile turned to a grimace. "Right now the thought of food makes me gag."

Brian stood. "Okay, I can't make you." He snagged his car keys from the dresser and shoved them in his pocket. Glancing at her from the foot of the bed, he said, "Now, about supper…"

"I'll talk to Mom. She may have planned to fix something." Leslie flashed a wry smile. "She'll disown us if we give Emma any more junk food. I'll call you this afternoon and let you know. Okay?"

Brian nodded and walked back to her. He

leaned forward to kiss her lightly on the lips. "We'd better be off. My first patient is scheduled for eight-thirty, and I need to run by the hospital to make rounds before that. Emma," he called at the door. "Come kiss Mommy goodbye."

In seconds, the towheaded little girl came bouncing into the room, dressed in denim overalls and a red T-shirt. Although Leslie had combed her hair earlier that morning, it was already falling into disarray. She repositioned Emma's barrette before kissing her head.

"Be good at school, and remember that Nina will pick you up about lunchtime." The toddler nodded and giggled.

"All right, baby," Brian interrupted. "Let's go. Hop in your car seat, and I'll buckle you in." Leslie gave Emma another peck on the cheek, and the toddler ran out of the room, heading for the kitchen door leading to the garage. Brian leaned over and kissed his wife again. "Do you need anything before I leave?"

Leslie pointed to her laptop and the pile of books beside the bed. "No, thanks. I've got plenty to do. I need to grade some papers and read a little. I'll be able to stay sane for a while."

He grinned. "I love you. Call me later."

"I love you, too." She blew him a kiss.

BY TEN O'CLOCK Leslie was bored. Since she was allowed to go to the bathroom and take occasional trips to the kitchen, she fetched a glass of lemonade and was headed back upstairs when the doorbell rang.

She frowned. It was rare for anyone to come to the house during the day. In keeping with the directives of her obstetrician, she slowly walked to the front door. Peering through the peephole, she saw two uniformed police officers accompanied by a man in a dark suit.

Police? Her thoughts raced, and her heart rate rose. Her hand was trembling slightly when she opened the door.

The expressions on the faces of the three men accentuated her fear. One of the uniformed officers spoke. "Ma'am, I'm Sergeant Hunton, from the Dallas Police Department. Are you Mrs. Carpenter?" His voice was slightly tremulous.

Leslie felt the blood leave her face. She gave a tiny nod.

The man in the suit said, "Mrs. Carpenter, I'm Jerry Zeiger, one of the chaplains for the DPD. Can we come in?"

Leslie's legs were wobbling so badly she barely managed to step aside to let the men in.

The chaplain took her arm and led her into the living room. "Please sit down, ma'am."

She glanced toward the two uniformed officers, who remained standing just inside the door. Neither looked at her. Her hand was visibly shaking now as she reached out to move a cushion before sitting on the edge of the sofa.

THE CHAPLAIN SAT beside her and took her hand in his; hers was icy. He had to force himself to look at her directly. "I'm so sorry," he said in the quiet, calm tone common among clergymen. "We have some bad news.... There was an accident. A delivery truck ran a red light and collided..." He paused and watched the young woman with growing concern. At that moment, he actively hated his job. He sighed, then said, "Ma'am, your husband's car was hit and he was killed instantly."

Leslie shook her head from side to side. She swallowed twice before she managed to whisper, "Emma?"

The chaplain held on to her hand, trying to give even a small amount of support. He no longer looked at her directly; instead, he stared at their hands. "Mrs. Carpenter, I am so sorry, but the little girl was killed, too."

Even though he was expecting it, Zeiger was still affected by the wrenching sound of her sob. Pulling away from him, the young woman doubled over and buried her head in her hands. He wanted to comfort her, but he knew she would find little solace for a long, long time. And he understood too well that she'd never forget this moment. She would never totally recover.

THAT NIGHT, SHE lost the baby.

CHAPTER ONE

THE FIRST THING Leslie Carpenter noticed as she stepped off the British Airways jet in Nairobi was the smell. It was earthy, rich with the scents of soil, manure, tropical flowers and sweat. After being confined in the stuffy, crowded 747 for more than ten hours, she welcomed it.

Leslie shouldered her large canvas tote and joined the slow line of passengers. She was struck by the odd mix of people carrying loose clothing, bags, sacks, briefcases and children as they made their way down the corridor into the terminal. Most were African, with a significant number of white and Asian faces in the crowd. These, she surmised, were tourists or expatriates, although a smattering appeared to be businesspeople.

As she headed toward the immigration officials working at glass-enclosed desks, Leslie noticed soldiers scattered throughout the processing area. They were dressed in camouflage fatigues and carried wicked-looking machine guns. She could see at least three from her location in the passport control line, and their presence reminded her of the acts of terror that were relatively common in Eastern Africa. She took a deep breath and told herself the situation had calmed in recent months.

After getting her passport stamped, she followed the crowd to the baggage-claim area. The conveyer belt was already laden with suitcases, boxes, foam containers wrapped with duct tape, duffels and even heavy black garbage bags. Various emotions tugged at her as she watched the carousel, feelings she hadn't experienced in many months. She recognized excitement and anticipation along with nervousness and more than a twinge of fear. Feeling very alone, she wondered for the twentieth time—*What am I doing?*

The incongruity of standing in the capital of a developing country hit her, and not for the first time. For the past year and a half she had depended on her family and friends in Dallas. Their love and patience, along with her compassionate colleagues at the nursing school, had helped her through the tragedy that had shattered her life. The very idea that she could leave them and fly halfway across the world struck her as preposterous—even now that she had done it.

It had taken months to recover from the emotional assault that followed the accident. Living with her parents had helped.

More than a year had passed when a colleague mentioned the need for a volunteer nurse-practitioner to run a rural clinic in Africa for six months, allowing a long-term missionary to return home for a much needed sabbatical.

Leslie had contacted the East Africa Mission office in Atlanta, and less than five weeks later, she tearfully kissed her parents, sisters and closest friends goodbye at Dallas's DFW airport, promising to email as often as possible.

Now, following two ten-hour flights, she was in Nairobi.

She located her bags and stood in the slow line for Customs. After presenting the required forms, she took a deep breath, straightened her shoulders and moved toward the exit.

Anna MacDonald, also known as Mama Joe—the nurse who would be heading home for sabbatical—was supposed to meet her at the airport and accompany her back to the village clinic. Leslie had seen pictures of the veteran nurse and, scanning the faces, she quickly spied the petite woman in the crowd. She was easy to spot, with her white face, silver-gray bun and black-framed glasses, standing beside a smallish, middle-aged white man. Leslie waved to the pair and was relieved when they waved back. Mama Joe and her companion hurried forward and, without hesitation, she scooped Leslie into a warm hug.

"Hello, dear! You must be Leslie. I'm Mama Joe. We are so happy that you've come!" Her voice was a little deep and a bit raspy, with the hint of a Southern accent. "You're a wonderful answer to my prayer." She pulled back and smiled, taking Leslie's hand. Behind the heavy glasses, her eyes were a soft brown.

"I'm very happy to meet you, too, Mama Joe." Leslie hoped the warmth in her voice matched that of the older woman. "I can't believe I'm actually here, and I can't wait to get started at the clinic."

Mama Joe's smile widened, and lines creased her tanned face. "We'll be heading out for Namanga—our village—later this afternoon. I'll be able to show you everything before I leave in a couple of weeks." She indicated the man beside her. "Leslie, this is Dennis Williams. Dennis is the regional director of the East Africa Mission."

Leslie shook his hand. "Yes, Mr. Williams, we spoke on the telephone a few weeks ago. It's good to meet you."

"Call me Dennis, please. Thank you again for helping out at the last minute like this. We feel very lucky to have you take over the clinic for the next six months." He took her suitcases and headed toward the exit. "If you aren't too tired, we could show you a little of the city, have lunch with my wife—then our driver can bring you back to catch your flight to Namanga."

"The village is a couple of hours south of here by plane," Mama Joe explained. "It takes six hours to drive because the roads are riddled with potholes, so we fly when we can." She took a quick breath and continued, "I came up this morning with Ben Murphy. He's one of the pilots who help us from time to time. We're supposed to meet him here at three."

Leslie glanced at her watch. It was a little after ten. It had been more than twenty-four hours since she left Dallas for London. After a three-hour layover at Heathrow, she'd been able to doze with her head propped against the small window of her red-eye flight. Yet, despite the grueling trip and minimal sleep, she was wide-awake. "That sounds terrific!" She smiled. "I'd love to see Nairobi."

Leslie accompanied Mama Joe and Dennis toward the busy terminal's exit. She'd passed her first hurdle and she felt welcomed by her new colleagues. *Maybe,* she thought, *I've made the right decision after all....*

THE TRIP FROM the airport was like nothing Leslie had ever experienced. In the parking area, she was introduced to a young Kenyan named Marcus who chauffeured the mission's van. "I rarely drive," Dennis explained. "I've lived in Nairobi for more than five years, but I still can't get used to driving on the left."

Mama Joe acted as tour guide, pointing out the various sights. As they neared the city, the trees and lush grassland quickly gave way to signs of human habitation. People walked and jogged on a roadside path, their numbers growing as the van progressed. Mama Joe explained, "Most people don't have cars. They grow up running everywhere. That's why so many of the great runners are from Kenya."

Leslie watched in amazement as the van passed men in dress pants and sometimes even suits jogging toward town, often carrying briefcases or backpacks. The women wore dresses or skirts and blouses of batik cottons in a rainbow of colors. A lot of them carried bundles, often on their heads, and babies in cloth slings on their backs. Many pedestrians lugged wooden carts filled with bananas, mangoes and other fruits, building materials, chickens, bolts of cloth, and what appeared to be car parts. She stared when she saw two men leading a Cape buffalo.

Leslie tried to absorb the sights of the engulfing commotion when they reached the city. The streets were crowded with trucks, cars and buses, many of which appeared decrepit, with rusting fenders and duct-taped bumpers. With surprising frequency, their relatively new and well-maintained van was passed by large passenger vans overflowing with people. Following her stare, Mama Joe laughed. "Those are *matutus,* Kenya's primary means of public transportation. The vans are supposed to hold about fifteen people, but as you can see, they typically carry at least twice that number."

Leslie shook her head slightly in sympathy as she continued to look through the window. Drivers here were aggressive—really aggressive. She watched in astonishment as a rust-covered car swerved around them and nearly cut them off, narrowly avoiding a head-on collision with a car in the right-hand lane. Leslie clutched the seat and glanced at Mama Joe and Dennis. They didn't seem the least bit fazed by the darting traffic, sudden stops and starts and blaring horns. With slightly nervous resignation, she determined to avoid watching the traffic ahead and concentrated on the sights from her window.

The city's skyline loomed. Modern skyscrapers were interspersed with two- and three-story buildings that appeared to date back to British colonial rule. Occasionally ramshackle structures were adjacent to office buildings, and a variety of crowded shops and stores could be seen only a few feet off the busy street.

"I'm surprised there are so many tall buildings," Leslie said as they approached the city center. "Nairobi reminds me a little of Chicago or even New York."

Dennis nodded. "Nairobi is very cosmopolitan. Of course, the majority of people are African. But because of British colonization, there's a large contingent of Europeans here. And there are a lot of immigrants from South Asia, particularly India and Pakistan."

"This is *very* different from where we live," Mama Joe added. "In our area, there aren't many who aren't African. Mostly farmers. We also take care of quite a few Masai—the nomads who tend cattle."

Leslie wondered anew about the conditions she'd be exposed to in the rural area. She had vaguely pictured mud huts with thatched roofs and cooking over open fires.

They drove out of the primary business district and entered a residential neighborhood. As they progressed down a tree-lined street, the houses grew rapidly in size until they became mansions on huge lots surrounded by high walls. "We are very fortunate," Dennis said. "The building that houses the East Africa Mission was donated about fifty years ago by a wealthy family who returned to England."

Marcus turned the van through a gate and parked in front of a large Victorian. Inside the old brick walls, Leslie saw a lush lawn, edged by deep beds with layers of flowers. As they walked to the front door, Leslie recognized the sweet smell of honeysuckle and lilac. Dennis held the door open for the two women. "The main offices of EAM are on the first floor," he explained. "My family and I live on the second."

Two African women were seated at desks in the first room of the mansion. The young women smiled shyly at Leslie as they were introduced, revealing beautiful white teeth which contrasted strikingly with their very dark faces. Mama Joe stopped to chat as Dennis led Leslie through the lower floor.

A slightly plump woman with gray-tinged brown hair met them at the top of the stairs. Before Dennis could make the introductions, she took Leslie's hand. "Hello, I'm Connie. I'm so glad you had time to come by." She pulled Leslie into the living room. "Please sit down. I know you're exhausted—that trip is a killer!" Leslie sat back in a cushioned chair with the lemonade Connie had handed her and surveyed the room with its enviable collection of Victorian antiques. It gave her the impression that she was in a parlor in southern England rather than in a missionary's home in central Kenya.

The disconnect was vaguely perplexing.

At Connie's suggestion, Leslie spent a few minutes in the modern bathroom freshening up before lunch. She changed into the spare blouse from her carry-on bag. It was slightly wrinkled but clean. The high humidity had caused her wavy, dark brown hair to curl, so she brushed it into a heavy ponytail and confined it with a large barrette. There were faint dark rings under her large blue eyes. She sighed. Only a good night's sleep would remedy that.

Lunch was anything but exotic: fried chicken, mashed potatoes and salad. The only nod to their being in equatorial Africa was the selection of fruits for dessert—mangoes, pineapples and papayas.

Between bites of flavorful mango, Leslie asked, "So, why are you called Mama Joe?"

"I haven't thought about that in quite a while." Easy humor shone in the crinkled corners of the other woman's brown eyes. "Well, when we first came to Namanga, our kids were very small. As a sign of respect, I was not called by my given name, but by the designation 'Mama.' 'Joe' is my oldest son, so I was 'Mama' of 'Joe,' which became 'Mama Joe.' I've been known by that name for about forty years." She chuckled. "I doubt many people even know my name is Anna!"

At Leslie's prompting, Mama Joe recounted how she and her husband had traveled to Kenya in the late 1960s as newlyweds. "We raised four children here," she said. "In 1994, we retired and moved back to Alabama, but when my Daniel died just a few years later, I decided to come back where I could be useful."

Leslie sat quietly, thinking about how closely Mama Joe's reasons for coming to Kenya mirrored her own.

She wanted to help the people here, too.

She wanted to find a place where she could be useful again.

She only hoped she could find that in Africa.

CHAPTER TWO

THE COMBINATION OF jet lag, exhaustion and lunch slammed Leslie during the drive back to the airport. The van was nearing the airport when she awoke, surprised she'd slept through the crazy Nairobi traffic.

Marcus offered to wait at the van with Leslie's bags while the women located the pilot who would take them on the final leg of the journey. "Ben told me to meet him at the Rift Valley Bar around three o'clock." Mama Joe gestured toward the rear of the terminal. "It's over there. Back near the gates."

They were making their way through the crowd when they heard a voice call loudly, "Mama Joe! Mama Joe!" A woman dressed in a bright yellow-and-orange cotton skirt and blouse ran toward them and grabbed Mama Joe's hand.

"Mary!" Mama Joe exclaimed. The two embraced, and they conversed for a moment in Swahili before Mama Joe introduced Leslie.

"This is Mary Keino, a dear friend of mine. Mary worked with me many, many years ago, even before we settled in Namanga." She leaned toward the Kenyan woman, and they talked for a moment more. Mama Joe laughed at something Mary said, then turned to Leslie. "I would really like to visit for a moment. She's telling me about her grandchildren." She motioned in the direction of the bar. "Would you mind going to find Ben and letting him know we're ready?"

Leslie smiled. "No problem. I'll be right back." She swiftly covered the remaining distance and was at the door of the Rift Valley Bar before it occurred to her that she'd failed to get Ben's description. She considered retracing her steps to ask Mama Joe, but glancing across the long terminal, she rejected the idea. Surely she'd be able to recognize their pilot.

The dim lighting forced Leslie to pause a moment just inside the bar to let her eyes adjust.

The patrons—mostly men—were seated at tables haphazardly scattered across the limited floor space. At the table nearest the door sat three well-dressed Indian or Pakistani businessmen. Two couples, probably tourists from Japan, were seated at another table. At one end of the long bar to the left, a white man slouched against the counter, talking with two women perched on stools. An older American-looking couple sat at the other end of the bar.

Leslie frowned. She had expected to find a lone man; so as far as she could tell, Ben wasn't here.

As she snaked her way among the crowded tables toward the guy tending bar, she caught bits of conversation. The businessmen seemed to be having an intense discussion. Their conversation grew more heated, and as she passed she saw one man trying to convince the angry guy to keep his voice down. The third man stared at her, his expression livid and his gaze eerily disconcerting. Leslie tried to seem uninterested as she continued forward.

The tourists, by contrast, were quite sedate. They talked in low tones and did not acknowledge Leslie or the group arguing at the next table.

The trio at the bar were speaking—or flirting, rather—in French. The man glanced her way as she approached, and his eyes lingered on her with undisguised interest. When he saw he had her attention, he lifted his glass toward her and gave her a nod—as if suggesting that she join the party.

Annoyed, Leslie returned his leer with a glare, much to the satisfaction of the two women, who seemed to realize they were losing his interest. She pointedly dismissed him and turned toward the bartender, who was taking an order from the older couple.

While she waited, Leslie overheard the pretty brunette say something in rapid French. Her tone was unmistakably petulant. Out of the corner of her eye, Leslie saw the guy shrug. He leaned over and pushed aside a strand of hair to whisper something to the second woman, an attractive blonde. She nodded coquettishly and then glanced at Leslie before all three laughed, drawing the attention of the tourists and the businessmen.

Leslie's cheeks reddened. She tried to appear unaffected as she glanced down at her clothes. She knew she looked wrinkled and shabby. Absently, she reached up to smooth back a strand of hair that had escaped the barrette.

Flustered, she noticed that the man seemed unusually tall and muscular for a Frenchman. Her stereotype was reinforced, however, by his gold-streaked brown hair, which looked like it would reach his wide shoulders if it hadn't been pulled back into a ponytail. She huffed silently; she had never liked long hair on men.

The women burst into more laughter as he finished a story. Grinning, he reached over and flicked the dangling earring of the blonde, then he took a drink from his glass and turned in Leslie's direction. His face was deeply tanned, and his leering grin revealed straight white teeth. He was casually dressed in khaki pants and boots, and the sleeves of his white shirt were rolled past his elbows. His eyes were an odd pale green, closely resembling the color of a Coke bottle. Feeling as if she'd been caught staring, she quickly looked away.

Trying to ignore the group at the bar and the stares of the other patrons, she glanced toward the corner of the room. She was surprised to see a man sitting alone at the table farthest from the door, drinking coffee and reading a book—somehow she had missed him. He wore a navy suit with the gold braid and buttons of a pilot.

Leslie made her way to his table, relieved to escape the obnoxious trio and the attention of the businessman with the creepy stare.

"Excuse me."

The pilot appeared to be in his forties, with

neat, dark hair that was graying at the temples. He glanced up from his book and removed his glasses. “Yes?”

Leslie held out her hand. “I’m Leslie Carpenter. Mama Joe said I should find you and let you know that we’re ready to go.”

The man frowned. “I’m sorry. You must be mistaken. I do not know anyone named Mama Joe.” Although his English was flawless, his accent was European, most likely German.

Leslie glanced at the insignia on the breast of his coat and saw a Lufthansa name pin. Her hand fell to her side and she blushed. “E-excuse me. I—I’m sorry. I thought you were someone else!” She started to back away.

He gave her a nod. “It is no problem.” Replacing his glasses, he returned to his book.

BEN MURPHY HAD a long-standing practice of observing his surroundings, so he noticed Leslie the moment she entered the bar. Although his attention appeared to be focused on his companions, he was keenly aware of her as she made her way through the room. His initial glance revealed a young woman wearing the rumpled clothes of a traveler. When she approached him, he registered a woman in her late twenties, of average height, with a slender, almost thin, build.

He turned slightly to get a better look and did a double take when he saw her eyes. Despite the dim light, he could tell they were a dark, rich blue, highlighted by heavy lashes and expressive eyebrows. She looked directly at him for only an instant, but he was caught off guard by his reaction. He had an odd feeling of vertigo as his heart rate soared and his vision seemed to narrow in on her face.

Unwilling to dwell on the young woman with the extraordinary eyes, Ben dismissed her. Collecting his thoughts, he returned his attention to his companions while keeping an eye out for Mama Joe and the new nurse. He'd been told few details about the substitute, and idly pictured a woman of about fifty, with graying hair, sturdy legs and a critical disposition.

Maintaining his part of the conversation, Ben discreetly watched as the young woman wandered back toward the bar after a short discussion with the commercial pilot seated in the corner. She pointedly ignored Ben, which he found both irritating and amusing. At a tap on his wrist, he leaned toward his new friends, only to be taken aback by the woman with the blue eyes watching him. Rarely did anything or anyone startle him, but *she* did. That fact bothered him, mostly because he didn't understand it. His life depended on his ability to focus. So, when he found himself unbalanced by the eyes of a strange woman, it was unnerving. He couldn't peg whether unnerving was good or bad, but he didn't like it.

Ben kept his expression impassive. She couldn't know that his heart rate had climbed and his head was swimming a little. With considerable effort, he shook off the moment in time to glimpse Mama Joe entering the bar.

"Excuse me, please, Monique. Helene," he interrupted in flawless French. "Ladies, there is the dear friend I am waiting for. *Au revoir.*" He paid the tab and gave an apologetic shrug to the two women before walking away.

As Ben approached the older woman standing at the door, he realized Monique's derogatory comment about rich old cougars was for his benefit. He ignored the insult and smiled at the gray-haired nurse with sincere affection.

He was halfway to the door when he sensed someone following him.

LESLIE'S PATH TO Mama Joe was suddenly blocked as the Frenchman cut in front of her. Abruptly, he turned toward her. His movement was so quick and unexpected that she couldn't stop. Her momentum carried her forward, and she inadvertently rammed into his chest.

He was as hard and immovable as a brick wall, and Leslie would have fallen backward if he hadn't caught her. She was suddenly aware of the large hand that dug painfully into her upper arm. After quickly regaining her balance she discovered that everyone in the room was staring at them.

Mortified, Leslie shook off his hand and took a small step back. "What do you think you're doing?"

"Keeping you from falling on your butt, lady.... And you're welcome." His words were low, almost a growl.

Unceremoniously, Ben turned his back on her and strode the final steps to Mama Joe. He smiled and bent to kiss her on the cheek. "Did your nurse get here okay?"

Mama Joe peered around Ben to Leslie, who cautiously walked toward them. "Didn't you meet her? It looked like...um..."

Ben rolled his eyes and sighed audibly. Mama

Joe recognized the awkwardness of the moment between the two of them. "Ben, Leslie, uh... well...perhaps we should be going. Marcus is waiting at the van."

Leslie forced herself to hold out her hand in an attempt at dignity. "I'm Leslie Carpenter. Mama Joe sent me to find you. I guess I didn't recognize you." She managed a slight upward movement of her lips, which she hoped resembled a smile.

Ben paused a second before he shook her hand. With a tone that reeked of insincerity, he replied, "Charmed." He quickly turned back to Mama Joe. "I'll find Marcus and get the bags. Meet me by the general aviation gate in a couple of minutes." Without waiting for a reply, he headed toward the terminal entrance.

Leslie felt a need to explain as she walked with Mama Joe toward the portion of the airport that managed noncommercial aircraft. "I didn't realize who Ben was because he was with two women. And they were speaking French." She shrugged. "I assumed they were tourists."

Mama Joe nodded and patted her on the arm. "Oh, I see. That makes sense because Ben was born and raised here. In Kenya—like Europe—most everyone knows more than one language.

In the city, people typically speak Swahili, English and their own native dialect. Many people also speak French, because most of central Africa was colonized by France and Belgium." She paused for a moment before adding, "On the coast, around Mombasa, many people are of Indian or Pakistani heritage, so they also speak Hindi, Urdu or Arabic."

As they reached the general aviation gate, Mama Joe continued, "Ben learned French at the boarding school he attended with my youngest son, Nathan. But Ben is something of a linguist. In addition to French and Swahili, he speaks at least three tribal dialects. That can be very helpful living here. I'm afraid I'm not much for languages—I've had to get by with just Swahili."

Leslie listened absently as Mama Joe's conversation shifted to her children. "Joe also went to the boarding school. He's a pastor now, and he and his wife, Sandra, have three children. They live in Mobile, and I can't wait to see them."

The far end of the terminal was much less crowded, and the women sat together facing the entrance to wait for Ben. Leslie's weariness had returned, and she merely nodded at appropriate times as Mama Joe continued the one-sided conversation.

"Nathan and Ben were good friends. They finished high school here and went to the States for college, like most MKs—that's what we call missionary kids. Ben was a little different, though, because he went to live with his grandparents in Kansas when he was about fifteen. He always had this hankering to fly airplanes and play football. He eventually got an appointment to the Air Force Academy and became a quarterback. All-Conference or something like that."

Leslie had to blink quickly and bite her cheek as she grew drowsier. Mama Joe seemed oblivious to her predicament and continued to recall Ben's athletic exploits.

After a few minutes, Leslie glimpsed Ben through droopy eyelids. Seeing him helped restore some measure of alertness, and she focused on the tall man walking toward them, carrying her two large suitcases. Ordinarily, she would have felt guilty, knowing how heavy her bags were—although he seemed to be managing easily. She'd had enough of Ben Murphy. So what if he *could* speak six languages and throw a football? She knew what he was—a player.

Her thoughts suddenly took a different turn. What had he been drinking at the bar? Could he be *drunk?* A twinge of alarm compounded her annoyance, and she debated whether to say something to Mama Joe.

Ben barely glanced at Leslie as he led the way toward the section of the airport where privately owned aircrafts were secured. He paused by the door and handed a uniformed official a form. A conversation in Swahili followed before the clerk stamped their paperwork and gestured for them to proceed.

They followed Ben into the bright sunlight, passing a number of planes of varying models, sizes and vintages before Ben stopped near a single-engine, high-winged Cessna. The plane was pale beige with a dark green stripe, and it appeared to be well-maintained. He unlocked the plane and heaved Leslie's bags into the cargo hold. She was thankful she hadn't packed anything breakable, and as she witnessed his disregard of her belongings, her irritation reached a new high.

In silence, Ben opened the passenger door and adjusted the seat forward. He stepped back and motioned for Leslie to climb into the rear seat. "Be sure to watch your step." His tone was short, and his gesture hinted at annoyance.

Leslie moved forward to comply, but Mama Joe took her arm. "No. No. Here, let me ride in the back. The view is much better from the front!"

Leslie looked at the narrow opening leading to the rear seat and recognized that it would be difficult to maneuver into. She started to protest, but Mama Joe waved her away. "I may be old, but I'm agile!" Ben assisted the elderly nurse as she stepped up and crawled deftly into the rear of the plane. He readjusted the front passenger seat and then stood back to allow Leslie room to board.

She shifted her large canvas bag to her left shoulder and placed her right foot on the small metal step welded to the landing-gear strut as Mama Joe had done. She was determined to appear as coordinated and capable as the woman who was almost forty years her senior, and she grasped the door to pull herself up into the plane. But her bag slipped off her shoulder and the strap snagged on a small hook that held the seat belt. She let go of the door's frame to free the strap, but became unbalanced. Groping frantically for something to hold on to, she found nothing but air.

A well-placed hand to her bottom caught Leslie. Ben held her weight easily with one hand as he loosened the strap of her bag with the other. Then he pushed her into the seat. He watched as she cleared the door before closing it firmly. Without comment, he turned and walked toward the back of the plane.

Leslie felt her face turn scarlet. She couldn't believe that for the second time in less than an hour, Ben's quick response had kept her from falling flat on her rear. She clenched her teeth as she settled into her seat. In humiliation she realized that she could still feel the pressure of his hand.

She took deep, calming breaths and studied her surroundings. The plane was compact. The front bucket seats were separated by only a few inches, and a dizzying array of dials, gauges, knobs, indicators, switches and buttons comprised the instrument panel.

"Have you ever flown in a small plane before?" Mama Joe asked, leaning forward.

Leslie turned awkwardly in the confined space to face the older woman and shook her head. “No, this is my first time.” She wondered again if she should mention Ben’s drinking.

Her nervousness must have been evident, because Mama Joe patted her arm. “There’s no need to worry. Ben’s an excellent pilot. He was in the air force, you know. Besides,” she added cheerfully, “it’s much safer than driving.”

Leslie wanted to answer that it wasn’t the flight she feared—it was the pilot’s level of sobriety. She managed to keep her concerns to herself and merely nodded in reply.

Leslie watched Ben walk around the plane, examining the fuselage as he commenced his preflight inspection. At least he didn’t *seem* drunk. “Do you need to fly often in your practice, Mama Joe?”

“Oh, every now and then. If a call is nearby and the distance can be traveled in a few hours, I’ll have Titus take me—he’s my driver. But for an emergency, or if it’ll be more than three hours by car, I’ll fly if I can.” She took a breath. “It seems like it goes in clusters. Sometimes I’ll stay near Namanga for weeks without being called away, and at other times I’ll fly to distant villages or to Nairobi several times in one week. There’s really no way to predict it.”

"Does Ben always take you when you fly?" Leslie tried to keep her tone casual.

"About half the time. He's freelance, and for the most part he ferries supplies and equipment all over East Africa. Sometimes he flies tourists from one game park to another." She leaned forward and added conspiratorially, "I don't think he likes flying tourists, but it pays well."

"So, how much does he charge you?" Against her will, Leslie found herself watching him inspect the propeller. His shirt stretched across his wide chest as he reached up to run his hands along the length of the blade.

Mama Joe smiled. "Oh, he doesn't charge us. If we need him, and if he's around, he'll take us wherever we want to go for free." She looked at Leslie and added, "But if he's off somewhere, we call one of the guys from MASS—that's Mission Aviation Support Services."

"Are they nearby?"

"Andy Singleton works out of Mutomo, about seventy miles northwest of us. Ed Jones is in Tsavo, about fifty miles southeast. The problem is it takes at least an hour for them to get to Namanga. Ben is local. Also, if we use Andy or Ed, they won't be available for others. Besides, we have to pay a small fee for their services—just enough to cover fuel and maintenance, but it adds up." She frowned slightly. "Now that I think about it, I'm not really sure how Ben manages to work for free."

The conversation halted as the object of their discussion opened the pilot's door and climbed in. All three were silent as Ben finished his preparations; Leslie watched as he flipped several switches and turned some knobs. He pulled a pair of headphones from under his seat and put them on. The propeller began to revolve, and within seconds the cabin was filled with a loud roar. Ben pushed a button on the flight control, and Leslie heard him speak to someone in the tower through the microphone attached to the headphones.

"Roger that, Ground," he said. "Clear for taxiway Delta. Stop short of runway one-eight."

Ben taxied the plane toward the end of the runway, and they waited in silence as another plane took off. It was a little unnerving to be sitting in such a small aircraft among the much-larger cargo and passenger jets. Over her shoulder, she saw that Mama Joe was reading a book and didn't seem the least bit nervous. She shifted and glanced at Ben. He was wearing dark glasses and appeared to be idly watching the other planes on the runway.

Suddenly he spoke, startling her. "Roger, Tower. Centurion, November-Four-Two-Alpha-Romeo cleared for takeoff." With that, he pushed in the throttle and released the brakes. Within seconds, they were in the air. Even before they had reached the end of the enormous runway below, he turned the control and the plane banked gently to the right. It straightened briefly and then turned toward the left, all the while in a gradual climb.

The view from Leslie's window was spectacular. She was awed by the striking beauty of the land and the brilliant colors. The greens of the grass and foliage seemed deeper, and the cloudless sky more brilliantly blue, than any she had ever seen.

They had been airborne about fifteen minutes when Ben lightly touched her arm.

"Look just below us," Ben said loudly. He banked the plane sharply to the left and pointed down. Her eyes followed where he indicated, and she saw a large herd of zebras. As she watched the animals move gracefully through the high grass, Leslie forgot her concerns.

Ben circled and descended to bring the herd

into view again. As he maneuvered the plane, Leslie had to shift her gaze from looking out of the left window back to the right, and, as she did, her eyes met his. She smiled with sincere appreciation and said "Thank you," pitching her voice so that he would hear.

Something in Leslie's expression made Ben's heart accelerate. She'd looked at him with childlike amazement, and her lovely eyes, which had held an unmistakably desolate look and then irritation, were shining. The discomfort he'd felt in the bar returned. Unconsciously, he rubbed his hand against his leg. He forced his attention back to the instrument panel, adjusting the directional gyros to guide the small aircraft home. But after engaging the autopilot, he found his mind drifting, and he wished she'd look at him with the same excitement she had just shown a herd of zebras.

Irritably, he shook the thought away. It was her eyes—her spooky eyes. He didn't like what they did to him. He frowned as he stared at the controls. No, he didn't like it at all.

Intent on the views from her window, Leslie did not see the flicker of response that crossed Ben's face, or the furtive glances that followed. But Mama Joe did.

Concerned, she watched the man she had known since childhood. She'd been worried for him since his return to Kenya almost three years before. It had been disheartening to see how much he'd changed from the friendly, eager-to-please and focused youth she had known, and she was keenly aware of the rumors that followed him.

She was well acquainted with his solitary lifestyle, had heard reports of heavy drinking and knew he was often seen with the daughters of wealthy tourists. His questionable employment led to periodic absences from Namanga, and the words *smuggling* and *guns* were frequently used in conversations about him.

His reaction to Leslie surprised her. He was unable to hide his interest, but she sensed a pronounced wariness in him, too. And she knew that the young woman was vulnerable. Indeed, she appeared emotionally fragile, and she certainly didn't seem prepared to handle a relationship with a man like Ben.

Mama Joe watched the pair and recognized curiosity mixed with animosity. Close proximity to each other for the next six months could be extremely painful, maybe even devastating, for both. She began to silently pray.

She was still praying when the Cessna landed an hour later.

CHAPTER THREE

NAMANGA'S AIRPORT CONSISTED of a single narrow grass landing strip. Leslie noticed a sheet-metal shed that held tanks for aviation fuel along with a small office and a dilapidated hangar for the Cessna. Two planes rested alongside the hangar, but as far as she could tell, they were long past airworthiness. The lone man on duty waved to Ben while approaching the plane as it taxied toward the hangar.

Mama Joe indicated the smallish, middle-aged man. "That's Charles Endebbi. He and his son manage the airstrip and do some mechanic work. Ben's plane is the only one based here, but quite a few tour operators use the field because it's close to several national parks."

As Ben cut the Cessna's engine, a Jeep approached, driven by a sturdy man of indeterminate age. "There's Titus," Mama Joe said as she waved to the newcomer. "He's been my driver for more than a decade."

A considerable amount of gray was scattered through his short black hair, but Titus's dark face was smooth and youthful. He helped both women from the plane. As they were introduced, he gave Leslie a nodding bow and welcoming smile.

Mama Joe turned to Ben, who had been giving instructions to Mr. Endebbi. "Thanks again for the ride, Ben. Are you sure we can't take you home?"

"No, thanks. I've radioed Simon. He'll be here in a few minutes."

Although they had barely spoken, Leslie was anxious to be free of the playboy pilot. However, she followed Mama Joe's example and held out her hand. "Thank you for picking me up."

Ben accepted her hand but dropped it quickly. "No problem." His eyes were focused on her left shoulder. After the terse response, he turned away to help Titus with the luggage.

They drove from the airport in the aging Jeep that Mama Joe laughingly assured Leslie was more reliable than it looked. "We've had this old Jeep longer than I want to admit. It hasn't let us down yet, and Titus keeps it running like a clock."

The terrain around them contrasted starkly

with Nairobi. The Jeep bumped and jolted on an unpaved road through a vast savanna. The land was dry and dusty and vegetation consisted primarily of tall brown grass and stunted thornbushes. She recognized flat-topped acacia trees and bottle-shaped baobab trees from the books she had read to prepare for her journey. Some of her earlier unease returned as she studied the surroundings, and she fleetingly wondered if it was too late to go back.

Mama Joe interrupted her brief moment of panic. “We’re only about twelve miles from the landing strip,” she said over the rumble of the Jeep. “We should be at the clinic in about twenty minutes. It’s located a few miles from town, which is a relatively short walk by Kenyan standards.”

They saw no other vehicles, though occasionally they passed locals walking or jogging along the road. The women were conservatively dressed in bright-colored *kangas,* and most had two or three children in tow. The men wore long, Bermuda-type shorts or khaki slacks and T-shirts. Most wore shoes or leather sandals, but a few were barefoot. Whenever they met someone, without exception, the local people smiled and waved to Mama Joe and Titus.

Dusk was fast approaching when they arrived at the clinic complex and Leslie got her first look at her home for the next six months. She was encouraged and relieved as she examined the fairly large compound in the waning light. There were two main buildings surrounded by an eight-foot cinder-block wall. "Titus and his wife, Naomi, live there," Mama Joe said as she pointed toward the smaller dwelling. "And the clinic and my apartment are in here."

The Jeep stopped before the larger building—a long, low, sturdy structure. A slender Kenyan woman with short graying hair and excellent posture had come out of the clinic and waited on the covered, screened porch.

"This is Naomi," Mama Joe said with sincere affection as she stepped up to the porch. "Naomi has been nursing with me for more than a decade. The clinic couldn't operate without her."

Naomi was obviously pleased but embarrassed by Mama Joe's praise as she shook Leslie's hand. She was wearing what Leslie later learned was a Kenyan nurse's uniform: a blue-striped dress with a white collar and apron. "I am very much looking forward to working with you," she said shyly. Her velvety brown eyes were friendly, and Leslie liked her immediately.

"In addition to Naomi," Mama Joe told her, "the clinic employs a bookkeeper and receptionist named Elizabeth, and a woman named Agnes who helps with cleaning, cooking and laundry. They've already gone for the day, but you'll meet them early tomorrow."

Mama Joe turned to open the freshly painted screen door and stood to one side. "Well, this is it." She flipped on a light and invited Leslie in. "It's nothing fancy, but it works."

The arrangement reminded Leslie of pictures she had seen of clinics from the 1950s. The large waiting area held a receptionist's desk, tall filing cabinets and rows of neatly arranged chairs; the open, airy room smelled of bleach and alcohol. The worn but spotlessly clean linoleum creaked a little as she wandered over to one of the large, curtainless windows.

"There are three examination rooms on this side of the building," Mama Joe explained as she led Leslie to the back of the main room. She opened a door to reveal a small room furnished with an examining table, and she pointed out a glass-and-metal cabinet against the far wall. "Each exam room has a locked cabinet, which holds our supplies and medications. In the hall is a large storage closet where we keep other equipment and items that we don't use as frequently."

Leslie skimmed the contents of the cabinet and found it to be well stocked. Bottles and jars of medications were clearly marked. Boxes of exam gloves, dressing materials, suture sets and similar supplies took up the middle shelves, while disinfectants and cleaning implements were neatly lined up on the bottom. "This looks great, Mama Joe."

Leslie followed the two women through a door at the rear of the clinic into the living quarters. A generous kitchen with a small eating area took up one side of the apartment; on the other side were a 1960s-era bathroom and two bedrooms. "Our electricity comes from propane tanks and generators that are located behind the clinic," Mama Joe explained as she showed Leslie around the homey, nicely provisioned kitchen.

Leslie nodded appreciatively. "I must admit I'm relieved to know that everything looks pretty normal." She grinned a little sheepishly. "I was afraid that things would be a lot more primitive—like cooking over campfires."

Mama Joe and Naomi laughed. "We have to be fairly modern," Mama Joe explained. "In addition to holding my milk and eggs, the refrigerator is needed for some of our medications and vaccines, and we need electricity to filter water and run the autoclave." Her smile faded. "AIDS is such a threat, we have to be able to sterilize equipment. Later on I'll introduce you to the generators and water filtration system."

Titus entered the kitchen carrying Leslie's bags and proceeded toward the two bedrooms, which were accessed through a short hall off the kitchen. "Titus and Naomi have been working for over a week to get your room ready." Mama Joe gestured for Leslie to follow him, and under her breath she whispered, "I hope you like blue!"

The warning was appropriate. Titus set her bags down in a room with cinder-block walls that had been painted a soft blue. Blue-and-white gingham curtains adorned the windows, and the single bed was covered with a lightweight blue cotton spread.

"How did you know that blue is my favorite color? This is wonderful!" Leslie exclaimed as she gave Titus and Naomi a smile of thanks and shook their hands in appreciation. She managed to suppress a grin as she looked around the baby-blue room, grateful they hadn't chosen pink.

As Leslie lifted one of her bags onto the bed and started to unpack, Mama Joe pointed to the mosquito netting hanging from a hook above the bed. "Other than vigilant attention to HIV precautions and the water filtration system, using that net is probably the most important thing to remember. Long-termers don't generally use drugs to prevent malaria because of the side effects. Instead, we rely on insect spray and nets. If, God forbid, we do get malaria, we just treat it."

Leslie nodded, studying the netting. "I'll be careful." She hung several shirts in the small closet. "Have you had malaria?"

"Yes, a couple of times. It's not fun, but with the right antibiotics, we can treat it quickly and effectively. But always sleep with the net.... Oh, and another thing. It'll help keep the spiders away." Mama Joe turned to walk toward the kitchen. "While you unpack, I'll come up with something for supper."

Leslie frowned as she watched the retreating nurse. Glancing warily around the room, she whispered, "Spiders?"

LESLIE'S FIRST DAY in the clinic was a trial by fire. Over a breakfast of scrambled eggs, toast and fruit, Mama Joe outlined the course of a normal day. "Titus opens the compound gates at seven. There are almost always people waiting. We have some scheduled appointments, but most patients are walk-ins." She took a bite of toast. "Once or twice a week we'll get calls on the telephone or radio to assist people from other villages within a sixty-mile radius. Those are usually emergencies, like accidents or difficult births."

"When do we stop?" Leslie pushed the eggs around her plate. Her appetite was negligible. She ran her hands across her khaki skirt. Although she had several years of working as a nurse-practitioner in clinics, she felt ill equipped for her new role.

"Normally, things start to slow down midafternoon. We try to be finished by five or six."

Before she began to see patients, Leslie met Elizabeth and Agnes. Elizabeth, the receptionist/bookkeeper, was a couple of inches taller than

Leslie and very slender. She was probably in her late twenties or early thirties, with a beautiful complexion and very short kinky hair. Agnes, the clinic's housekeeper, was a bit older—Leslie guessed she was probably about forty. Barely over five feet, she was slightly plump, at least by Kenyan standards.

Leslie quickly learned that Agnes's English was somewhat limited, but Elizabeth's was very good. "Whenever you need help translating or have a question, please ask, and I will drop everything." Her eyes were sincere, and her smile was infectious. Agnes was much shyer, although just as welcoming, and both women proved to be eager to help Leslie settle in.

Throughout the morning and afternoon, Leslie was introduced to a vast array of maladies, many of which she had only read about. During the first part of the morning, she followed Mama Joe and Naomi and quickly learned how to treat malaria, dysentery, scabies, intestinal worms and an assortment of venereal diseases. The variety of cases was amazing, and prenatal checkups were interspersed with the suturing of small cuts and treatment of dermatological complaints.

For the most part, the problems were routine

and could be managed with simple instructions, basic first aid and, occasionally, medications. The day flew by, and it was after six when the last patient left.

"Whew!" Leslie exclaimed as she looked around the empty waiting room. "That was exhausting! Is it like this every day?"

"No. Sometimes we get *really* busy," answered Mama Joe. Seeing Leslie's astonishment and slight panic, she grinned. "Just kidding. Actually, this was a fairly heavy day. Normally we see about thirty or forty patients. Today we saw more than fifty."

"That's a relief," Leslie replied. "I don't know how we'll manage this many patients without you."

"We always seem to take care of everyone. If it is really busy, we'll work faster."

Leslie helped the other women prepare for the next day before realizing she was starving. Thankfully, Agnes had prepared a hearty supper of vegetable soup with bits of cut-up chicken and rice. She and Mama Joe sat at the kitchen table, eating hungrily, all the while talking about different cases and how to manage various problems.

That night—after checking her room for spiders—Leslie crawled into bed exhausted. As instructed, she carefully arranged the netting to insure she was completely covered. In the quiet darkness, she allowed her thoughts to settle...and realized she was happier than she had been in a long time. She was smiling as she fell asleep.

IN THE SEVEN YEARS Leslie had been a nurse, she had never lost a patient. On the second day of practice at the Namanga Clinic, she lost two. She had been warned multiple times before she took the assignment that death was common, and she thought she was prepared. She was wrong.

Leslie slept well and awakened refreshed. She felt confident and quickly began seeing patients alone, occasionally seeking Mama Joe's or Naomi's advice on how to manage a new problem. The morning went smoothly, but around noon, an expressionless young woman carried a small baby wrapped in a colorful cotton cloth into the exam room. The woman gestured to the infant and said something; Leslie recognized the Swahili word for *baby*. She nodded, smiled and indicated the exam table. As the woman placed the infant on the table and unwrapped it, Leslie felt a chill. A quick visual inspection revealed an emaciated face with half-closed eyes and loose skin. Gently, she touched the infant's chest and discovered an unnatural coolness. There was no hint of movement. As she positioned her stethoscope to listen to the baby's heart, she yelled, "Mama Joe! Naomi!" The other nurses appeared within seconds.

"I don't hear anything," Leslie whispered to Mama Joe as the older nurse picked up the limp form and gently rubbed its back, trying to elicit movement. Like Leslie, she pressed her stethoscope to the tiny chest. Less than a minute passed before she looked up at her colleagues and shook her head. Naomi discreetly left the room to return to her own patient.

Mama Joe spoke with the infant's mother for a few minutes. Although Leslie didn't understand the words, she was struck by the mother's lack of emotion. Was she, Leslie, more disturbed by the baby's death than its mother? As the woman watched, Mama Joe carefully rewrapped the child in the cotton cloth. She handed the tiny bundle back to the mother and embraced her. Then the woman shuffled out the door to walk back to her village where she would bury the child.

When the woman had gone, Mama Joe turned to Leslie. "She told me the baby had been ill with diarrhea for a few days. She went to the local healer at first, and the baby was getting better. But this morning the baby was sick again. She wouldn't eat at all and only cried a little. That was when the mother decided to bring her here." Sorrow was evident in her tone, and she rubbed her eyes. "She had to walk about ten miles.... Obviously, she was too late."

Leslie remained quiet, and Mama Joe helped her clean the exam table with a strong disinfectant. Noticing Leslie's silence and shocked expression, she sighed and shook her head. "Sometimes there is nothing we can do to help. But, if she had brought the little one to us yesterday, we probably could have saved her."

A tear ran down Leslie's cheek. "It's so sad... so unnecessary."

Mama Joe gathered her into a comforting hug. "Yes it is. But we have to maintain perspective. We do everything we can to stop the sickness and death, and much of the time we can." She blinked back her own tears and added, "Leslie, this is something we have to learn to cope with. We don't accept it, but we do cope with it." Mama Joe pulled away and headed toward the reception area. "I need to show you what to do in the event of a death." Together they filled out the forms that were required by the Health Ministry and gave them to Elizabeth to post.

Leslie wiped away tears as she pondered the day's lesson. In Kenya, death was common. Give the body to the family and fill out two forms, and that was the end of the process. She desperately wanted to sob, but she followed Mama Joe's example and went back to care for her next patient, knowing there were many more who needed help.

LATER THAT AFTERNOON, a boy of nine or ten burst through the front door. He had obviously run to the clinic and was panting heavily. Elizabeth called to Mama Joe, and, after talking with the boy for a minute, the older nurse grabbed her bag and motioned for Leslie to follow. "Titus!" she yelled from the front porch. "We need to go to town." In a very short time the Jeep was at the door, and the two nurses climbed aboard with the young boy.

"What's happening?" Leslie asked as they bounced down the unpaved road.

Mama Joe's answer was hushed. "The boy's

father has AIDS. He's been sick for more than two years. The family is very poor and can't afford for him to go to a hospital. Evidently, he is much sicker, and the boy's mother sent for me."

A short time later, the Jeep pulled in front of a small wood-and-mud dwelling at the edge of the village. Mama Joe entered the home without knocking, and Leslie followed closely behind her. The interior of the hut was dark and overly warm, illuminated and vented by two small windows. The odor was a nauseating mixture of cow dung, human excrement, body odor and decay. Leslie cupped her mouth and swallowed hard to keep from gagging.

Her eyes adjusted to the scanty light, and she saw an extremely frail man covered by a thin blanket lying on a cot in one corner. An equally frail woman sat on a short stool near the head of the bed. Her jaundiced eyes watched intently as the two women entered the hut.

Mama Joe whispered a greeting as she approached the cot. She reached out and touched the woman, then the man, on their heads. She asked a few questions, which were answered by the woman in a bare whisper. Mama Joe glanced toward Leslie and motioned for her to come near the cot, and Leslie knelt by the meager bed to assess the dying man. His eyes were closed and sunken, and a wet, rasping noise told them he struggled to breathe.

Mama Joe knelt beside Leslie. Her voice was barely above a whisper as she said, "This is Mr. Kanjana. His high fever is most likely caused by pneumonia." They briefly discussed a treatment plan, and Mama Joe drew up medications for inflammation and pain into two syringes. Although Mr. Kanjana did not flinch at the prick of the needles, Leslie cringed as her colleague injected the medications into his skeletal thigh.

The nurses tried to get the patient to sip some water, but he did not have the energy to swallow. Mama Joe held his fragile hand for a while, and Leslie watched as she said a prayer in Swahili. A few minutes later, Mr. Kanjana's breathing seemed to ease, and Mama Joe rose and drew the wife away from the cot. Safely out of the husband's earshot, Mama Joe spoke to Mrs. Kanjana for a moment. With a tiny nod, the woman returned to sit beside her husband.

"The medications will allow him to breathe a little easier, but, judging by the breathing pattern, he probably won't live but a few more hours." She spoke quietly to Leslie, who glanced at the pitifully thin woman seated by the cot. "I told her I would stay with her. Why don't you go back to the clinic? Titus can take you home and then come back for me."

Leslie desperately wanted to go back to the clinic. She desperately wanted to leave the stinking confines of the tiny house filled with death. Instead, she looked into Mama Joe's calm brown eyes and whispered, "No. I'll stay." Tears threatened to fall, but she managed to blink them back. Squaring her shoulders, she said, "Tell me what to do."

As Mama Joe predicted, it was over in less than two hours. The nurses helped Mrs. Kanjana clean the body and cover it with a new cloth. There was nothing left for them to do but fill out the requisite forms when they returned to the clinic.

The frail woman stopped them as they were leaving. Her yellowed eyes were filled with gratitude, and she whispered something in Swahili. Mama Joe simply nodded, and Leslie did the same. As she waited, she tried to avoid thinking about the loneliness the widow would now have to endure, and she struggled once more to blink back tears.

Dusk had fallen and, once outside, Leslie

gulped in the warm, clean air. She was surprised to see that a number of men and women had surrounded the dwelling, waiting patiently for them to emerge. Those nearest to Mama Joe nodded with apparent respect but gazed at Leslie with curiosity. The young boy who had fetched them stood with two other children near the door. Their expressions were stark.

On the drive home, Mama Joe explained that the Kanjana family had already lost two children to the scourge of AIDS. "Mrs. Kanjana doesn't have long. She's taking antiretrovirals, but they've only slowed the disease a little." She sighed audibly. Her lined face showed fatigue, and she closed her eyes.

As soon as they arrived at the clinic, Leslie excused herself and rushed to the bathroom where she was violently ill. Afterward, she scrubbed her hands and face and rinsed her mouth, all the while trying to regain her composure. When she finally returned to the kitchen, she found Mama Joe seated at the table drinking a cup of hot tea. A second cup had been prepared for her, and she sat down and sipped it gratefully.

Leslie interrupted the silence a few minutes later. "How do you do it?"

Mama Joe smiled sadly. "Just when I think I can't take it a moment longer, when I can't bear to see one more child die, or treat one more case of some dreadful, preventable illness, or when I think I can't face walking into the clinic one more time—something happens. Sometimes it's something big and impressive, like saving a life or delivering a baby. But it's usually something little, like a smile from a child or a grateful look from a parent."

Laying her roughened hand gently over Leslie's, she said, "I wish I could tell you it gets easier, but it doesn't. You just do what you can and leave the rest to God." She reflected for a moment before adding, "After all of these years, I still find myself asking *why?* But we can't expect answers. I've learned to try to help whenever I can and to fight death any way I can. We don't always win, but we can always help ease pain and suffering."

Mama Joe gave a tired smile. "Leslie, Dennis Williams told me your story—about your husband and daughter…" She wiped away a tear and continued, "I believe that you were sent here for a purpose, and I'm glad you're here. You can understand what others experience…

You've been prepared in a very hard way to do what needs to be done. And you *can* do it."

"I want to be strong, and I really do want to help." Leslie sniffed. Her smile was faint. "You're a very good inspiration…"

At that, Mama Joe placed both hands on the table and pushed back her chair. "Agnes made supper for us and left it in the oven. I'm kind of hungry."

Thirty minutes ago, Leslie doubted she'd be able to eat for a long while. But words of encouragement from a brave woman had helped. She wiped the tears away and blew her nose. The corners of her lips turned up slightly. "I don't know if I can eat much, but I'd love another cup of tea."

CHAPTER FOUR

SUNDAY BROUGHT A badly needed respite from Leslie's first hectic week at the clinic. Her confidence and knowledge of the practice had improved significantly. Her Swahili, in contrast, was developing much more slowly. Mama Joe and Naomi were encouraging, however, and Elizabeth and Agnes were patient. Overall, she was pleased with her progress. The days were busy and enormously rewarding. Time off from seeing patients, though, was welcomed.

Unless she was called away, Mama Joe was adamant that Sunday mornings were to be spent at the local church where the service was led by a missionary family named Merdian. "Paul and Judy and their adorable children have been here for almost three years," Mama Joe explained during breakfast. "They're working on translating the Bible into one of the tribal languages—like Ben's parents used to do." She smiled proudly. "Paul is highly respected by the local people, and most everyone calls him 'Preacher'—even those who don't come to church. His wife, Judy, is wonderful, too—she's a terrific cook." She sipped her coffee and added, "Oh, that reminds me. They've invited us to lunch."

The service was unlike anything Leslie had ever experienced. The church consisted of a large, tentlike structure with a concrete floor and permanent metal roof. The sides were composed of fiberglass panels that could be removed to allow for ventilation and replaced during the rainy scason. Folding chairs were arranged in long rows, and Leslie estimated that the structure could easily hold two hundred.

The nurses arrived early, but the church was already half-full. Mama Joe spied the preacher on a wooden stage, where he was trying to get a stubborn microphone to cooperate. "There's Paul!" She waved in his direction.

The preacher motioned them forward. As he jumped off the stage to greet them, Leslie determined that Paul Merdian was probably in his middle thirties, even though he was mostly bald. He was of medium height and sported a full brown beard, a few shades darker than the remaining close-cropped hair that encircled his head. He grasped Leslie's hand enthusiastically when Mama Joe introduced them. "Judy and I have been looking forward to meeting you. We've heard very good things about how you're adjusting."

Leslie blushed. "Oh, that's nice to know. I still feel like I have a lot to learn, and Mama Joe's only going to be here a little more than a week."

Paul smiled. "Don't worry, you'll do fine. Titus and Naomi can help you out of just about any problem. And Judy and I are always here." His gray eyes were warm and friendly, with deep laugh lines at the corners. Leslie got the impression that he smiled a lot.

While they were speaking, a petite woman with shoulder-length blond hair and a cheerful disposition joined them. Mama Joe hugged the newcomer, who introduced herself. "Hi, Leslie. I'm Judy. I can't wait to hear about what all is happening back in the States." Judy's complexion was slightly pinkish and her features were fairly nondescript. Nonetheless, her lively blue eyes and a smile that rivaled her husband's made her particularly attractive.

Judy's warm reception reassured Leslie and she instinctively knew they'd be friends. "Thanks for inviting us to lunch." She smiled and added, "I'll be glad to trade you all I know about what's going on at home, if you'll coach me on adapting to life in rural Kenya."

Judy laughed. "You've got a deal!"

Leslie gestured toward the children playing tag outside the tent. "I think I can guess which are your children." A boy and girl, deeply tanned but still obviously white, raced around the area, standing out among the twenty or so African children. A much smaller boy with pale brown hair toddled with them, trying to keep up.

Judy grinned proudly. "Our older son is Johnny. He's eight. Beth will be seven in a couple of months, and Stephen just turned two."

Leslie smiled and continued to watch the children, swallowing hard at Stephen's toddler stride—for a moment, an image of her little girl sprang to mind. But the memory was not as painful as it had once been. "They look…ah… energetic. I'm guessing you stay pretty busy."

Paul wiped his forehead in mock weariness and sighed audibly. "Busy doesn't begin to describe what I have to do. All the cooking and cleaning and teaching…just kidding. Judy's remarkable. She does most of the kid-rearing, including teaching them at home." His pride and affection were evident. “Better excuse us. We need to get started. We’ll catch up with you after the service and head to the house.”

Leslie and Mama Joe found seats near the front of the tent. They were surrounded by colorfully dressed villagers. Glancing around the gathering, Leslie was pleased that she recognized a few faces. Mama Joe greeted a number of the people in the congregation.

The service lasted nearly three hours, and Leslie loved every minute. Singing dominated the first hour. Some songs were in English, but most were in Swahili or one of the regional dialects. Judy accompanied many of the hymns, playing an aged, upright piano with obvious skill. But most of the African songs were sung a cappella, and Leslie was captivated by the villagers’ complex harmonies. At times it seemed like there were three or four different songs being sung simultaneously, but the melodies blended into a joyous whole. Scripture readings were interspersed with testimonies from those in the congregation before Paul gave a message. The service closed with more singing.

While Paul finished his duties at the church, Mama Joe and Leslie went home with Judy and the children. The Merdians lived only a short distance away, and, like the clinic, their home consisted of a group of buildings surrounded by a high cinder-block wall. The wood-frame house was one story and painted white. A wide porch fronted it, complete with comfortable-looking rockers. Leslie stared appreciatively at the carefully cultivated yard of thick green grass. Colorful beds of flowers surrounded the porch, a testament to the diligence of Paul, Judy or both. She saw red and yellow gerbera daisies and white and pink impatiens interspersed with snapdragons and hibiscus. Off to one side was a commendable rose garden with at least two dozen bushes sprouting blossoms of various colors. The sweet smell of the garden reminded Leslie of home.

Mama Joe agreed to help Judy in the kitchen while the children gave Leslie a tour of the house. "This is where I sleep," Johnny said as they entered a small room at the back. He proudly pointed to the handmade desk and bookcases, which were crowded with children's books, readers and workbooks. A computer was pushed to one side. "These are my books. Mom teaches us school stuff every morning and makes us work really hard."

"Yep," added Beth. "I'm in the second grade

on some things with Johnny, but mostly I do first-grade lessons."

Johnny continued, "Stephen doesn't read yet 'cause he's still a baby. But sometimes we read to him and show him pictures. He likes that."

Leslie was charmed. Her heart tugged again when she saw one of the books she had read to Emma. She managed to blink back tears and refocused her attention on the children. "Maybe we can read a story after lunch."

Leslie picked up the toddler, who had been pulling at her dress, and he grinned at her shyly. Not wanting to be left out, Beth grabbed Leslie's free hand. "Miss Leslie, do you like puppies? Our dog, Lady, had puppies last week."

"They don't walk yet, and their eyes aren't completely open," Johnny said, "but they're really cute. Want to go see 'em?"

"I would love to see the puppies. We can go after lunch, but right now I had better go see if your mom needs any help." Smiling, Leslie set Stephen back on his feet and left the children to play in their room.

As Leslie passed through the combination living and dining room, heading toward the kitchen, the front door opened. Expecting Paul, she waited with a smile of greeting. Instead, she was surprised as a tall, lean man entered the house, and she found herself face-to-face with Ben Murphy.

Ben was dressed exactly as he had been at their previous meeting, in khaki slacks and white shirt. As before, his hair was pulled back in a short ponytail. That, coupled with his swarthy tan, light green eyes and expressive mouth, gave him the appearance of a pirate. She sighed inwardly, dismayed to concede he was extremely good-looking.

Ben managed to hide his surprise at meeting Leslie in the Merdians' living room. His gaze swept over her quickly, and he felt an odd catch in his chest. Today her hair was down, falling around her shoulders in shiny, mink-colored waves. Her simple red dress had short sleeves and skimmed her ankles. Though it was modest, it was appealing. He watched with annoyance as her smile disappeared. Twin bright spots on her cheeks rivaled the red of her dress.

After what seemed like an eternity to both, Ben broke the silence. "Paul invited me for lunch." His voice was flat and his face void of expression.

"Oh. I see. Well, hello then." Leslie searched for something to say, but her brain appeared to have ceased functioning, and she just looked at him and grew more flushed.

Ben did a little better. "So, how are you settling in?"

She acknowledged the question but could not quite manage a smile. "Pretty well. There have been some…ah…challenging times. But so far things have gone all right. Mama Joe is a terrific teacher." Her expression brightened a little when she mentioned her mentor.

Ben knew it was his turn again, and he was pondering what to say when someone bounded up the front steps. Both gratefully turned as the screen door opened and Paul entered. Grinning broadly, he shook hands with Ben. "Really glad you could come. You haven't been around much lately."

Relieved to have a diversion, Ben responded to the preacher with genuine affection. "Hey, are you kidding? Do you think I'd pass up an opportunity to eat Judy's cooking?"

Paul beamed at Leslie but continued to address Ben. "Judy and I thought it would be good for you to meet our newest missionary." Paul crossed the room to shake Leslie's hand in much the same manner, and she was glad he didn't seem to notice the awkwardness of the scene he had entered.

"Ben and I have already met. He flew me from Nairobi," Leslie explained, then deftly changed the subject. "I'm really looking forward to getting to know you and Judy better. I've already made friends with Johnny, Beth and Stephen. After lunch they're going to show me the puppies."

As if on cue, all three children entered the living room and saw Ben. The elder pair ran to hug him. Grinning mischievously at them, he scooped Johnny up and proceeded to hang the boy upside down by his ankles, eliciting giggles of delight from all three.

"Me, too! Me, too!" Beth cried.

From his inverted position, Johnny scoffed, "Heck, no. Uncle Ben can't do this to you. You're wearing a dress."

Ben set the boy on the ground, scooped up the little girl, and said, "Well, maybe you can't be turned upside down, but I can give you a big hug, can't I?" Beth grinned and threw her arms around Ben's neck; then Stephen held up his arms and was hauled into the mix.

Ben's ease with the Merdians surprised Leslie. He was obviously very fond of Paul and his family, and the feelings were reciprocated. She couldn't imagine they had much in common—well, other than living deep in the African savanna.

LUNCH WAS VERY informal and, as predicted, delicious. Roasted chicken was served over curried rice mixed with bits of mango and pineapple. Conversation was easy, and Leslie learned a great deal about her hosts. Paul and Judy had been high school sweethearts from Indianapolis and married right out of college. "We shared an interest in church ministry and African culture," Paul told her. "Even early in college, we were focused on going to Kenya."

"It took several years before we realized our dream," Judy confided. "Paul had to complete seminary, and by then we had Johnny and Beth. Stephen was born in Kenya." Judy smiled fondly at Mama Joe. "He was delivered right here in this house."

Over lunch, the two men shared tales of a recent hunting expedition in which they had shot several eland. Leslie looked at them quizzically. "I didn't know you could hunt in the game parks."

"Oh, definitely not the endangered animals

like elephant and rhino, and not the big cats," Paul explained. "But they have hunting seasons for antelope, much as they do at home for deer. If herds aren't thinned, they can quickly overgraze the parklands. And eland meat is really quite good. We'll have some next time you come over."

Leslie grimaced. "That's what I was told about buffalo and ostrich. I'm still not a believer. But this chicken is delicious." She glanced askance at her hosts and added, "It is chicken?" Everyone laughed.

As the others were finishing lunch, Judy got up to put Stephen down for his nap. With pleading looks at their mother, Johnny and Beth asked if they could be excused. "Yes, you may. Stay within the wall, though!" With a rush and the slamming of the screen door, the two disappeared.

At Judy's insistence, the group settled in the living room with cups of coffee. Conversation drifted to discussions about the customs of the region and their experiences while living in Kenya. Leslie was fascinated. Ben was surprisingly pleasant, although he rarely addressed her directly. His comments were informative and enlightening, and he answered questions with honesty and wry, self-deprecating humor.

Ben appeared to grow a little more at ease with Leslie as the conversation progressed, and during a lull, he tried to draw her in with a question. "So, Leslie, do you have a fiancé or boyfriend crying in his coffee at home while you spend six months here?"

Leslie recognized Ben's attempt to put a crack in the wall that had been evident from their first meeting. Nonetheless, the question caught her off guard, and she answered awkwardly, "Uh, no. Only my parents and sisters and a few close friends."

Ben flashed his most engaging smile. "Oh, come on. With those big blue eyes, I can't believe you don't have some man pining away, waiting anxiously for you to come back." Because Ben's attention was focused on Leslie, he missed Mama Joe's warning frown.

Leslie glanced at him, then quickly averted her eyes to stare at a book on the coffee table. "No, really. There's no one waiting at home."

Judy perceived Leslie's distress and intervened. "How about dessert? I have pineapple cake or banana cream pie."

Not willing to be sidetracked by his hostess, Ben misinterpreted the flicker in Leslie's eye and her sudden wariness. Teasingly, he persisted, "Oh, I get it. You're probably like me—you know, off to see the world. No strings attached. Not interested in settling down."

Mama Joe caught Leslie's flush. Unfortunately, she was too far from Ben to kick him. Following Judy's lead, she said, "Pineapple cake sounds delicious. Leslie, why don't you help Judy?"

Suddenly it became imperative for Ben to know more about Leslie. Her vagueness and obvious discomfort made him even more curious, so he ignored the other women. Mild sarcasm was apparent when he said, "But you really don't look like an adventurer. You look more like a soccer mom or—"

"Ben, drop it." Mama Joe's interruption was blunt, but her demand had the intended effect. A startled silence ensued for a few seconds.

Leslie finally looked directly at Ben. She took a deep breath and said, "I had a family." She clenched her jaw and continued. "My husband and daughter were killed in a car accident about twenty months ago. Actually, twenty months, one week and three days." Her voice was hushed and matter-of-fact, her face totally blank.

Their eyes remained locked until he blinked and looked down at his hands in embarrassment. Very quietly he said, “Leslie, I’m sorry. I didn’t…” He studied the coffee table and contemplated crawling under it. “I didn’t have any idea.”

Although she was stunned, Judy managed to interject herself into the conversation. “Leslie, I’m so sorry. How awful for you.” Tears formed in her eyes.

Leslie nodded to her and gave a little shrug. “Let’s not talk about it.” Abruptly, she stood up. “The kids wanted me to look at the puppies.”

Paul and Judy started to rise, too, but she motioned for them to stay seated. “No, please. It’s okay. Why don’t you go ahead and have dessert? I need a minute.” Without waiting for a reply, she let herself out.

ALONE IN THE WARM SUNSHINE, Leslie felt a sense of relief. She strolled through the lovely garden, absorbing the delicate scents. The peaceful space gave her an opportunity to calm her emotions. Determined to recover her enjoyment of the day, she followed the sound of children’s laughter to a shed near one corner of the walled compound. Inside she saw the two children sitting beside a large black dog. The dog was lying on her side, and Leslie counted eight puppies greedily nursing.

Beth jumped up and grabbed Leslie's hand, drawing her into the shed. "Her name is Lady, and she's really nice. You can pat her, but don't bother the puppies while they're eating."

The dog looked up with friendly brown eyes, and her tail thumped slightly in welcome. Leslie smiled while holding out her hand for Lady to sniff. "Hello, there. What a lovely family you have." The dog's tail thumped again, and Leslie rubbed her behind the ears. Sitting down in the dirt beside the children, she asked, "Do the puppies have names?"

Johnny pointed to the largest puppy. "I call that one Horton, 'cause he eats the most." He pointed out one of the others. "That one is Sam. His name is really Sam-I-Am, but we just call him Sam."

Beth decided it was her turn and indicated a brown-spotted white fluff of fur. "This is Dora. She's named after a character in one of my favorite books."

The children introduced the remaining puppies to Leslie. After they finished eating, Leslie watched as the children gently picked up the small animals and stroked their coats. "Their eyes are just starting to open. Mom said it will take a couple of days, but then they can see," Johnny explained.

Spending time with the children helped restore Leslie's good mood, and soon she felt it was time to rejoin the others. She rose. "I probably need to see if your mom needs help cleaning the kitchen. Thank you for showing me the puppies."

She was still smiling when she stepped outside and turned toward the house. She stopped short, however, when she became aware of a man standing only a few feet away. The bright sunlight momentarily blinded her, but what she could make out alarmed her. Her heart rate soared as her vision cleared. A Masai warrior in tribal clothing was staring at her.

He towered over her, and she guessed that he was well over six-and-a-half-feet tall. Red cloth, the exact color of blood, draped his body. The drape covered one shoulder, and the cloth formed a skirt that reached just below his knees. A wide collar made of tiny red, white, green and blue beads adorned his neck, and a kind of leather necklace, decorated with claws of some sort, reached past the middle of his chest. She blinked again when she saw the spear he carried in his right hand—it was even taller than the warrior. His expression was fierce, and he watched intently as she took an involuntary step back toward the shack.

A wave of fear nearly overwhelmed her. She swallowed hard and managed to squeak, *"Jambo."*

The man's eyes did not leave hers. *"Jambo."* His voice was a deep growl.

A giggle from the shed reminded Leslie of the children, and she felt a moment of panic. *Johnny and Beth!* She had to get the man away from the children. Her eyes held his as she started to move slowly toward the house, and she was relieved when his attention remained on her rather than on the shed. Her limited Swahili had deserted her, so she spoke in English. "What do you want?"

He did not move but simply stared at her. She could read nothing in his coal-black eyes.

She tried again, grateful that her voice sounded stronger. "The preacher? Do you want to see the preacher?"

He shook his head slightly. "No." She was struck again by the deep timbre of his voice.

"No. I want to see the pilot." His cadence was slow and the English was heavily accented.

Another giggle from the shed drew the attention of both Leslie and the warrior. Before Leslie could shout a warning, Johnny appeared at the door with Beth close behind him. As Leslie tried to gather breath for a scream that she hoped would be heard in the house, Johnny spoke. "Hey, Simon. Do you want to see our puppies?"

Pushing past her brother, Beth reached for the hand of the amazingly tall man. "We have eight puppies, and Johnny and I help take care of them."

The Masai warrior grinned down at the little girl. As soon as she saw the change in his expression, Leslie felt a rush of relief so strong that she felt faint. The man's face was split by a smile revealing large, astonishingly white teeth, with a gap in front almost wide enough to hold another tooth.

The deep voice responded to the child's question. "I am sorry. I cannot stay now, Missy Beth. I must get Ben. I will see the small dogs another time."

"That's okay. Uncle Ben's in the house." Still holding the man's hand, the little girl pulled him in that direction. "We just ate lunch. Did you eat? I bet Mom has some extra food if you're hungry."

"I'll go tell Mom." Johnny ran ahead, and within seconds he bounded up the front steps.

It took the better part of a minute for Leslie to control her breathing and follow the two children and the giant to the house. She was simultaneously relieved and acutely embarrassed. She'd read about the Masai tribesmen in preparation for their trip and knew they were friendly. But even though she'd seen pictures, this man's appearance had been startling—and so fearsome that she had been terrified.

Leslie continued toward the house and watched as Ben and Paul met Simon on the front porch. Paul gave the warrior a hearty handshake, and his friendly smile met Simon's gap-toothed grin. She noted that Ben and Simon did not shake hands; despite the distance, she discerned an obvious ease, even affection, between the two men. Paul asked a question in Swahili, and Simon nodded. A brief three-way conversation followed, and then the men turned in unison to look at Leslie.

Paul motioned for her to join them, and they

stepped aside to allow her onto the porch. "Leslie, this is Simon Osagie. He works with Ben."

Leslie held out her hand. "It's nice to meet you, Simon."

"It is my pleasure, Miss Leslie." Despite his thick accent, she had no trouble making out the words.

Ben watched her closely. "Simon thinks that he frightened you. He wants to apologize." Normally, Ben would have been amused, but after his earlier behavior he was uncharacteristically reserved.

Leslie gave Simon a shy smile, then addressed him directly. "No. No. It's fine. I was alarmed when I first saw you, but I see that was foolish."

Ben tried to soothe her discomfort. "It can be pretty startling to see the Masai in full regalia. Simon usually wears T-shirts and Bermudas. He dresses this way for special occasions."

Simon watched her for a moment and then looked back at Ben and said something. Ben shrugged in reply, and both men looked at Leslie. Simon's expressive face showed curiosity, but she could not read Ben's.

Mama Joe and Judy joined the group on the porch, and both women greeted the giant warrior with affection. Judy asked him into the house for coffee, but Simon shook his head and indicated Ben's Jeep. Ben explained, "There was a wedding in Simon's family. He came here to get a ride home and to remind me that I have to get ready to fly out tomorrow. We need to be on our way." Both Mama Joe and Judy hugged the pilot, and Paul shook both men's hands. Simon gave them all a nodding bow.

For a moment Ben's eyes met Leslie's, and he looked like he wanted to say something. Finally, he copied Simon and simply nodded. "Leslie." Then, without waiting for an acknowledgment, he turned and followed Simon to the Jeep.

CHAPTER FIVE

"LESLIE! LESLIE, HONEY, wake up!" Mama Joe knocked loudly before barging into the bedroom. "You need to get ready for a delivery."

Leslie opened her eyes and blinked. It was still dark outside, but the light from the hallway allowed her to focus on Mama Joe's face through the mosquito net. "Okay…okay…" She sat up in bed and swept her hands at the netting, trying to find the opening. "What time is it?"

"About six." Leslie was surprised to see that the older woman was ready for work. "Get dressed and come have coffee and a bite, and I'll fill you in." Mama Joe closed the door as she left.

Leslie crawled out of bed and—after checking the floor for spiders—quickly got ready. She joined Mama Joe in the kitchen. True to her word, Mama Joe had a cup of coffee and toast with jam waiting. Gratefully, Leslie took a sip of the rich black coffee and sighed with pleasure. "Okay, what's up?" she asked.

"Father Christopher just called."

"Father Christopher?"

"Oh. Didn't I mention? He's a priest—a very old friend—who has a mission in the Lake Magadi region. He works with the Masai people." Mama Joe paused for a second and took a sip of her own coffee. "A woman in their area just went into labor. She has already lost two infants at birth, and so Father Chris wants us to help with the delivery rather than relying on the village midwives."

Leslie nodded. "That makes sense. Where's Lake Magadi?"

"It's not far. Only about seventy or eighty miles."

Leslie sipped her coffee. If the woman was in early labor, they should have plenty of time to travel eighty miles. "Sure. When do we leave?"

"Er...well, that's the thing. It won't be us—it'll be you."

Leslie's cup stopped halfway to her mouth. "What?"

"Honey, I'm leaving tomorrow. I've worked with you for two weeks now. You've delivered four babies during that time, and I know you can do this." Mama Joe took a bite of toast, then added, "Besides, I haven't started packing."

"But..."

"It'll be over before you know it. Just a quick flight down and—"

"Flight?" Leslie set her cup down with a start. "But if it's only eighty miles..."

"The road in that direction is terrible, so driving is out. I've already talked to Ben. It's all set. You need to meet him at the airstrip in about half an hour."

"Are you sure?"

"Don't worry, you'll do fine." Mama Joe patted Leslie's hand and then turned to gather the dishes.

Titus drove her to the airstrip, where she saw Ben already working to prepare the Cessna. She thanked Titus and walked toward the plane, carrying her bag close to her chest as if it were a shield. Ben had been squatting down to inspect one of the tires, and when he finished that task, he rose. She felt his eyes on her, and for some reason, her heart started to pound and her mouth went dry.

Ben frowned. "Where's Mama Joe?"

"She needs to take care of things before she leaves tomorrow. She wants me to handle the delivery." Leslie knew she sounded defensive. Did he think she wasn't capable?

"Oh, right... So it's just us?" He did not look pleased. He opened the passenger door and then stood back. She threw her bag inside, then reluctantly allowed him to assist her—she did not want to chance a repeat of her first attempt to climb into the plane. A short time later they were flying west toward the Great Rift Valley. The entire flight was made in silence.

THE BIRTH WENT WELL. The baby boy weighed slightly more than seven pounds, quite large for a Kenyan infant. To avoid the common complication of neonatal tetanus, Leslie clamped the umbilical cord with a small plastic clip and cut it with a sterile pair of scissors, ignoring the ceremonial knife offered to her by the attending midwife. In broken but improving Swahili, she told the mother and midwife how to keep the cord area clean and to not put *anything* on it, specifically cow dung. She prayed silently that her instructions would be heeded.

Successful births were always uplifting, and, despite her fatigue, she was smiling as she left the tiny hut and stepped into the afternoon sunlight. Her good humor was dashed a little, though, because the first person she saw was

Ben. With her bag in hand, she continued forward to the Jeep that had been provided by Father Christopher.

THROUGHOUT THE DELIVERY, Ben had waited just outside the door, squatting in the shade with the anxious husband. After nearly five hours, he watched as Leslie walked to the borrowed Jeep. Her thick brown ponytail sagged, and all around her face, wisps of hair had escaped the confines of the cloth-covered rubber band. She was flushed with heat and fatigue, and her white cotton shirt was damp with perspiration; the tail was no longer neatly tucked into her waistband. He observed her rifling through her canvas bag to locate a bottle of water, which she used to wash her hands. Then she splashed some on a bandanna and wiped her face.

He felt a gnawing in the pit of his stomach that had nothing to do with hunger. Ben dreaded the flight home. He knew she didn't like him and she hadn't wanted to fly with him. He sighed and stood up. Glancing at his watch, he realized that it was midafternoon. She hadn't eaten anything in hours.

Leslie didn't hear Ben approach and startled a bit when he reached past her to open his olive canvas duffel bag. He drew out a clear pint-size bottle filled with amber liquid and a label indicating that it was some type of bourbon. He also found two candy bars and offered her one.

She took the proffered candy and murmured, "Thank you." She glanced at the bottle disapprovingly and turned away to store her bags in the vehicle. Her irritation grew when she caught him grinning at her. She didn't know if he was deliberately trying to aggravate her or if he simply did not care what she thought of him. Hoping that he would recognize her displeasure, she silently climbed into the Jeep and motioned for the driver, who was waiting nearby.

During the twenty-minute drive to the landing strip, Leslie and Ben didn't talk. Ben spoke freely with the driver, however, and Leslie observed him take at least three drinks from the bottle. He even offered her a sip, which she frostily declined. She might have imagined it, but she thought he was enjoying her discomfort as she saw traces of humor in his eyes. That annoyed her even more.

They finally made it to the airstrip, and Leslie was anxious to be off before Ben drank more. She was gathering her bags and not watching where they were going when the driver brought the Jeep to an abrupt halt. He said something nervously to Ben, and Leslie lifted her gaze to where the Cessna waited on the grassy strip. Less than fifteen feet away from the plane three men were lounging near a beat-up truck. They were dressed in olive-colored military garb, and each carried a rifle.

Her attention returned to Ben when he whispered, "Damn." She became even more concerned as the focus of her anxiety shifted from the sobriety of the man beside her to the guns of the men standing beside his airplane. Leslie knew nothing about firearms except that they were dangerous, and these looked particularly worrisome.

Ben and the driver exchanged a few words, then he glanced at her. "Act deferentially to me, and don't look directly at anyone." He nodded to the driver, who steered the Jeep toward the three men; beads of sweat appeared on the driver's brow. As the vehicle came to a stop, Ben said through his teeth, "Help Mr. Bostmati take the bags out, and wait here until I tell you what to do. Mr. Bostmati is going to leave." He did not look at her.

Ben's manner startled Leslie and she studied the men near the plane. She started to question him, but he didn't pause. Ignoring her, he got out of the Jeep and walked toward the men with a confident swagger. She listened as he addressed them in Swahili. Deciding it was best that she follow his instructions, she helped the obviously frightened driver unload the bags. As soon as he was back in the Jeep, he took off in a cloud of dust, causing Leslie's concern to edge into fear.

The conversation between Ben and the three men went on for several minutes. At first, Ben did most of the talking. She assumed he was explaining their purpose for being in the area. As she watched out of the corner of her eye, Leslie saw that soon the men were nodding with him in agreement, and then they were laughing. The men glanced her way as he talked with them, and she got the impression that once again the laughter was at her expense. Unsure of how to respond, she stood in silence, compelled to wait for Ben to tell her what to do next.

After about ten minutes, he turned to her and said loudly, "Woman, put those bags in the hold of the plane and bring out the two bottles of whiskey stored there."

Woman? Her eyes grew wide with indignation, coupled with mounting fear. She opened her mouth to answer.

Ben saw her hesitation. In an angry tone he belted out, *"Just do it!"*

Leslie recognized something new in Ben's expression. In a moment of intuitive clarity, she caught a glimmer of apprehension in his otherwise nonchalant, bravado-based sneer. With all thoughts of disagreement instantly gone, she hurried to comply.

Turning his back on Leslie, Ben engaged the men in conversation, and soon they were laughing again.

As instructed, Leslie loaded the three bags into the cargo hold, then dug through a wooden box and found two bottles of liquor. Quickly she crossed to him and stood a few feet to the side, waiting for him to acknowledge her. One of the men glanced her way, and finally Ben took the bottles.

Curtly, using precise, clipped English, he said, "Get in the plane and wait for me. I will join you after a break with these men." When it appeared that she was going to say something, he added, *"Now."*

Without looking at any of the men, including Ben, Leslie obeyed.

The interior of the plane was hot. Leslie grew more uncomfortable by the minute. From her seat she could clearly see the three armed men, and she watched as they opened the bottles and shared them. Ben pulled the open bottle out of his pocket and took a long swig.

As time passed, the plane got hotter and the laughter got louder. Trying to be quiet, Leslie partially opened her door to allow air to circulate. Now she could hear bits of the conversation. She caught occasional words that she knew in Swahili and even rarer words of English. As far as she could tell, they were talking mostly about guns and alcohol. Finally she heard Ben say the word "airplane," followed by other phrases including the Swahili words for "night" and "travel." He moved as if to get into the plane, but one of the men stopped him. They exchanged a few words.

Leslie felt her jaw clench as Ben appeared to answer a question angrily, and a brief argument followed. Finally, he nodded, reached into his pocket, and pulled out a handful of Kenyan shillings. She watched as he counted out several of the larger bills and handed the money to one of the men. With that, he opened the door and climbed into the plane.

Ben did not acknowledge Leslie as he prepared to take off. She noted that the armed trio seemed to have lost interest in the plane and its occupants. Ben had left the two bottles with them, and they were focused on consuming the remainder of the contents as they waited for the plane to depart.

Ben did not bother with his routine preflight check. He simply started the engine and taxied to the far end of the field. In less than a minute they were airborne, and immediately the cabin of the small plane cooled.

Relieved at not being detained or worse, and much more comfortable in the cool air of the higher altitude, Leslie relaxed a little. She stared straight ahead, but her attention returned to Ben when she heard him give out a deep "Whew!"

"What?" she responded edgily.

His eyes were focused on the dials and indicators on the flight panel, but while holding the control of the plane with one hand, he reached into his pocket with the other and pulled out what remained of the bourbon. He took a drink and then surprised her when he grinned. In a voice loud enough to be heard over the engine's roar he said, "That was a little nerve-racking, wasn't it?"

With each passing mile, her apprehension and irritation had lessened, replaced by relief and then curiosity. "What just happened?"

His answer was surprisingly nonchalant. "Oh, just some local government thugs, shaking us down."

Leslie was incredulous. "*What?* You mean those men were officials?"

Ben nodded and took another sip.

"And you *bribed* them?"

He glanced at her and then shrugged. "Yeah… so?"

She didn't answer but turned to gaze out the window, bewildered. She wasn't sure Ben was much better than the thugs.

Ben huffed audibly at her response. When she glanced back to face him, he rolled his eyes and said, "And what was I supposed to do? Demand to see some paperwork? Appeal to their softer side?" His tone grew more impatient and his words grew louder. "Explain my rights as an American? Dazzle them with my charm and good looks?"

He was practically shouting. Hell, he thought as he finished the tirade—that was pretty much what he had done. He'd ingratiated himself with fast talking and jokes, along with a couple of bottles of bourbon and about $200, to be allowed to leave. He was simultaneously glad that she didn't realize the precariousness of the situation and irritated that she didn't understand how lucky they were to get away for only a couple hundred dollars and two bottles of cheap booze. He mirrored her response as he turned to stare out of his window.

Leslie recognized that she was being unreasonable. She sighed. "Ben, I'm sorry. I know I should be happy to be out of there. I just wasn't expecting...well, I wasn't expecting *that.*" She rubbed her forehead with her hand and sighed again.

Ben's temper evaporated. He glanced at her. "Look, I get it. I know it's a shock, but that's just how things are done here." He took another swallow from the flask.

Her irritation returned in a heartbeat, and in the sternest voice she could muster, she said, "I *really* wish you wouldn't drink any more of that until we land."

Ben simply grinned and held the bottle out to her. "Here, have a drink. It'll make you feel better."

Leslie ignored the offered bottle and said flatly, "I don't think so."

Ben persisted. "Come on. Just one sip and you'll feel much better. I promise."

Leslie considered that the more she drank, the less would be available for him, so she grabbed the bottle and unscrewed the cap. Bracing herself, she took a gulp and immediately choked on the contents. She coughed repeatedly, and tears filled her eyes. Despite the noise of the plane's engine, she heard him chuckle.

"I've never seen anyone react quite that way to sweet tea."

Trying to clear her throat, she took another sip. When she could speak again she asked, "You mean this stuff has never been anything but tea?"

"Did you actually think I would drink and fly?"

"You know I did! And you said nothing to make me think any differently!" She crossed her arms and glared at him, "I can't believe you wanted me to think you were drinking!"

"Let me get this straight. You *were* mad because you thought I was drinking, but now you're mad because I *wasn't?*"

"Yes! I mean, no! I mean…oh, never mind." She took another drink, and the irony of the incident suddenly hit her. She began to giggle.

The tension of the day abruptly eased, and she laughed out loud. She glanced back at Ben and shook her head. “You know,” she managed to say, “I really hate to admit it, but you were right. I feel *much* better now.”

The glint in his normally piercing green eyes softened, and his reluctant smile was genuine. “You should laugh more.”

He held her gaze for a few seconds, then stopped smiling. “Leslie, contrary to village rumor and popular belief, I don’t have a death wish. Although I hesitate to use the word never, I would *never* fly under the influence of alcohol. Please rest assured.”

Leslie knew he was attempting to make her feel safer. Despite her original misgivings, her opinion of him rose a little. She tried to think through this revelation. She hadn’t been the only one to see him “drinking,” and he hadn’t done anything to disabuse others of the notion. Why would he put up that kind of facade? Obviously he went to considerable lengths to have people think the worst of him.

They continued the flight in silence, and she studied him surreptitiously. As usual, his long hair was held back from his face in a neat ponytail. No doubt it was much neater than hers just now. His white cotton shirt was considerably sweat stained from waiting for her in the sweltering heat and then talking with the officials. Likewise, his khaki pants were dusty from the events of the day, but had probably been freshly laundered when he donned them that morning. Growing progressively less discreet in her observations, she noticed his hands. The nails were well trimmed, and there was no hint of the inevitable grease and dirt often associated with aircraft mechanics or men living in the African bush.

There was no doubt that Mama Joe and Paul and Judy were comfortable with Ben and even respected him. She had been troubled trying to understand why—but now she was starting to see.

AS THE FLIGHT CONTINUED, Ben was lost in his thoughts. His opinion of Leslie had also shifted during the afternoon. Through the high windows and frequently opened door of the mud hut, he had remained attentive as she cared for the young woman in labor. Her words were authoritative without being judgmental. She had not scolded the young mother or her attendants; nor had she acted condescendingly. She couldn't change generations of tradition in an afternoon, but there were things she tried to do to improve the health of the people, and he respected her for it. She understood that centuries of tradition, superstition and misinformation had left the villagers extremely vulnerable. She knew there were some things that could not be changed and some that did not need changing. She just wanted to help.

She hadn't commented on the heat and the dust, and she didn't utter a word of complaint. Nor had she asked him for anything. He knew she was uncomfortable with him, and, rather than putting her at ease, for some reason he wanted to irritate her, and he wasn't really sure why. He glanced at her and saw that she was watching his hands. He wondered what she thought of him. Normally, he worked very hard to preserve his carefully cultivated image, but he had let her know one of his closely guarded secrets. Again, he wasn't sure why. Had he shared the bottle with her to ease her mind, or did he subconsciously want her to know that he wasn't a drunk? He didn't want to explore his motivations any further, so he focused on getting home instead.

Beside him, Leslie slowly relaxed, leaning

against the plane's door, both emotionally and physically drained. Minutes later, she fell asleep to the drone of the engine.

THAT EVENING, LESLIE related most of the day's events—omitting the part about the non-bourbon-containing flask—to Mama Joe as she helped the older woman pack for her early-morning departure. Trying to sound casual as she folded a sweater, she commented, "Ben's a little unusual. Why does he live out here?"

Mama Joe placed the sweater inside her suitcase and gave Leslie a side glance. Turning back to the pile of clothes, she answered the question with one of her own. "So, Ben Murphy has got you curious, huh?"

Leslie didn't really want to admit her interest, but after a little pause, she said, "Yes, I guess."

Mama Joe sat down facing Leslie. "Leslie, I truly don't know. It's like he's come here to get away from things that happened to him at home."

"What things?"

Mama Joe looked pensive. She seemed to be trying to gauge how much to explain. "I knew Ben when he was a kid. He was sweet and easygoing, with a wonderful sense of humor. He got along with everyone. As I told you, he was a gifted athlete at the Air Force Academy, and he graduated near the top of his class. He did so well that his first assignment was to learn to fly bombers."

She took a breath. "When he was about twenty-five, he married a girl named Glenna. According to gossip among the missionaries here in East Africa—unfortunately, we do gossip sometimes—she was a lawyer, and gorgeous. And she and Ben were supposed to be a perfect couple. But something happened early in their marriage, and Ben gave up flight training and was transferred to Washington. For about two years, he worked at the Pentagon and went to graduate school." She paused, as if for effect. "Then Glenna left him."

Mama Joe shifted and sighed deeply. "Leslie, most of the rest is rumor and conjecture. I'm only telling you this because you're going to be here, working with him, and you deserve to know as much—or as little—as everyone else does. Evidently Ben was devastated. He distanced himself from his friends and became a loner. Despite those changes, everyone who knew Ben was amazed by what happened next."

"What happened?" Leslie's voice was very quiet.

"Well, about six months after Glenna's departure, there were allegations of an affair between Ben and a married female officer. I heard that Ben was accused of insubordination and fraternization. There were rumors of actions being taken and charges being filed. The story is that he was dishonorably discharged and barely escaped charges of sexual harassment and a court-martial."

Leslie was taken aback. But, on reflection, it wasn't a stretch for her to believe that Ben had been engaged in some type of affair with a married woman. After all, she had seen him in action. And yet, vaguely, she was aware of being disappointed.

"Do you believe the rumors?" Leslie asked. She did not want the story to be true.

Mama Joe shrugged. "I'm not sure. He's changed a lot. It's as if he's here because he has nowhere else to go. Like I said, maybe he's trying to escape from something. But now that I think about it, I wonder if he's looking for something instead…"

CHAPTER SIX

TWO MONTHS PASSED in a blur of activity. Leslie was relieved at how easily she settled into the lifestyle and the work. For the most part, she was comfortable providing care to the clinic patients. Occasionally it was necessary to ask Naomi for assistance or advice on how to manage a problem, but those instances were becoming rarer. And although she still relied on Elizabeth or Agnes for help with translation, she was pleased that her command of Swahili, while still limited, was growing.

Early one workday near the beginning of her third month, Leslie was summoned for an urgent phone call. “It is Dr. DeMerode from Médicins Sans Frontières,” Elizabeth explained. “He and his wife operate a clinic in Nyeri.”

Before leaving, Mama Joe had briefed Leslie on other clinicians with whom she had occasional contact. Among those she mentioned were Dr. Jean-Baptiste DeMerode and his wife,

Christine, who were on the staff of Doctors Without Borders.

"Nyeri?" she asked.

"It is about one hundred kilometers on the other side of Nairobi," explained Elizabeth as she passed the phone to Leslie. "Near the Rift Valley."

"Hello. This is Leslie Carpenter," Leslie said into the receiver.

"Mrs. Carpenter, I am Dr. DeMerode. Mama Joe told me to contact you as I would her, should we need assistance." His French accent was heavy and his word usage a bit odd. "We have a problem with a measles outbreak in three villages. Many ill children are contracting pneumonia. We are trying to contain the outbreak and prevent serious complications." He paused and then added, "My wife and our assistants cannot cover all of the needs. We have lost two children and fear that we may lose more. Will you help?"

Desperation and fatigue were evident in Dr. DeMerode's voice, and Leslie quickly answered, "Yes. I'll be very glad to come help you. Let me arrange transportation and I'll call you back to let you know when to expect me. Where do I need to go?"

He gave her the location of the hospital and contact information. "I will await your call," he concluded.

Since Mama Joe's departure, Leslie's practice had stayed primarily near the clinic in Namanga, though twice she had been called on to travel to points more distant. On both of those occasions she had flown with Ben. After the incident with the corrupt officials, their relationship had thawed a bit. Although he was cordial, he seemed to want to maintain distance, which was fine with her. For the most part, their encounters were relatively formal, with few social niceties and little conversation.

Leslie was still not completely comfortable in his presence. On those few occasions when he was near, she'd been disquieted to catch his light green eyes closely monitoring her actions. Why was he watching her like that? Did he think she was going to do something stupid?

Leslie tried to contact Ben, but she learned from Mr. Endebbi at the airstrip that Ben was away and not expected back for a week. "Shoot!" Leslie said as she hung up the phone, vaguely aware that she was sorry he wasn't available. "Elizabeth, where are the names and numbers of the Mission Aviation Support pilots

Mama Joe told me about? Let's see if we can find someone else."

They were able to reach Andy Singleton, who informed Leslie that he would be at Namanga's airstrip in two hours. He assured her that they would be able to make the trip to Nyeri by dusk. Leslie called Dr. DeMerode to let him know the arrangements. With mingled excitement and apprehension, Leslie gathered supplies and a few personal items and in short order was flying to northern Kenya.

Andy Singleton was the direct opposite of Ben. He was in his late fifties and very friendly and talkative. He and his wife had lived in Kenya for about ten years, and he was both knowledgeable and competent. Flying with Andy was calm and nonthreatening. The trip to Nyeri went smoothly, and he assured her that he'd be glad to come collect her when she was ready to return.

The DeMerodes were in their late forties, and they were not French, as Leslie had assumed, but Belgian. Jean-Baptiste was tall and quite thin, with salt-and-pepper hair and a reserved, somewhat pessimistic demeanor. Christine was a very attractive woman with chin-length black hair and pretty, amber-colored eyes. Unlike her husband, she was gregarious and cheerful, despite the dire circumstances of their meeting. Fortunately, their English was excellent, and they were able to quickly assimilate Leslie into the care of the children who had contracted measles.

The next several days sped by. The team was responsible for dozens of sick children and surrounded by panicked parents and relatives. The first day Leslie worked directly with Dr. DeMerode or Christine, whom she learned was also a nurse. After that, she worked either with them or with one or two of the Kenyan nurses.

The team labored through waves of fatigue to battle the scourge of measles. They dosed children with medications to reduce fever and treat secondary infections. When children were struggling with pneumonia, they constructed oxygen tents and suctioned their airways to allow them to breathe more easily. They also took turns roaming through the nearby villages in concentric circles, moving outward away from the hospital. In the villages they gave measles booster shots to children as they searched for cases that had not been diagnosed.

The workdays lasted eighteen to twenty hours. When she could no longer function safely, Leslie retired to their temporary quarters, a small tent that had been erected behind the hospital. She ate when she could and washed her hands dozens of times each day, until they were raw from the abrasive soaps and disinfectants.

The first morning Leslie was in Nyeri, one child succumbed to pneumonia. But the hard work and round-the-clock care proved to be successful, and no other children died from the dreaded disease, although many became very seriously ill.

Late one evening after the outbreak had begun to wane, Leslie shared a rare moment of relaxation with Christine outside of their tent. The two women had become friends during their brief but busy time together. Each sipped a cup of tea as they lounged in relatively comfortable camp chairs, their tired feet propped on a wooden box that served as a table. Although it seemed like forever, Leslie realized that only five days had passed since her arrival. No new infections had been identified for more than forty-eight hours, and all of the children with pneumonia and other secondary infections were recovering. While the women rested, Jean-Baptiste was making the final rounds of the evening, examining the children who were still hospitalized. Thankfully, their number had dropped to only a handful.

"We must have a celebration," declared Christine. She placed her cup of tea on the box and leaned forward. "Jean-Baptiste and I will drive to Nairobi tomorrow to pick up supplies." Her lively amber eyes were more animated than Leslie had seen them before. "We can take you with us, and your pilot can meet you there. We will go to dinner and have a nice wine to celebrate the end of the outbreak. You can stay at your mission." She grinned at Leslie and added in a conspiring manner, "And I will make Jean-Baptiste take me to a hotel for the night! I want a proper bed with linen sheets and room service!"

Leslie chuckled at her new friend's plans. After a very busy three months, followed by the exhausting past several days, an evening at a restaurant and a night in a converted mansion sounded like a vacation. "A good restaurant and wine would be wonderful right now." She rose and gestured toward the office located in the hospital building. "I'll go contact Mr. Singleton to see if he can meet me in Nairobi the day after tomorrow."

AS PLANNED, LESLIE traveled to Nairobi with the DeMerodes. They dropped her at the headquarters for the East Africa Mission, where she would spend the night. That gave her a few hours to visit with Connie and Dennis Williams before dinner.

Since she'd only brought work clothes with her, Leslie borrowed a dress from Connie for the occasion. The violet linen sheath was a little large, but it complemented her eyes beautifully. Connie also had a pair of black sandals that Leslie could wear comfortably. They were much more fashionable than the dusty loafers and athletic shoes she'd brought with her from Namanga.

Deciding to celebrate in style, Christine made reservations at the French Room, an exclusive restaurant located within the Serena Hotel. Dinner was set for seven, and the Williams's driver, Marcus, dropped Leslie off at the hotel after making arrangements to return in three hours.

Leslie sighed in appreciation of the comfortably air-conditioned hotel as she passed through the lovely lobby and descended the marble stairs to the lower level. Entering the restaurant, she paused to look around and absorb the ambience. After spending the previous five days caring for critically ill children in fairly primitive conditions, it was jarring to stand in a beautiful room surrounded by well-dressed patrons. The tables were covered with crisp, white linen cloths and featured real silver, lighted candles and fresh flowers.

She spotted Jean-Baptiste and Christine already occupying a table set for three near the center of the room. The Belgian couple rose when she approached, and both brushed multiple air kisses near her cheeks. “I am to be envied, because I am with the most beautiful women in Kenya,” Jean-Baptiste boasted to no one in particular. Christine giggled and patted his arm, then motioned for Leslie to be seated.

Over the next two hours, Leslie realized that she had misjudged Jean-Baptiste. In Nyeri he had been working twenty-hour days to protect the lives of more than a hundred children. Now, with that weight removed, he seemed to be another person. Before, he had been grim and often brusque with her and others, but now he was much more animated. His smile was infectious, and his easy humor seemed to subtract fifteen years from his face.

He poured a French Bordeaux into crystal glasses. “I wish to propose a toast,” he said, raising his glass. “To our new friend, Leslie. Our greatest blessing for coming to our rescue and helping save many lives."

Leslie blushed and nodded in acknowledgment, hiding her embarrassment behind a sip of wine. "Thank you. I'm glad you called me and very happy that I could help." She reached toward Christine and clasped her hand to affirm what she was saying. "It was my pleasure to work alongside the two of you."

Dinner was superb, and the conversation with Jean-Baptiste and Christine was enlightening and entertaining. Leslie learned they were originally stationed in the Congo, which had a long and tenuous history with Belgium. After a number of years and several locations later, they'd been asked to relocate to northern Kenya. "Our children were getting ready to go to university, and we liked the idea of living in a more accessible area. And this country is more stable," Christine explained.

"Tell me about your children," Leslie said. With that prompting, the couple entertained her with stories of raising their teenage children in both Belgium and Africa, and the time passed quickly.

As the dessert dishes were being removed and coffee was served, Leslie checked her watch.

"Marcus will be here shortly," she said. "Please excuse me for a few minutes." She left to make her way toward the ladies' room.

As she returned to the table, she had to pause near the door to the restaurant to allow a group to enter. Absently she noted that they were an unusually multicultural party. The four women gained her attention first. They appeared to be either European or American and wore lightweight silk or satin cocktail dresses, which were several inches north of knee-length. They all sported jewelry of impressive size but questionable authenticity, and wore considerable makeup and very high heels. Each of the women was attached to a businessman.

While waiting for the group to pass by, Leslie observed that the first three men to enter were Korean or Japanese. They were small and rather thin—older than the women—and all wore well-tailored business suits. The last man stood out, mostly because he was a head taller than his companions and outweighed any of the men by at least fifty pounds. He was also the only white male in the group. A bit more casually dressed than the other men, he wore a sport coat and no tie, and his ponytailed, brownish-blond hair contrasted sharply with the black hair of the other men. Although his back was to her, she immediately recognized Ben Murphy.

From her position behind the door, Leslie saw that Ben's arm was draped around an attractive blonde. As they walked through the entry, he was leaning slightly, apparently engrossed in something she was saying. Uncharitably, Leslie silently surmised that it was much more likely the woman's diamonds were real than her hair color.

As Leslie watched, Ben replied to the blonde. Idly, he brushed aside a strand of bleached hair before he straightened to study the entrance of the restaurant. Before she could look away, he caught her staring at him. For some inexplicable reason, she felt her heart beat faster and her face redden when Ben's gaze latched onto hers. Annoyed at her response, Leslie wasn't sure how to react to the unplanned encounter.

Ben was obviously with colleagues and on a date—if you could call it that—but Leslie had been raised to always acknowledge an acquaintance. She hesitated momentarily but, after a breath, took a step in his direction.

Ben's expression did not change. There was no hint of recognition and no acknowledgment of her presence. As she started to move in his direction, he deliberately turned his back to her. Leaning forward, he engaged the attention of the three other men, asking a question that Leslie was too far away to hear. At that point, the men and women seemed to group around him, cutting off any access.

Leslie realized she'd been snubbed. Seething, she strode back to the table where the DeMerodes were waiting.

She tried—she hoped successfully—to hide her consternation. She managed to carry on her part of the conversation but watched furtively as the maître d' seated Ben's party at a corner table. Although she had no way of being certain, it appeared that one of the Asian men was the host, and Ben seemed to be an important guest. From a distance Leslie thought that the men were in an earnest discussion with one another, and the women were left to their own conversations. She became more convinced by the moment that the women were hired, invited to join the men as decorations and after-dinner entertainment. And she was dismayed to find that for some reason she cared what Ben did with his own time.

She turned her attention back to her hosts and watched Jean-Baptiste sign the credit-card receipt. "Thank you once more for dinner," she said, trying to regain her earlier sincerity. It truly *had* been a wonderful evening. "It was lovely and much needed!"

Jean-Baptiste stood aside to allow Christine and Leslie to precede him as they exited the restaurant. "No, no!" he replied. "We want to thank you. Had you been unable to come…well, the outcome would have been different on many cases. We are grateful to have met a new colleague and friend." They paused at the juncture between the entry to the restaurant and the lobby of the hotel, and he shook her hand, his face solemn once more.

"Excusez-moi." A voice interrupted from the doorway. Ben stepped hastily forward with his hand extended. "Jean-Baptiste, it is my pleasure to see you again."

Jean-Baptiste allowed his surprise to show. He smiled and shook the offered hand. "Ben Murphy. It has been at least a year since we have seen you."

"Oui!" Ben replied, and turned to Christine. He took her hand, and she presented her cheeks, which he air-kissed three times. *"La belle Christine,"* he said with aplomb. A conversation ensued in rapid French, which Leslie

tried to follow. She understood the gist: Jean-Baptiste and Christine appeared to be explaining the measles epidemic and its resolution. She watched as Ben nodded his head—he appeared genuinely interested and sympathetic. There was a pause, and Jean-Baptiste said something and then gestured toward Leslie. The three turned toward her.

Still smarting from Ben's earlier snub, Leslie debated her response. Ben took the option from her when he held out his hand and said, "Yes, Mrs. Carpenter. It's nice to see you again. I understand that you've been helping the DeMerodes work through a difficult situation."

Leslie felt her face redden as she shook his hand. She quickly pulled her hand away and murmured, "I was glad that I was able to help." She looked into his eyes for only a second, then diverted her gaze to stare at his chin. She knew her response had been abrupt, so she added, "The people of Nyeri are fortunate that Christine and Jean-Baptiste were there for their children." Her smile felt awkward and forced.

"Do you two know each other?" Christine asked.

Ben did not wait for Leslie to reply. "Yes. I flew Mrs. Carpenter—er, Leslie—to Namanga when she first arrived, and a couple of times since then."

"Oh. I see. Of course, that makes sense. I recall that you know Mama Joe well." Christine sounded a little disappointed.

Another short discussion ensued in French before Ben took a short step back. "I fear that I must return to my colleagues." He kissed Christine's cheeks and shook Jean-Baptiste's hand again. "It was nice to see you, Leslie," he said. Although he didn't touch her, his gaze found hers and held it. This time, something deep and unreadable flickered in his eyes. He seemed to be about to say something else; instead he blinked, then gave a slight nod and reentered the restaurant.

As she watched the departing man, Christine chuckled and said something quietly to Jean-Baptiste. She leaned over to Leslie and whispered, "His colleagues." She grinned. "He seems to have a lot of friends with long hair."

Jean-Baptiste responded with an exaggerated nod. Christine jabbed a teasing elbow in his abdomen and giggled. "The only thing I think he is more concerned with than his 'friends' is his work." She turned her hand palm up and rubbed her thumb across her fingers in the universal sign for money. "He seems to be doing very well with it."

"How do you two know Ben?" inquired Leslie, trying not to sound overly interested.

Christine paused to consider, then answered, "Well, the American and European communities are really quite small in Kenya. Most everyone knows everyone else, or we know someone who does." She took Jean-Baptiste's hand and started toward the hotel's lobby. "Also, Ben is a very handy person to know. When we first moved here from the Congo two years ago, there was an outbreak similar to this one. Except then it was polio." She shuddered in recollection. "Ben was able to help us. He worked very hard to obtain vaccines, supplies and other aid."

"Yes," interjected Jean-Baptiste. "If Ben had not come to our assistance then, the results of the epidemic would have been much worse." He smiled at Leslie. "Many children would have died or been crippled had he not helped."

Leslie was eager to learn more, but they had arrived at the hotel's entrance. She waved when she saw Marcus parked nearby. Christine and Leslie hugged tearfully, and Jean-Baptiste took her hand and kissed her cheeks, thanking her once more. "Please call me again," she said in parting. "I'll be happy to come to work with you anytime."

"The sentiment is mutual," Jean-Baptiste replied. "Give Mama Joe our regards when she returns."

LESLIE HAD DIFFICULTY falling to sleep that night. She was comfortably settled in a lovely guest room at the East Africa Mission house, but her mind seemed to repeatedly return to the events of the evening rather than the hectic, trying and tiring days she'd spent fighting measles. She kept recalling the expression on Ben's face in that brief second before he'd turned his back. Was it her imagination, or was it a look of yearning? She chided herself, thinking that more likely it was regret or embarrassment. But as she reflected on what she'd seen in his eyes, it seemed as if he were reaching out to her—like he wanted something from her.

She tried to brush those thoughts aside and focus on the coming day and her trip back to Namanga. She was mostly successful and, after a few minutes, fatigue took over and she fell into an exhausted sleep.

CHAPTER SEVEN

ONE AFTERNOON, near the end of her third month in Namanga, Leslie heard a vehicle pull into the compound. The sound was unusual, given that almost all of their patients walked—or ran—to the clinic. From the exam room where she was completing a follow-up visit with a new mother, she heard a man's deep voice ask, "Where's Mrs. Carpenter?"

Elizabeth was in her customary spot at the desk, and Leslie could hear an exchange in Swahili, but the distance prohibited comprehension. She refocused her attention on her patient, but an urgent knock interrupted her. Without waiting for a response, Elizabeth opened the door and said, "Miss Leslie, please come."

Elizabeth's expression alarmed Leslie. Apologizing to the new mother, she hastily followed the clerk into the waiting area, but stopped abruptly when she saw Ben Murphy. She hadn't seen him since the encounter at the restaurant several weeks earlier and had forgotten how imposing he was. His eyes shone vividly in his deeply tanned face. She read impatience in his expression, along with something she had rarely observed in him—concern.

He closed the distance, obviously in a hurry, and grabbed her elbow to pull her toward the door. "You need to come with me. I have a client who may be having a heart attack." His words were terse.

She stopped and tried to pull away. "Wait just a second. I need—"

He refused to let go of her. "Maybe you don't understand," he interrupted. "You need to come *now*."

She yanked her arm again. "Let go. I have to get some things."

"Oh. Sorry." He finally released her and followed as she retreated into the storage room. "He's a tourist." His tone was more conciliatory. "Probably about sixty-five. Evidently he has some history of heart problems."

His description compelled Leslie to hurry. She quickly collected a blood-pressure cuff and an assortment of medications and supplies, then stuffed them into a large canvas tote bag that she slung over her shoulder. Grabbing the portable defibrillator, she thrust it at Ben. “Here. I may need this.”

As they neared the door, Ben inquired, “If he has to be evacuated to Nairobi, can you come?”

Leslie hastily considered the possibility, and, frowning, she nodded. She paused at the door to give instructions to Naomi and Elizabeth. “I’ll be back as soon as I can. If I haven’t returned by this evening, assume we’ve flown to Nairobi.”

Outside, she saw two men sitting in the back of Ben’s Jeep. They were similarly dressed in newish, pressed khaki shirts and slacks. The older man had thinning, iron-gray hair and appeared to be in his sixties as Ben had suggested. He was obviously ill, leaning heavily against the younger man. As she approached the Jeep at a rapid walk, the younger man’s eyes pinned her, and he barked, “Are you the doctor?”

Leslie barely glanced at him as she crawled into the back of the Jeep and wedged herself between the front and rear seats. “I’m a nurse-practitioner,” she answered absently, her attention on assessing the patient. She gently shook his shoulder. “Sir, can you open your eyes?”

The man complied and gave her a faint smile. His face was grayish in color, and he was sweating heavily. He looked to be about average height, but was at least thirty or forty pounds overweight. She rummaged through her canvas bag and pulled out the blood-pressure cuff and stethoscope. "How long have you been having chest pain?" she asked as she wrapped the cuff around the man's arm.

"A little last night." His voice seemed weak and his breathing shallow. "But it's bothered me quite a lot today."

She finished taking his blood pressure and then said to Ben, "Hand me that case." When he did, she opened it and removed two pads. "Sir, I'm going to check your heart rhythm," she explained as she started to unbutton the man's shirt.

"Wait a minute!" snapped the younger man. "We want a doctor, not a nurse!" He reached out and grabbed her wrist.

His tone and inflection struck Leslie as haughty and she bristled. Impatiently, she shook him off. "Well, I'm what you've got right now. If you'll help instead of getting in the way, perhaps we can get him to a doctor!"

Ben shouldered his way past the younger man and helped pull back the patient's shirt. He said, "Look, Justin, Mrs. Carpenter is the only health-care provider within a seventy-mile radius. She has a lot of experience. I assure you, she can handle it."

Both men watched as Leslie slapped one pad on the patient's chest and the other on his left side before connecting wires directly into an opening in the unit. She activated the combination electrocardiogram and automated defibrillator and watched the screen for about a minute. She looked up at Ben and said, "We need to go." Although her words were calm, her eyes communicated urgency.

Ben held her gaze briefly then nodded. Absurdly, she felt a wave of satisfaction at his declaration of confidence and quick response to her instructions. He actually meant what he'd said to the younger man and wasn't merely trying to placate him. Then she shook off the feeling—why did she care what Ben Murphy thought?

Ben jumped into the driver's seat, and the younger man moved to join him in the front. As they pulled out of the compound, Ben made belated introductions. "Leslie, this is Bill Cooper and his son, Justin. I picked them up earlier at Amboseli Preserve to fly to Kilimanjaro. But before we got to the airstrip, Bill complained of chest pain, and then he blacked out for a minute." He was pushing the Jeep as quickly as possible down the dusty, rough road. "Bill and Justin, this is Leslie Carpenter."

The older man opened his eyes, which were light brown and a little watery and red rimmed. "Nice to meet you, Leslie." His voice wavered somewhat, and Leslie glanced at the heart monitor again.

"Mr. Cooper, do you have a history of heart disease?"

"Yes. I had a heart attack about five years ago—"

"My father has had a couple of heart attacks." Justin interrupted his father, turning to face the occupants in the rear seat and watching Leslie's actions like a hawk. "He had an angioplasty two years ago by the best cardiologist in Seattle. He stopped smoking and has been fine since." His tone made it sound as if it was her fault that his father was having chest pain—and that she was little better than dust because she wasn't a doctor. She took a deep breath and worked hard at holding her temper, electing to ignore him.

"Justin, I can give my own history." Mr. Cooper waved his hand in the direction of his son, perhaps trying to calm him. "He's right. I had an angioplasty with a stent. They told me I didn't need surgery. Just stop smoking…lose weight…

exercise more." Despite his obvious discomfort, he managed a weak grin. "I stopped smoking."

Leslie couldn't help but like Bill Cooper. She patted his arm in a gesture of reassurance. "Have you taken any meds today?"

"Just my cholesterol pill." He seemed to be short of breath. "I didn't bring my nitro pills with me.... Stupid, I know...but I haven't had any problems in two years."

"Mr. Cooper, I can't tell if you're having a heart attack, but you're obviously having angina, and your heart rhythm indicates some premature contractions." Leslie took his blood pressure again and glanced at the monitor. "Are you allergic to any drugs?" He shook his head and closed his eyes. She rummaged in her bag and pulled out two small bottles. She handed him a tablet. "Here, chew this. It's aspirin." When he had finished chewing the pill, she handed him another. "Nitro. Under your tongue." He nodded and obeyed.

Ben made good time, and when they arrived at the airfield Bill Cooper's pulse had slowed to almost normal and his color had improved. Charles Endebbi met them at the hangar, and he and Ben began to prepare the Cessna.

Obviously impatient to be off, Justin Cooper left the confines of the Jeep to monitor the process, mostly staying out of the way. For the first time Leslie studied the younger man and noted that he was probably in his late thirties. He was of average height and solidly built, although not heavy like his father. He glanced anxiously back toward the Jeep. She climbed from the vehicle to try to reassure him. As she approached, Justin whipped around, and she got her first good look at him. His appearance was striking. His features were even and refined, and his dark hair, although thinning slightly, was nicely groomed.

"Mr. Cooper, your father should be fine," she said. "His heart rate and rhythm and blood pressure have stabilized, and you'll be in Nairobi in less than two hours. Ben can call ahead and have an ambulance meet you and drive him to a hospital."

Justin Cooper's light brown eyes flashed with intelligence and agitation. "You *are* coming with us, aren't you?" It was as much a command as a question. His stare was intense.

"I really don't think that will be necessary. As I said, his condition has stabilized." She frowned. "I'm needed here, and I couldn't get back tonight because the airfield isn't lighted—"

"I don't care! I'll pay you to come with us. I'll pay Murphy to fly you back tomorrow." His attitude was unrelenting, and Leslie got the impression that he was used to getting his way.

She straightened her shoulders. "Look, Mr. Cooper, it's not about getting paid. I don't work for money. If I thought your father needed me, I'd come. But I have responsibilities here." Plus, she thought, she would have to endure Ben's company, something she'd successfully avoided for the better part of a month. She blinked at that random thought—was that part of her hesitation?

"Ms…er…Leslie, my father is a very important man. Insuring his well-being should be your primary responsibility." As if to emphasize what he was saying, he placed both of his hands on her forearms and gave her a small shake.

Leslie didn't respond well to being bullied and was growing increasingly irritated. She took a deep breath in an attempt to control her temper. "I need to go assess him again. We'll talk more in a minute." She pulled away and hastily returned to the Jeep.

BEN FURTIVELY WATCHED the exchange between Leslie and Justin Cooper. Both Coopers, as he'd been informed several times during their brief acquaintance, were prominent lawyers from Seattle. Their clothing appeared costly, and both wore expensive watches that were inappropriate for the African bush. Either they hadn't read the guidebook warnings about the high rate of theft of such items, or they didn't care. He shrugged. Obviously they were wealthy enough to set their own agenda and hire charter pilots.

For some reason he did not pause to examine, he was annoyed to witness what appeared to be an intense discussion between Leslie and Justin. Objectively, he knew the lawyer was good-looking, in a smarmy, refined kind of way. But he had an unmistakable air of superiority that grated on Ben. As he started to turn away, he saw Cooper grasp Leslie's arms and hold her briefly. He was overcome by a wave of jealousy so powerful that he became light-headed. Without considering what he wanted to accomplish, he started toward them. He had taken a few steps in their direction when Leslie broke the contact and returned to the Jeep.

Ben stopped abruptly and rubbed his hands over his face. *What is wrong with you?* he chided himself. *Get your act together and get the man to Nairobi!* He managed to refocus his attention and, ignoring the others for the time being, he helped complete preparations.

At the Jeep, Leslie watched the heart monitor for a minute. The patient's heart rate was down, but there were still some worrying irregularities. "Mr. Cooper, how are you feeling now?" she asked as she took his blood pressure.

"The pain is definitely better, and I don't feel quite as nervous or nauseous."

She turned as she heard someone approach. She expected Justin Cooper, but it was Ben.

"How's he doing?"

"Better. His heart rate and blood pressure have improved, so he's stable enough to travel." She glanced from her patient to Ben, but when she saw the intensity in his green eyes, she blinked and looked away. "He definitely needs to get to a hospital as quickly as possible. Are you ready?"

"Yeah." He nodded, not taking his eyes from her face. "Let's go."

"Uh…Ben, I'm not sure that it's necessary for me…"

"You're kidding, right?" His voice was incredulous. "Get in the plane. I'll assist Mr. Cooper. You should ride in the rear seat with him."

He turned his back to her and leaned toward the patient.

"Wait just a minute!" She grabbed his arm and pulled him around. She dropped her voice. "Where am I going to stay? How will I get back?" She was startled to find that, standing this close, she was forced to lean back to meet his eyes. She did not recall his being that much taller than she was.

He looked down at her hand on his arm and sighed. "Look. There's a Hilton a couple of blocks from the hospital. You can stay there." His eyes rose to latch onto hers. "And don't worry. I'll bring you back first thing in the morning."

Between Ben and Justin, it appeared that arguing was futile. Although she was confident that Mr. Cooper would make the trip with no further problems, Leslie conceded that it would be good for her to accompany him anyway—just in case. Reluctantly, she nodded and climbed into the plane.

TWO HOURS LATER, Bill Cooper was loaded into an ambulance and driven to Nairobi's most modern hospital, the Aga Khan. Ben found a taxi, and the trio followed. At the hospital, Leslie accompanied her patient as he was evaluated by the staff, and soon he was whisked away to the coronary care unit, reportedly in stable condition.

Leslie shifted the large canvas bag from one shoulder to the other as she made her way back to the hospital lobby to find Ben. Her work was done and she suddenly realized that she was tired and very hungry. It was nearing dusk, and she had not eaten since breakfast. She hoped to persuade Ben to stop for dinner before going to the hotel.

"Leslie! Wait!" She turned to see Justin Cooper jogging toward her, skillfully dodging people in the crowded lobby.

"Dad and I didn't get a chance to thank you," he said as he halted beside her. He took her hand in both of his; his light brown eyes were now warm and friendly. "The doctor said that his blood enzymes are good and that the nitro and aspirin probably prevented something really serious. If he does okay tonight, we're going to fly to the States tomorrow or the next day." His tone was sincere.

Leslie smiled. "That's great news. I'm just glad I was able to help." There was an awkward pause, and she tried to remove her hand, but he didn't let go. "I'll try to stop by in the morning before we leave."

Justin's eyes raked over her with a new type of interest. This change in manner and the look in his eyes made her much more uncomfortable than his earlier arrogance had. "Say, why don't I try to say thanks properly?" he asked. "We haven't really had an opportunity to break the ice." He smiled, revealing perfect white teeth. "Since we're both stuck here for the night, how about a drink? And then we can talk about dinner."

"Uh, well…" His suggestion made her nervous. It sounded like a date and she hadn't dated since Brian's death. She looked down at her rumpled skirt and simple white blouse—her standard uniform for the clinic. "I don't have a change of clothes," she managed, fairly certain he wouldn't be deterred by the excuse. On reflection, though, maybe dinner with Justin would work out. She was hungry, and she only had about twenty dollars worth of Kenyan shillings in the bag.

Glancing toward the hospital's entrance, she spotted Ben and waved to him with her noncaptured hand. He approached and gave a brief nod to Justin. Leslie was confused by Ben's angry expression; she wasn't sure what was wrong, but he didn't look happy.

Justin, too, was caught off guard by the intense glower in Ben's green eyes. Feeling momentarily threatened, he dropped Leslie's hand and took a step backward.

Ben eyed them both before he concentrated on Justin. "How is Bill?" Despite his heated stare, his voice was mild.

Leslie glanced uneasily from one man to the other. Although Ben seemed reserved, she sensed an element of menace directed toward Justin. She tried to deflect the tension by answering. "He's going to be fine. Right now he's in the coronary care unit, but Justin just told me that they'll probably fly home either tomorrow or the day after."

Ben continued to watch the other man as he listened. Cooper nodded in agreement with her explanation but didn't comment.

Clearing her throat and wishing for enlightenment, Leslie turned to Ben and said, "Justin just mentioned going to get something to drink… and…well, maybe dinner." She looked back at Justin and added, "We all need to eat."

Justin recovered quickly. With a short laugh he responded, "Yeah, sure. Murphy, you probably helped save Dad's life. I guess I owe you dinner, too."

Probably? Leslie didn't really like Ben, but there was no doubt that his quick decision to commandeer her, coupled with his ability to get Mr. Cooper to Nairobi in a short period of time, had been more essential to saving the man's life than anything she had done. She blinked and glanced back at Ben, disconcerted to see that his attention was on her.

Desperate to break the awkwardness of the situation, she took a breath. "Uh, Ben, you mentioned a hotel nearby. Could you help me check in? I'd like to wash up a little. Then perhaps we can meet Justin in an hour or so."

"Yeah. Sure. Actually, I've already gotten us both rooms at the Hilton." Ben turned to their companion for a response.

Justin gestured toward the bank of elevators across the lobby. "That should work. I need to check on Dad first."

"The hotel is a couple of blocks south and one block east of here," Ben replied. "You can find it." He motioned to the door. "Let's go, Leslie."

Feeling as if she were being herded, Leslie gave Justin a friendly smile. "Then it's settled.

We'll see you in about an hour in the lobby at the Hilton."

"I look forward to it." Justin seemed to have tuned out Ben. His eyes skimmed over Leslie appreciatively, and his tone was more than a little flirtatious.

Ben took her elbow and all but dragged her through the hospital exit. Leslie had to practically jog to keep up with him as he pulled her down the brick steps, away from the large building and onto the sidewalk.

Finally, she slid to a stop. "Wait just a minute!" Making no attempt to hide her irritation, she tried to loosen her arm, but his grip did not slacken. Her canvas bag slipped off her shoulder, and she repositioned it.

He wheeled around to face her and huffed, "What now?" His tone was just as irritated.

Leslie took a few seconds to absorb the busy city avenue. The air was still warm outside, despite the darkening sky. The sidewalk was packed with people jostling about, and the street was crowded with cars, motorbikes and the ubiquitous *matatus*. Horns blared, signaling the displeasure of impatient drivers.

She returned her attention to Ben. "Lighten

up for a second, will you? Why did you pull me out the door like that?"

"Leslie, he's married!" Ben squeezed her arm and glared at her.

She shook her head and gaped at him in confusion. *"What?"*

"Cooper is *married!*" Ben was practically shouting.

Leslie simply blinked. "Oh… Well, okay… So what?"

"*So what?* He was coming on to you!" Ben finally let go of her but continued to glare.

"No, he wasn't!" she snapped back. "And even if he was, it's none of your business!" Absently, she rubbed her arm. "And besides, how do you know he's married?"

"He was wearing a ring earlier. He probably took it off for your benefit!" Ben gestured toward her in an aggravated manner; his tone had quieted only slightly.

Leslie glanced around and saw that they were attracting attention. She sighed and tried to calm them both. Softening her voice, she held up a hand in a motion of peace. "Ben, I don't care. It doesn't matter, except that I feel sorry for his wife. I just want to eat something and then go to bed." She shrugged and added tiredly, "Look,

I'll never see him again… And besides, *you're* coming with us."

Ben closed his eyes for a second and took a deep breath. "You're right. Sorry. I guess I was bothered that you might fall for his line."

"You've *got* to be kidding!" Her exasperation welled up again. "I've seen *you* in action, Mr. I'll-take-two-Frenchwomen-here-and-a-bleached-blonde-there! And *you're* warning *me* about some guy I have absolutely no interest in?" She huffed her annoyance and barely avoided rolling her eyes. She could not believe his hypocrisy. How dare he suggest that she might fall for some sleaze or be interested in a married man?

Ben rubbed his eyes with one hand and sighed. "Oh, hell." His frustration evaporated. "Thanks for pointing out the irony." Suddenly, and unexpectedly, he grinned. "You know, I could eat, too. And since Cooper is paying, steak sounds good."

The grin caught Leslie off guard. It was genuine, and it changed his face—in a way she liked. He wasn't classically handsome like Justin, but he was extremely attractive. His green eyes glittered with mirth, and his expression was boyish. She was charmed despite her own misgivings.

With a slight nod, she laughed as she commented, “As long as it’s not eland or Cape buffalo, that sounds like a plan. Lead the way.” She followed as he started up the street.

CHAPTER EIGHT

THE PAIR HAD COVERED about two blocks when Leslie fell a few steps behind Ben. The variety of people on the street fascinated her, and she slowed her pace to take in the sights, sounds and smells. Besides, Ben's stride was long, and she was too tired to scamper along beside him. A number of vendors displayed all kinds of foods; some she recognized, some she didn't, and some she regretted that she did. Did they *really* eat monkey? Other vendors showed clothing and sandals, one was selling small appliances, and several were hawking cigarettes.

She was captivated by the schoolchildren in their colorful uniforms. Sometimes they tagged along behind parents, but many were in the custody of older siblings. She stopped and watched three small boys being herded by what appeared to be a bossy older sister. She was holding the hands of the two younger boys and trying to keep the oldest moving forward—not entirely successfully, as she had to repeatedly call to him to follow.

Smiling, Leslie looked up and realized that Ben was nearly half a block ahead of her. She had taken a couple of quick steps in his direction, intending to catch up, when suddenly she was struck hard from behind; the blow knocked her to her knees. A rough hand to her back shoved her farther down onto the dirty sidewalk, and her canvas bag was yanked from her shoulder.

Stunned, she pushed up on her hands and knees just in time to see a skinny man running back toward the hospital clutching her bag. "Stop him!" Her first cry barely reached a few yards, but she jumped to her feet and started after the man, furious. Her second shout was much more effective. "Stop him! Stop that man! He has my bag!"

She had taken only a few steps and was preparing to shout again when she was grabbed from behind, immobilized by two strong arms. A hand clamped over her mouth, and a voice growled in her ear, "No! Shut up!"

Abruptly, anger transformed into terror, and she frantically tried to break away from the powerful grasp.

"Stop it! Be still! It's me!" Ben's voice was insistent, spoken directly into her ear.

She stopped struggling and jerked her head, trying to convey that she understood. He released her and she whirled to face him. Her anger returned, and she pointed in the direction of the hospital. "He stole my bag!"

Since she had been looking at Ben rather than watching the thief's progress, she missed what happened next. She heard loud yelling, followed by running feet, then the sounds of muffled groans and thuds. She turned toward the noise.

"Damn it! Wait!" A low string of oaths came from Ben as he pulled her roughly back, trying desperately to turn her away from the melee. But he was too late—she had seen the mob and what they were doing. And despite Ben's efforts to shield her, she could hear the noises coming from about a hundred feet away.

A crowd of at least twenty men and women had descended on the thief. He was down on the ground, and they were taking turns kicking and punching him. In that brief glimpse, she saw that his eyes were closed and he was bleeding profusely from his mouth and nose.

Frantically, she tried to pull away from Ben. "No! Ben, no! We have to stop them!"

His face was implacable as he held her tightly, struggling to keep her eyes averted. "Honey, we can't," he whispered in her ear. "There's nothing we can do now."

Leslie started sobbing and managed to turn her head toward the mob, which had grown even larger and more vocal. As she watched, a young boy, probably about ten or eleven years of age, appeared to rise from their midst. Incredibly, he was carrying her canvas bag. Leslie ceased struggling, but she was still sobbing when the boy reached them. Grinning, he proudly presented the bag to Leslie, and she robotically took it from him. Ben let go of her long enough to reach into his pocket to grasp a handful of shillings. He did not stop to count them, but simply thrust the money at the boy before he grabbed Leslie's arm to drag her away from the ugly confrontation.

Stunned, Leslie clasped the bag to her chest and continued to cry as she allowed Ben to pull her down a side street. The noise of the beating had attracted considerable attention, and a large group of people had gathered around to watch or participate. Fortunately, the gawkers ignored Ben and Leslie, and they moved unhindered away from the throng.

BEN WANTED TO put as much distance between themselves and what had transpired as quickly as possible. Walking rapidly, they covered several blocks, turning a couple of times to move in different directions. The streets became considerably less crowded, and they could no longer hear the sounds of the beating. Finally, he stopped and turned to Leslie.

"Oh, dear God!" His whispered response was panicked. She was covered in blood. The canvas bag was wet with thick streaks and large splotches, which evidently had come from the thief's wounds. Leslie clutched the bag to her chest and, as a result, some of the blood had rubbed off on her hands and bare lower arms and permeated her blouse. One of her cheeks was smeared. She was no longer crying, but her eyes were oddly vacant. Ben could recognize the signs of shock.

Blood. In most circumstances, a little blood was no big deal. It was certainly not a big deal to Ben, who'd been exposed to various injuries and even death on many occasions. And blood would not bother Leslie, whose passion and livelihood involved dealing with the substance on an almost daily basis. But Ben had lived in Kenya for years and knew that blood could bring death. AIDS was pervasive, and exposure to even just a drop of contaminated blood on an open wound could infect. Ben also knew that a significant percentage of Kenyans had the virus.

Ben had observed both Mama Joe and Leslie enough to know that they were extremely cautious about avoiding direct contact with body fluids, always wearing gloves, aprons or gowns, and sometimes even masks, to protect themselves. He had taken precautions himself whenever he anticipated being exposed. Anything less would be stupid. But Leslie wasn't in any shape to think through all that right now—he doubted she even realized there was a problem.

Hastily, he scouted the area. They were near an outdoor café that was rather quiet, with only a few patrons this early in the evening. Keeping hold of Leslie's arm, Ben drew her to a cloth-covered table that appeared to have been recently vacated. On it was a half-empty glass of soda and a nearly full glass of water, sitting next to a couple of used plates and coffee cups. Swiftly, trying to avoid attracting attention, Ben moved the dirty dishes onto a chair. He stripped off the tablecloth and held it toward Leslie, who was staring blankly in his direction.

"Honey, drop the bag onto the cloth." He was grateful that she did not question him or argue, but merely obeyed. He wrapped the cloth around the bloody bag and set it on the table before reassessing Leslie. "Hold out your hands," he commanded. When she complied, he poured the remains of the soda on her hands and forearms; this was followed by most of the water. He wet a napkin and gently washed the smear off her face. Her blouse needed to come off, but there were too many people around, and he had nothing to replace it with.

He grabbed the cloth holding the canvas bag in one hand and Leslie's damp hand in the other and pulled her in the direction of the Hilton. Their circuitous route from the mob beating had not taken them far out of their way, and they reached the hotel in only a few minutes.

Hugely relieved he'd reserved rooms earlier, Ben steered Leslie straight to the elevators. Fortunately they were alone in the car, and he pushed the button for their floor. He took those seconds to assess her again and was alarmed by her white face and blank expression. He realized that she had not said anything since witnessing the brutal beating.

They exited the elevator, and he quickly led her down the corridor to the room where he'd stored his backpack a short time earlier. He opened the door and ushered her into the room before he closed and locked it.

Just inside the room, he dropped the tablecloth containing the bag and grasped Leslie by her shoulders. "Honey, we need to get you undressed," he cajoled. She shook her head, apparently not understanding, so he tried again. "Leslie, there's blood on your shirt. You need to take it off and go have a hot shower." He reached up and started to unbutton the buttons, but realized he would have to deal with the blood. To avoid further contamination and speed the process, he simply yanked the tail out of the waistband of her skirt, and without an explanation, ripped the ends apart, rending all the buttons off at once. Her chest was fully exposed, covered only by her bra, which also bore splotches of blood where the fluid had seeped through.

The ripping of her blouse jerked Leslie from her stupor. She gasped loudly and pulled away from him, urgently trying to pull the garment back together. "What are you doing?" Her voice cracked, and alarm was evident in her expression.

Ben stilled her hands and managed to keep his voice calm and insistent. “Leslie, your blouse and bra are covered with blood. You’re risking exposure to HIV. You need to take them off and go have a hot shower.” His eyes held hers, and he was relieved that she seemed more alert.

“Okay.” She looked down at her tattered, bloodstained blouse and nodded. Her words were quiet and flat. “Yes, okay.” She turned her back to him and slipped off the blouse, and it fell to the floor between them. “The bathroom… Where’s the bathroom?” Her voice was devoid of inflection and her movements were erratic.

Ben’s mouth went dry as he stared at her nearly bare back. After catching his breath, he pushed past her, leading the way into the bathroom, trusting that she would follow. There he turned on the shower full blast and adjusted the hot water as high as he could stand it. Pulling a large towel from the adjacent rack, he turned back to face her and saw that she had followed as he hoped. But he was dumbfounded to find that she had blindly complied with his instructions and removed the bra.

He tried—he really tried—to keep his eyes on her face, but he didn't quite succeed. His breath caught. He could feel his face darken, and sweat beaded on his forehead. Seconds passed before he thrust the towel at her and walked quickly out of the room. "Use a lot of soap and shampoo. I'll find something for you to wear," he said as he practically slammed the door.

He waited outside the bathroom door until he heard her get into the shower. His hands were shaking as he silently berated himself. *Get a grip! She's not for you!* He knew he had to get his responses to her under control.

After he'd assured himself that she was okay and his heart rate had slowed a bit, he grabbed his backpack from the closet and rummaged through it, trying to find something she could wear. The best he could do was a pair of worn gym shorts and a clean cotton shirt. He left them on the bed and went to scrounge through the contents of the minibar, all the while listening to the sounds in the bathroom. He pulled out a beer, a Coke and a couple of candy bars.

He heard the shower cut off. Returning to the bathroom door, he snagged the shirt and shorts. He knocked lightly. "Leslie, I have some clothes that you can wear for now."

She cracked the door just wide enough to reach through and take the items from him. "Thank you." Her voice was barely audible.

A few minutes passed with Ben staring at the closed door. His mood was foul, and he was halfway through the beer when she emerged. The tails of his shirt fell nearly to her knees, and it was buttoned almost to the top; the sleeves were rolled up to her elbows. Her hair was wrapped in a towel, and she was holding the shorts with one hand. He took another swallow of the beer.

"Um, I'm sorry to bother you," she said. Her voice was still small and flat. "But I need a pin or staple or something to hold up the shorts." Ben set down the beer bottle with a thud and leaned over to dig through the backpack. Amazingly, he was able to produce a safety pin.

Leslie turned her back to secure the shorts. When she accomplished that small feat, she faced him and quietly asked, "Do you have a brush or comb?"

More time in the backpack produced a small brush, which Ben handed to her. "Thank you," she whispered, then returned to the bathroom. A short time later he heard the sound of the hair dryer. That struck him as a positive sign—she could manage something routine like grooming. He sighed with relief.

When the hair dryer turned off, he knocked on the door. “Leslie, come have a Coke and candy bar. Or if you want, I’ll call down for room service.” When she didn’t answer, he knocked more loudly. “Leslie!” There was no response, and he roared, “Leslie, I’m coming in!”

Fortunately, she had not locked the door, so he was able to enter without the added drama of breaking it down. But he was alarmed anew to see her staring at the mirror, her expression stark, tears streaming down her cheeks. “Oh, baby,” he mumbled. He drew her into the bedroom and gently pushed her to sit on the bed. Handing her a glass half-filled with Coke, he said, “Drink this.” Obediently, she took a sip while staring at the carpet.

His gaze followed hers and then moved across the room to where he had dropped her bag—the source of her extreme consternation. Quickly, he pulled the bag, tablecloth and all, onto the room’s small desk. Carefully avoiding touching any of the contaminated spots, he opened the bag and rifled through its contents, sorting through bottles of medications. He recognized the names on about half of the bottles and finally found one that would work—*Diazepam, five mg.* He opened the bottle and took out a tablet, glanced at Leslie and took out another. She had drunk about half of the Coke, and he held up the candy bar. "Would you eat a Snickers?" She shook her head. "Okay. Here," he said, holding out the medication. "Honey, they're Valium. I got them from your bag. They'll help you rest."

In slow motion, she took the tablets from him and swallowed them with a sip of the Coke. Finally, she looked directly at him; her eyes were tear swollen and bleak. "Ben, I don't know what happened.… I didn't mean for him… I didn't know…"

Fearing that she would start crying again, he sat beside her and gathered her into his arms, comforting her with his embrace. "I know, honey. I know. You didn't have any idea… I'm sorry I couldn't stop it for you." He cradled her head against his shoulder and rocked her back and forth for a long while. Finally, he smoothed back her hair and studied her. She had a bit more color, and her eyelids were starting to droop.

Ben pulled back the bedcovers and tenderly guided her down. He covered her with the sheet and blanket, saying, “Rest for now. We’ll talk about it in the morning.”

“Okay,” she whispered, and went to sleep.

CHAPTER NINE

BEN HAD FALLEN FAST, and he had fallen hard. He knew it was happening, and he had done nothing to stop it. Indeed, he did not want to stop it.

He sat beside the bed for a time just watching her sleep. He knew what he felt for her was not merely interest or infatuation. It was love. He admitted it, accepted it. He loved the way she looked, the way she talked and the way she cared for her patients. He loved the way she had felt in his arms and the way she smiled at him on rare occasions. She was smart, brave, caring, funny, fragile and precious. How could he not love her? It was so simple.

It was so extremely complicated. He scrubbed his face with his hands and sighed.

After making sure she was deeply asleep, he slipped out of the room to take care of several pressing issues. Because her blouse was ruined, he went directly to the hotel's boutique and selected a replacement. He didn't even glance at the price, just forked over cash when the saleslady gave him the total. That process was uncomfortable enough, so he was not about to buy a bra. But hers could not be worn in its current state, so he jogged a block from the hotel to a small store to buy bleach and detergent. On the way back, he bargained with a street vendor for a large nylon backpack to replace the contaminated canvas bag, then stuffed his other purchases into it.

Ben's final stop was the hotel bar. He was impatient to get back in case Leslie woke, so he was relieved to see that Justin Cooper had already secured a table near the door. The lawyer had obviously showered and changed and was sipping a cocktail.

Cooper remained seated when Ben approached him, so Ben pulled out the opposite chair and sat down without being invited, placing the recently procured backpack on the floor.

"Hello, Murphy. I wasn't sure you were coming." The men shook hands briefly. Justin's eyes conveyed annoyance, although his tone was cordial.

"Yeah, well…I need to let you know that the plans have changed." Ben leaned back in his chair. "Leslie won't be able to make it tonight.

She's not feeling well and decided to order room service."

"That's odd. She seemed okay an hour ago," Justin countered. Irritation and disbelief were apparent in his expression. He dropped his negligent pose and sat up straighter. His plans for the evening had been changed, and obviously he did not like it. "What room is she in? I'll go check on her." Pulling his wallet from his coat pocket, he gestured to the waitress.

"That won't be necessary," Ben replied. "I'll take care of her." He reached for the backpack and stood. "I trust that Bill will be able to leave tomorrow. Give him my best." With that, he effectively dismissed the other man and started toward the lobby.

Justin Cooper was rich and handsome. He was also an aggressive and successful attorney, and he rarely lost at anything. With his father in the hospital, he'd been planning to encourage Leslie to accompany him to his room after dinner. He was reluctant to give up easily.

Angered by losing control of the situation, Cooper paused for a few seconds then threw some shillings on the table and followed. They had covered about half the distance to the elevators when he called, “Hey! Murphy! Wait a minute!”

Ben stopped and turned. “What?” His face remained expressionless, although impatience was evident in the single word.

“Look, Ben,” he said. “Leslie is here because of me and my father. I promised her dinner, so I need to see about her. Where is she?”

Ben’s words were measured and authoritative. “Like I said…she’s not feeling well and has gone to bed. I’ll tell her that you were concerned. I’m sure she’ll want to check on Bill in the morning. Good night.” With a nod, he started toward the elevators again.

In a display of bad judgment, Justin persisted. “Hey. I’m not finished.” He placed a hand on Ben’s shoulder to stop him. He regretted his action immediately, however, when Ben swung around and faced him.

“What now?” Ben’s words were spoken quietly but with an undertone that was chilling.

Feeling the tension in the hard muscle, Cooper quickly dropped his hand and took a step backward as he stared into green eyes that were cold and flat. His experience and intuition finally recognized the warning conveyed in Ben’s expression. He perceived power and danger in the other man and understood that at that moment Ben represented a considerable threat.

Justin put both hands in his pockets, unconsciously signaling surrender. "Uh, tell her thanks again." He took another step backward. "And tell her I hope she feels better tomorrow." Without waiting for a response, he quickly headed back toward the bar, leaving Ben to watch his retreat in silence.

RETURNING TO THE room, Ben was relieved to find Leslie still sleeping soundly. Dining on two candy bars and a soda, he watched her with longing. He had no illusions that she returned his feelings. The man he had become would hold no appeal for a woman like her. He knew he was attractive to other women—women who wanted irreverent men, women who were captivated by danger and intrigue. But to him, their appeal was virtually nonexistent.

He knew the type of man who would attract her. Someone like her dead husband—solid, smart, temperate, devoted, and, he silently scoffed, gainfully employed.

He reached out and touched her cheek very lightly, not wanting to disturb her. He let his fingers wander to her hair and found that it was still damp. He stroked the dark waves before letting his hand drop to his side. He wanted to kiss her, but he did not dare—both for his sake and for hers. Instead, he slipped off his boots and shirt and lay down on the bed, remaining on top of the bedclothes, careful not to touch her again. He knew he had several hours before the medication wore off, and he needed to sleep, too. He could rest, content with the knowledge that she was here and she was safe.

Tomorrow he would take her back to Namanga, and then the worry for her would return. He was well acquainted with the dangers she faced. She could be preyed on by bandits and mercenaries. The savanna was rife with wild animals and snakes, and disease was everywhere. Even driving the pothole-infested streets posed a threat to her. But for now she was safe.

He went to sleep thinking of her beautiful eyes.

LESLIE OPENED HER eyes and experienced a moment of panic. She was lying on a bed in a hotel room covered by a lightweight blanket. Her thoughts cleared a little, and she recalled the shower and Ben giving her clothes and a brush. Then she turned her head and saw him lying on his side facing her, apparently sleeping. Hastily, she inspected her body with her hands and discovered that she was wearing his overly large shirt and gym shorts. Thankfully, he was still wearing his pants, and he was on the other side of the blanket.

She shifted her position only slightly, but Ben's eyes flew open and captured hers. His stare was alert, and he sat up. "Are you all right?" His voice was low, without a hint of grogginess.

She nodded. Hesitantly, she said, "Yes. I'm okay." She was surprised by the concern he displayed—she had expected him to be irritated or even angry.

He studied her a moment and, apparently reassured, he turned away and rose from the bed. He reached for the shirt he had draped over a chair. She was still dazed, but for some reason she was fascinated by the movement of the thick muscles in his shoulders, back and arms as he slipped on the shirt and started to button it. When that was accomplished, he turned to face her. His eyes were now wary, and he seemed uncomfortable. "I…uh… After you went to sleep last night, I went downstairs and got a few things." He gestured toward the closet.

Leslie sat up and looked around the room. A sudden wave of dizziness assaulted her, and she had to brace herself to keep from falling over. His expression transformed from wary to alarmed, and in two steps he was by the bed.

"You said you were okay," he growled with exasperation.

"I'm just a little light-headed." She blinked and gradually her head stopped spinning. "It's just that…" She rubbed her temples. "I'm so fuzzy."

"That's probably because you haven't eaten anything in at least twenty-four hours," he answered. "I'll order room service. What do you want? Pancakes? Eggs?" The words were abrupt, and his eyes did not leave her face.

Suddenly, in a tidal wave of memories, Leslie recalled last evening's events—being pushed to the ground and her bag being ripped away… screaming for the man to stop…the crowd yelling and hitting him…the bloody face. She was assailed with regret and shame. *The poor man! Was he badly injured? Did he… What if he died?* Shc swallowed hard and tried to blink back threatening tears. And then there was Ben… She looked up and saw that he was scowling at her.

"Leslie?" He gripped her upper arm to steady her. Anger, frustration, apprehension and something unidentifiable warred in his voice.

She remembered him washing her hands with soda and then practically carrying her to the room. Then he'd made her bathe before putting her to bed. Her blouse? Her bra? Dimly she recalled taking off her clothes to avoid the blood. She blushed and looked quickly away, studying her own hands resting on the rumpled sheet. What did Ben think of her now? And on top of everything else, he'd been compelled to stay with her. Obviously, he was annoyed at having to play nursemaid after she'd fallen apart last night. She didn't blame him; there must be a dozen places he would rather have been.

She sighed and, glancing up, she whispered, "Ben, I am so sorry…" Her voice broke. Tears flowed freely, and she brushed them away. "I know that I'm being a huge burden… I haven't thanked you…." She lifted her hand to cover his much larger one, which was now digging into her arm. His hand was warm and rough, and she touched it softly, trying to express gratitude.

His jaw clenched, and he snarled, "Look, don't mention it." He pulled away and strode back toward the desk. "What do you want for breakfast?"

Mortified by her own virtual collapse and confused by Ben's abrupt change in mood, she stared at his back. As if from a distance, she noted that his heavy, gold-streaked hair was still confined by a band and rested a few inches below the base of his neck. Oddly, she wanted to touch it. Her answer was very quiet. "Ben, I'm really not hun—"

He whirled back to face her. "You're going to eat breakfast if I have to shovel it in myself." His green eyes glared. When she flinched in response to his abrasive tone, he scrubbed his face with his hands and sighed. His voice quieted when he said, "Leslie, you've suffered a serious shock. You're weak, and you haven't eaten in at least a day." Accurately reading her continued reluctance, he tried a different tactic. "Look, we're not leaving until I'm convinced that you're not in danger of passing out."

Leslie was desperate to leave the hotel room and the company of the man who obviously wanted to be rid of her. She wiped at the tears again and squared her shoulders. "You're right. I'm sure that I need to eat something. Pancakes will help with my blood sugar…and maybe coffee will help clear my head."

She pushed back the bedclothes and slid over to the side of the mattress. As she did, the large shirt was pushed aside to reveal her legs; her hip was barely concealed by the equally large gym shorts. Ben swore under his breath and looked away to pick up the telephone.

Leslie paused for a few seconds to allow the room to steady before proceeding to the bathroom. Her hesitation brought his attention back to her, but she missed seeing the longing in his eyes as he watched her retreating form.

"Wait just a second," he called. When she turned and glanced at him, he gestured with his free hand. "In the closet… I got you a shirt last night. Yours isn't wearable." He punched the button for room service and added, "Also, I… um…bleached your bra…to make sure to get out the blood. Ah yes, room service…" He switched to Swahili and turned away to study the menu.

Leslie slid into the bathroom after retrieving her skirt and a bag marked with the hotel's logo from the closet. She found her bra draped over the top of the shower's glass door. She reached for it and discovered that it was pristine white and nearly dry. She shook her head and sighed in bemusement. For the life of her, she could not picture Ben Murphy washing out her underwear.

BEN SPENT THE next fifteen minutes trying to recover even a modicum of control over his responses to Leslie. He had awoken to her wide-eyed, confused stare. The humidity had caused her hair to wave in striking disarray, curling around her lovely face, and his reaction was immediate.

It had been necessary to leave the bed in haste to put as much distance as possible between them. When she sat up, she'd paled, and he was concerned that she would faint. He rushed to catch her, but touching her had been another mistake. He was furious. He couldn't look at her, couldn't touch her, could barely even talk to her without wanting to hold her in his arms and kiss her. As she changed in the other room, his heart was thudding, and he was sweating. If he could have viewed the situation objectively, he would have thought it comical. On almost a daily basis, he dealt with all types of sordid men—gangsters, thugs, murderers and terrorists—coolly and with confidence. But suddenly he found himself having a panic attack because of a pale, slender woman with big blue eyes.

He had shouted at her. He knew that she thought he was angry with her, and in a way he was. Indeed, her actions had landed them in this situation. And he recognized that it was imperative he get out of here—soon, before he did something *really* stupid like groveling at her feet and pouring out his feelings.

With considerable effort, he managed to calm himself enough to order breakfast.

BREAKFAST HAD JUST arrived when Leslie exited the bathroom. She was much more alert following her hot shower. She'd used Ben's brush to comb out her hair, but she had neither a band nor a clip, so it was necessary to wear it down. Along with shampoos and soaps, the hotel supplied packaged toothbrushes, so she was able to perform that little task. With grooming complete, having exchanged Ben's clothing for the new pink blouse and yesterday's knee-length skirt, she felt better equipped to deal with Ben.

He was standing near the window sipping coffee and watching her approach. She sensed that his anger had subsided. Perhaps the coffee had helped his mood.

Sporadic silence characterized their breakfast, as conversation was limited to essentials related to the meal. Leslie managed to eat about half her pancakes and drink a glass of orange juice. Feeling considerably stronger, she emptied the last of the coffee from the carafe into their cups. "Ben, if you don't mind, I kind of want to talk about…yesterday." She glanced up from the cup to catch his gaze. "Could you explain, um… What happened with that man?"

Ben finished the last of his omelet and leaned back. He was calmer and more in control now. He sighed and took a sip of coffee before he answered. "Beatings of that sort happen pretty much on a daily basis here. Kenyans, particularly those in the cities, deplore thievery—it's much too common. Plus, they don't really trust the police or court systems, so they're willing to take matters into their own hands." He toyed with a spoon, twirling it nervously between his fingers. "I'm not sure how accurate the tales are, but I've heard that at least one person is killed each day in situations like what happened yesterday. I saw something similar once before when a woman's purse was snatched. She started screaming, and the guy was surrounded by a mob in seconds."

Leslie waited, but he didn't continue. Her voice was quiet. "What happened that time?"

"Leslie, I don't think..." He placed the spoon on the table and frowned.

"What *happened?*"

He stared at his coffee and sighed. "The crowd dispersed quickly. The man was obviously dead. There was nothing anyone could do then, and nothing that could have stopped the people yesterday." His eyes were full of compassion. "I'm sorry you witnessed it."

"Ben, I didn't witness it, I *caused* it." Distress marred her words, and tears threatened again.

"No!" He spoke the word so adamantly that he nearly spilled his coffee. "No!" he repeated. He pushed his coffee out of the way and grasped her hands. "Stop thinking that! You didn't cause it. You just reacted to the man stealing your bag. The man...the crowd caused it. They were responsible. Not you."

His gaze moved from her eyes to their joined hands. "Look, if either of us is to blame, it's me. Leslie, I should have stayed closer to you. You dropped back to watch the kids... If I hadn't walked ahead of you, the man most likely wouldn't have grabbed your bag." He reached up and wiped a tear from her cheek. "Don't blame yourself," he added quietly.

Ben's tenderness and touch made Leslie nervous again. She pulled away and spent a minute tidying the room-service cart to avoid looking at him. Finally, he reached out and stilled her. "Leave that for now. We need to talk about something else."

She sat back and looked at him squarely. His expression was wary. "Okay. What is it?"

"Leslie, you got quite a lot of blood on your hands and face and shirt from the bag. The soda and water at the restaurant removed most of it, I think." His concern was evident. "But...Leslie, you know there's a possibility you might have been exposed to HIV. Guys like that—guys from the street—many of them are positive." Leslie watched as his worry became more apparent, and she rushed to dispel his apprehension.

"Ben. It's probably fine. What you did really minimized the exposure. Plus, I don't have any scrapes or cuts, and I don't think I got any in my eyes." She continued, "Regardless, Mama Joe keeps AIDS medications at the clinic, along with protocols on postexposure prophylaxis. I'll read them over and maybe even call someone back in Dallas to see if I need to do anything." She gave him a brief smile—of reassurance, she hoped. "You know, just in case."

He nodded but did not smile back. "Okay. That sounds like a good idea." He rose. "We need to be going."

She followed his example but reached out to touch his arm. "Ben, thank you again for…well, for everything. And I'm truly sorry for messing up your evening."

He whirled back to face her squarely. "Damn it! Would you *please* stop apologizing!" He took a deep breath when she stepped back in retreat. "Look, you didn't mess up anything." He rubbed his eyes and sighed deeply. There was nowhere he would rather have been last night than here with her.

"Leslie, it's okay. I should be the one to apologize." Holding her gaze with his, he touched her hand lightly in an uncharacteristically gentle gesture before turning away. "It's getting late," he added as he started to stuff items into his backpack. "We need to think about heading home."

Suddenly, she slapped her hand over her mouth and exclaimed, *"Oh no!"* Her eyes were huge. “Justin! I totally forgot about meeting Justin last night!”

Ben’s irritation evaporated. “Don’t worry.” He clenched his jaw to keep from grinning as he answered, “I took care of Cooper.”

CHAPTER TEN

IT WAS EARLY evening on a Wednesday in late April. The brief rainy season was waning, and Ben was grateful for a dry field when he landed the Cessna at Namanga. He'd been gone for nearly three weeks, traveling over the lowlands of Eastern Africa, meeting with various collections of greedy, selfish and often evil men. It was a relief to be home for a few days, where he could relax his vigilance. He'd radioed Simon earlier in the day, and the tall Masai was waiting patiently in the shade of the large metal shed. The Jeep was parked nearby.

Simon jogged forward as Ben taxied to a halt. Together, they unloaded two medium-size boxes and a large ice chest from the plane's cargo hold and placed them in the Jeep. Charles Endebbi's teenage son joined the men to help refuel and clean the plane before pushing it into the shed.

Ben needed to make a stop on his way home. The boxes, he explained to Simon, contained books and supplies Judy Merdian had ordered for the kids' schooling, and he knew she was anxious to get them. Because the Merdians lived near the center of town, Simon rode with Ben only a few miles before exiting the Jeep at a dirt path that snaked off into the savanna. It was difficult for the Jeep to traverse the area, and Simon and Ben both knew that with his loping run, Simon could cover the five miles to his home in about half an hour.

Johnny and Beth were playing on a tire swing in the yard when Ben's Jeep pulled up. Their smiles were wide as they ran to meet the visitor.

Johnny yelled toward the house, "Mom! Mom! Uncle Ben's here!" Together the children hugged the pilot when he squatted down to meet them.

"Did you bring us a sussie, Uncle Ben?" Beth asked excitedly. Her light brown hair had been pulled back into two no-longer-neat pigtails.

Ben laughed, and in a single motion he stood up and swung the little girl into his arms. "As a matter of fact, I did bring you something. I'll bet you can't guess what it is!"

"Is it something to play with?" Johnny questioned, tugging on Ben's shirt.

"Nope. You wouldn't want to play with it."

"Is it something to wear?" Johnny asked with a concerned expression.

"Nope. Nothing to wear." Ben grinned. "I'll give you a hint. It's something to eat!"

Judy had come out of the house and witnessed the exchange. Beth wiggled out of Ben's arms and ran to her mother. "Mommy, Uncle Ben brought us a sussie."

Judy smiled at the tired-looking man and gestured for him to come up to the house. "Ben, it's good to have you back. We've missed you."

"Boy, it's good to be home, Judy. This trip was grueling. I'm anxious to get to the house to rest, but I wanted to drop these by first." He walked back to the Jeep and lifted one of the boxes.

"Wonderful! Our new schoolbooks!" exclaimed Judy. She hurried forward to open the door.

Ben heard Johnny groan as he maneuvered through the door. "Oh, man. That's just books and school stuff." After Ben had carried in the second box, he turned to grin at the disappointed eight-year-old. "Hey, just a minute, dude. The surprise isn't books. Remember, I brought you something special to eat!" Returning to the vehicle, he reached into the large cooler. He pushed back what remained of the ice on top and pulled out two half-gallon cartons of ice cream. He turned to the two children, who were waiting anxiously only a step away, and handed them each a carton. Their eyes were huge.

"Wow! Ice cream! This is great!" Johnny cried loudly. "Mom, can we have some now?"

"Mommy, pleeease," whined Beth.

Judy looked at Ben and winked. "Kids, it's almost time for dinner…."

"Please, just a little?"

Judy sighed deeply. "Okay, but just a spoonful each. You can have a big bowl after dinner." She turned to Ben and asked, "Can you stay? Paul's in town helping Noah Mbruru with something on his computer and probably won't be back until pretty late. He'll be sorry he missed you."

"That's the best offer I've had for a month," Ben replied. "There's nothing much at home other than cans of beans. And since you're the best cook in Kenya…"

BEN PLAYED WITH the two older children while Judy finished dinner preparations in the kitchen. Through the door, she told him that Stephen was still napping. "Poor little guy," she explained,

"I took him to the clinic this morning because he didn't sleep much at all last night. I wanted Leslie to look at him, and sure enough, he has a bad ear infection."

Ben's stomach responded with a quiver when Judy mentioned Leslie. During the past several weeks he'd found himself thinking of her much too frequently. She had become a serious distraction, and he didn't need distractions. Even now, sitting in Paul and Judy's home, he swore he could smell the lotion she used on her hands.

He wandered into the kitchen. "So how are things at the clinic?" He was pleased that he'd succeeded in sounding casual.

Judy did not look up from her task of slicing a pineapple. "Oh, the usual. There was a crowd of people waiting. I saw a child with a broken finger, a woman with AIDS complications, and everything in between." She paused a minute and glanced at Ben. "Leslie seemed troubled, though. She was certainly not her usual self." Her frown conveyed concern. "Something seemed to really be bothering her."

Ben didn't try to hide his interest. "What do you mean?"

Judy scraped the pineapple pieces into a bowl. "It's a little difficult to pinpoint exactly. She seemed very happy to see us. She hugged me and the children, but she was edgy…like she would fall apart if someone just said 'boo.'" She shrugged. "I've never seen her like that. She's always upbeat and eager to talk with the kids and me. But not today. She looked like she'd been crying or was trying not to cry." She wiped her hands on a clean towel and turned to carry plates containing baked chicken, warm vegetables and homemade bread to the table. "The more I think about it, the more I'm worried."

She turned back to him, and her expression mirrored her words. "I should have tried to talk with her this morning, but I was tired from being up with Stephen. You know, if Paul were here, I think I would send him over to visit with her tonight, or I might even go myself and spend the night. But with the kids…" Her voice trailed off.

Ben helped her carry plates and cutlery to the table. Judy's concern was contagious. Was Leslie ill? Had something happened at the clinic? Had she received bad news from home? He tried to sound nonchalant. "I suppose I could stop by on my way home."

"Would you?" Judy looked relieved. "I was kind of hoping you might. It's probably nothing. She might just need someone from home to talk to… I get that way from time to time."

Ben left right after dinner. He offered to help with the dishes, but Judy shooed him on, telling him that he needed to see Leslie and get home before he collapsed. At Judy's suggestion, he took one of the cartons of ice cream.

"Don't you know that ice cream is a cure for virtually every kind of malady—mental or physical?" Judy exclaimed. Laughingly, she added, "The only thing more effective is chocolate!"

Dusk was approaching when Ben pulled up to the clinic compound. Titus had evidently heard the vehicle, and he appeared from the direction of his cabin to open the gate.

"*Jambo,* young Ben," the older man said. Ben returned the greeting and explained in Titus's dialect that he had brought Leslie a gift. Titus nodded and hid a knowing smile as he closed the gate behind the Jeep and Ben parked the vehicle in front of the screened porch.

Ben grabbed the ice cream out of the cooler and climbed the steps to the front door. He suddenly felt awkward, and his heart rate rose. He was annoyed by his nervousness, and he paused a few seconds before knocking.

THE DAY AT THE CLINIC had seemed interminable. The heat was stifling, and the dust seemed more pervasive than usual, despite the recent rain. Poverty, disease, ignorance and superstition had appeared insurmountable. And then there were the spiders....

After the last patient had finally departed, Leslie was uncharacteristically abrupt when she dismissed Naomi, Elizabeth and Agnes. The trio had gathered on the front porch, talking quietly together. She rushed outside to apologize and gave each woman a hug.

Finally alone, she lay down in her small room, wanting to rest for a few minutes before preparing something to eat. She removed her shoes and unbuttoned her shirt, hoping to cool off a little.

She was tired—physically and mentally. But her real problem was emotional. At her core, there was still a void where her heart used to be. Most of the time she was able to ignore it—but not today. The tears that had threatened all day were stinging the back of her eyes once more.

She stared at the stained ceiling and thought, *Time.* She needed time. She needed tomorrow to come. She closed her eyes and laid an arm over them, wishing she could sleep.

She might have dozed, for what seemed only a short time later, she heard a knock on the clinic door. She ignored it, but a few seconds later it was repeated. Again she ignored it. There was a third knock.

Her sense of duty surfaced enough to convince her that there must be some sort of problem or Titus would not have let the visitor inside the fence. *Oh, God.* She dragged herself to her feet. *Please let it be something simple. No death, please...*

She made her way to the front door—before coming to a full stop. Ben Murphy stood on the other side of the screen with an expression that was an odd combination of impatience and nervousness. As usual, his hair was more or less neatly caught back in a ponytail, and he looked like he needed to shave. Distantly she noted that, contrasting with his sun-darkened face, his eyes seemed greener than she remembered and were fatigued. His clothing was slightly rumpled, and his customary white shirt loosely covered his broad chest and shoulders. Leslie was momentarily alarmed as the thought crossed her mind that he was extremely attractive. She blushed at her own musings.

Not now—she couldn't deal with him now.

When she reached the door, she stood there a moment before speaking. Her response to seeing him combined irritation and fascination; she chose to react with irritation. Through the screen door she said, "What do you want, Ben? Do you need something? You don't look sick."

Ben was alarmed by Leslie's appearance and demeanor. She moved slowly and her pale countenance was virtually devoid of expression. Numerous wisps of shiny brown hair had escaped her ponytail, and her clothing was similarly in disarray. Her shirt was unbuttoned, revealing a white tank top, and the shirttail was pulled out of her waistband. Her feet were bare.

But he was exhausted, and her aggravation inflamed his. "Thanks, Les, it's nice to see you, too," he replied sarcastically.

Feeling duly chastised, she gave him a rueful smile that didn't quite reach her eyes. She sighed. "I'm sorry. I don't mean to be rude, but it's been a long day. I'm tired and not really feeling well." She stopped, hoping he would take the hint and leave.

She looked as fragile as a piece of crystal that would shatter under the slightest pressure, and Ben's concern intensified. He ignored her none-too-subtle prompt. "I just got back from

Mombasa and brought some ice cream with me. I left a half gallon at Paul and Judy's, but we thought you might like some, too." He held out the container.

Ben suddenly looked sweet and boyish, fearful that his gift might be rejected. Touched, Leslie smiled again, this time with more sincerity. She pushed open the door and invited him in.

He studied her expression and, after a momentary pause, walked past her into the clinic. "Leslie, I didn't mean to just barge in. I won't stay but a minute—"

"No, it's all right. Actually, I haven't eaten yet and ice cream sounds wonderful." She slipped past him and led the way through the clinic to the living quarters. When they reached the kitchen, she gestured to one of the chairs at the wooden table. "Here…sit down, and I'll dish up the ice cream. How about coffee or tea?"

As he handed her the ice cream, their hands brushed. Heat speared through his gut at the contact. She quickly withdrew the carton, and he saw her blush.

"Actually, tea would be nice. Oh, by the way, if you're interested," he added, "there is still some ice in the cooler. It came from a safe source."

That got a slight reaction from her. Clean ice was scarce, and the opportunity for iced drinks was severely limited. “Oh, yes, please. The heat has been awful, and iced tea would be wonderful.”

She put the kettle on the small stove to heat the water while he retrieved the ice chest from the Jeep. He was grinning when he returned carrying the cooler. “Look what else I found,” he said as he handed her two large bars of chocolate. She looked puzzled, so he explained, “Melt the chocolate in a small pan over the boiling water. Presto! Chocolate sundaes!”

He was finally rewarded with a real smile. “I don’t know if I can handle this,” she said with sincere enthusiasm as she took the candy bars. “Iced tea and chocolate sundaes on the same day!”

Ben sat at the table and watched her prepare the treat. His fatigue melted like the chocolate. At her prompting, he told her a little about his excursions during the past three weeks, describing the people he had flown and sights he had seen, but omitting details of most of the encounters and transactions. Gradually, her bleak mood lightened.

While they were eating the ice cream and

melted chocolate, he entertained her with stories of his exploits during his years in Kenya. "...then, there was this time when I accompanied Simon and three of his brothers on a hunt for a rock python. The snake had eaten some of the family's chickens and was suspected of polishing off a baby goat. So these four Masai showed me how to track the thing, and in no time we discovered the snake hole in the foothills near their homesite."

He took another bite of ice cream. "Our little hunting party waited outside the hole for three *days* before one of Simon's brothers spotted the snake. He yelled, and we all went running toward him. I was in the lead with my rifle, but then I saw the snake slithering toward us. It was—and I'm not making this up—about twenty feet long, and it weighed more than I do. Plus, it was *fast!* My first thought was, 'Well, *hell,* that is the biggest thing I've ever *seen!*'"

He grinned, looking sheepish. "I took a couple of shots at it, but missed by a foot—which was hard to do because it was so big. Anyway, it kept coming in our direction, moving a lot faster than we could run."

Leslie leaned forward, wide-eyed and intent

on the story. He paused to scrape the last of the chocolate onto his spoon and lick it.

"Well, what happened?" she inquired impatiently when he didn't immediately continue.

"So there I was, jogging backward as fast as I could—I wasn't about to turn my back on the thing. I kept praying that I wouldn't fall on my butt. I shot again...missed again. All the while Simon and his brothers were laughing so hard they could've hurt themselves." He stopped again, drawing out the story to enjoy the animation on Leslie's face. Her blue eyes crinkled at the corners as she grinned at him.

"Don't tell me. It caught you and tried to strangle you, right?"

He laughed and shook his head. "Thad—Simon's youngest brother, who by the way is a foot taller than me, and I'm over six-three—trotted up beside me and calmly threw his spear." He sighed dramatically. "He caught the snake right behind its head—practically severing it. It was a great shot, particularly since he was laughing so hard."

"And then?" Leslie asked, realizing that she was having fun. This was a side of Ben she had only glimpsed before. He was self-deprecating and almost boyish, and he didn't seem the least bit embarrassed to be the brunt of the joke.

"Well, of course we had to cut it open to look for the gold."

"Gold?" She looked skeptical.

"Yep. You see, a Kenyan legend says that gold stones can be found in the bellies of pythons." Ben shook his head, feigning disappointment. "Unfortunately, there was no gold. But the guys ended up skinning the thing, and then taking the meat back for the family. It fed them for a week."

"Let me guess," Leslie broke in as she tried to keep from choking on a sip of tea. "It tastes just like chicken?"

"Nah. It tastes like snake." He grinned, then glanced around the empty room as if to be certain no one would overhear. He leaned toward her and said in a stage whisper, "Actually, I didn't eat any. Just the thought of it—ew! But don't tell a soul, or I'll have to hurt you." He was rewarded with a laugh.

When their laughter died down, the awkwardness returned. Ben glanced outside and saw that it was completely dark. "Well, I guess I had better be going," he announced, and stood to leave. He could tell that she was feeling better. Whether it was the ice cream or the company he didn't know, but her fragile demeanor had practically disappeared. He was relieved to see a faint light in her eyes and a bit of color in her cheeks.

The last thing Leslie had wanted that evening was a visit from Ben Murphy. But suddenly, she didn't want him to leave. She stood when he did and surprised them both when she placed a hand on his forearm and said quietly, "No, please. Don't go."

CHAPTER ELEVEN

Ben paused at her request. Watching her closely, he detected a hint of desperation. She laughed nervously and removed her hand. Picking up both glasses, she said, "How about another glass of tea? I think there's still some ice left."

The fragility had returned. Ben recognized at least part of the problem. She did not want to be alone. The past hour had given her relief from whatever had been bothering her, and he knew that she was reluctant to lose contact with another person. He was spent both physically and emotionally, but he could not leave her when she so obviously needed someone. "Sure," he responded. "That would be great."

He returned to his chair as she scooped the last of the ice from the chest and poured brewed tea into the glasses. Unfortunately, the easy camaraderie had vanished, and the silence that followed was uncomfortable. Ben carefully watched his glass, searching for something to say.

Abruptly, Leslie asked, "Do you ever get homesick?"

Her expression was reflective, and her gorgeous eyes appeared cloudy. Suddenly and uncharacteristically, he was afraid—overwhelmed by a profound fear. *Dear God,* he thought—*where she's concerned, my empathy is in overdrive.* He looked down at his glass again and silently contemplated. There was a line to be crossed, and whether she understood it or not, they were both standing at that line. He did not want to move. Ben knew there would be pain. Perhaps for both of them. He feared the pain for himself but, more compellingly, much more compellingly, he did not want it for her. From the core of his being, he wanted to prevent her suffering any more.

But as his eyes rose to frame her beautiful face, he realized that it didn't matter. She was already in pain. And maybe, just maybe, her pain could be eased.

Resigned, he crossed the line.

"Yes." The word was almost inaudible. "Yes," he repeated with more intensity as he looked into her deep blue eyes and nodded. "Only every day."

She watched him closely and sensed his sincerity. It was evident in the sadness of his smile and the depth of his emptiness. "What do you miss most?" It was her turn to gaze at her tea.

He looked out the window, staring into the darkness as if seeking inspiration. "What do I miss most?" he repeated quietly. He paused briefly then answered, "Seasons. I miss the spring. I miss autumn. I miss skiing." He gave a short laugh and turned his eyes back to hers. "I miss driving my car on highways that aren't littered with potholes, and not having to worry about driving at night. I miss going to the movies on a whim and watching Monday Night Football… And of course—" he grinned "—drinking water out of the tap without having to be concerned with what it's going to do to my large intestine. That's the first thing I'll do when I get home again—get a big glass of water right out of the faucet!"

Leslie chuckled. "No, a shower. I want to take a hot shower where I don't have to hurry and don't need to be concerned if I swallow a little water." He nodded and smiled.

They were silent for a spell, but this time the silence was easy. She appeared to consider his answers. "You didn't mention your family. Is there anyone at home you miss?" She saw a flicker of response before his face became impassive again.

He shrugged and answered matter-of-factly, "Just my folks. They live in a retirement community in Florida. They're in pretty good shape for being in their seventies. Shoot, Dad can probably outjog me, and Mom swims every day. But at their age, you never know when something could happen."

"No friends? No girlfriends?" She immediately regretted the question when she saw a muscle quiver in his jaw. She blushed but reached out her hand to touch his. "I'm sorry, Ben. I'm just being nosy. Never mind."

Unable to resist the opportunity, he turned his hand over to clasp hers and looked directly into her eyes. They were the dark blue of the sky nearing dusk, and once again he felt lost in them. His voice was quiet when he answered. "I was married once, but it didn't last long. She was from Denver, and we met while I was in flight training. We knew each other only a few months before we got engaged, but that wasn't the problem." He shrugged and frowned a little. "We each needed something the other couldn't give."

He looked down at his now-empty glass.

When she did not comment, he continued, "Our first assignment was in Del Rio. You're from Texas, so you probably know it's a dusty little town near the Mexican border. She hated it. She wanted me home, and I had to be gone a lot. We fought pretty much nonstop. I was committed to the marriage, so I requested a change of assignment. I left flight training and took a position at the Pentagon, thinking she would be happier in Washington. But then, in addition to my primary assignment, the air force sent me to grad school, so I still wasn't home much. We'd been in D.C. about a year when she left me for a partner in her law firm." He looked down at the small hand clasped in his and gave a rueful laugh. "Even I knew he was a better match for her than I was."

"Is that why you're here?" Leslie questioned.

"No, Leslie. Not directly, at any rate." He looked at her evenly but didn't add anything. She didn't press.

He squeezed her hand gently, then let go. Wanting to change the subject, he leaned forward, putting his elbows on the table. "So, now it's your turn. Other than long, hot showers, what do *you* miss?"

Leslie smiled sheepishly. "I hate to admit it

because it sounds so *female,* but I miss shopping. I would love to go to a mall." He smiled at her confession. Encouraged because the mood had lightened again, she continued, "I miss air-conditioning." She laughed out loud and said, "I *really* miss going to the supermarket and buying a chicken that's already cut up—minus its feet and head—and neatly wrapped in plastic... I miss peanut butter and pizza—thick, cheesy pizza." She giggled. "Gosh, it sounds like what I miss most is food."

He laughed as she wrinkled her nose at her own reflections. "But what about people? You haven't mentioned anyone either. Who do *you* miss most?"

Her smile dissolved. She paled, and Ben saw a wave of desolation wash through her eyes. She stood and carried her empty glass and bowl to the sink.

Here it is, he thought. *Here's what's troubling her.* Wanting to crawl under the table, Ben closed his eyes and sighed deeply. "Leslie, I'm sorry," he started, but she turned back to face him.

Leaning against the small cupboard, she shook her head. "No. It's okay." She shook her head a second time and bit her bottom lip. When she spoke, he had to listen very carefully because the words were so faint.

"They had blond hair...." She smiled slightly. Her eyes appeared to be focused inwardly as she remembered. She blinked rapidly, swallowed and started over. "They had blond hair and blue eyes. Brian's was a dark, ash-blond, but my little girl was a towhead. She was full of energy, bouncing all through the house... She loved to play on the swing set in the backyard and to read books...."

She paused. Ben remained silently watchful and waited for her to go on. When she continued to stare into space, he asked quietly, "What was her name?"

Tears appeared in her eyes, and she whispered, "Emma. She was soft and sweet and trusting and stubborn...." The tears began to flow in twin streams down her cheeks; she didn't acknowledge them. "I loved to sing to her at night and tell her stories. That's one of the things I miss the most—bedtime." She smiled sadly. "Every night I would give her a bath and then brush her teeth. Then we would tuck her into bed, and Brian or I would read a book. Then we would kiss her good-night." Finally, she brushed at the tears with the back of her hand. "Brian was a wonderful father."

Leslie reached for a clean towel to dry her eyes. Ben saw her hands tremble as she performed the simple task. He wanted her to talk. He wanted to listen. Indeed, he *needed* to listen. His voice was gentle. "Tell me about Brian."

Still avoiding looking directly at the man seated at the table, Leslie sat back down and wiped her eyes again. Her voice was heavy with emotion as she answered, "We met while he was a fourth-year med student. I had just finished nursing school and was working on the cardiac floor at one of the big hospitals in Dallas. Brian was very good-looking, and all of the young nurses had a crush on him. At first I wasn't really attracted to him because I thought he was too serious. But one evening he asked me to go out for coffee. We ended up talking until three in the morning." A sad light appeared in her eyes as she remembered. "I learned that even though he was serious, he was also smart, compassionate and funny. We fell in love that night."

The yearning in Leslie's expression and the simplicity of her statement cut through Ben's core like a sword. He recognized jealousy, which he knew was inappropriate, but that did not change the reality. *Dear Lord,* he thought, *I'm jealous of a dead man.* Ashamed, he turned his focus back to her.

She was saying, "We were married six months later. I started the nurse-practitioner program in the meantime, thinking that maybe one day we could work together. I got pregnant during the second year of his residency. It was an accident, but we were both happy about it, and just a little terrified. By that time, Brian had decided to become a pediatrician, and we figured he could get great experience at home." She brushed away another tear. "I was offered a position teaching nursing at the university, and I was able to do that even when Emma was a baby. Brian helped a lot."

She stopped again, apparently reluctant to continue. Unsure what to do, Ben reached out and gently wiped a tear from her cheek with his thumb. "What happened?" His eyes held hers, willing her to believe that he cared and wasn't just curious.

She swallowed. "I got pregnant again and had to be confined to bed for a few weeks. One morning Brian took Emma to school, and…a truck… He must not have seen the truck." She started sobbing. "The truck hit them… Then… because of the shock, I miscarried."

Tears stained her cheeks and her eyes rose to meet his. "It was two years ago today. Two years… Oh, God. I miss them so much."

She leaned over the table and buried her head in her arms. Her shoulders shook convulsively, and hoarse sounds came from her throat. Ben's heart broke for her, and tears formed in his own eyes. He could think of no comforting words. Finally, unable to simply watch, he stood and tenderly drew her up with him. She melted into his embrace. Her head rested on his shoulder; her arms circled his waist. He held her tightly and lightly stroked her hair. He closed his eyes and slowly rocked her back and forth.

When she had finally calmed, Ben pulled away. He placed one hand under her chin and angled her face up so he could see her.

Noticing his tears, her eyes widened with astonishment. Gently, she reached up and wiped the tears from his cheek, just as he had done for her earlier. Without taking his eyes from hers, he caught her hand and kissed her palm.

Shivers coursed through Leslie, and she placed her arms around his neck and pulled him to her. "Hold me," she choked. "Hold me again. Please...I need... Please."

At that moment, Ben would have done anything for her. There was no way he would turn down her plea. He held her gently, his hands lovingly touching her back and shoulders, roaming and caressing. His lips brushed her hair.

She raised her face and, in unspoken agreement, her lips found his. The kiss was soft, gentle and comforting. His hands rose to frame her face, and his lips moved to touch her cheeks and forehead before returning to her lips. Tension built, and the kiss deepened and intensified. Her cheeks had tasted of the salt from her tears, but her mouth carried the sweetness of the ice cream.

Emotion and energy coursed between them in waves, sparking something that strengthened with each rapid breath. Reflexively, his hands moved to caress her arms. Oddly, the contact with the softness of her skin startled him back to reality. That touch was like being burned to the core by something warm and precious, something elemental and essential.

Immediately, his hands stilled. He could not take advantage of her vulnerability.

He loved her too much.

Summoning what tiny shreds of self-control he could find, he wrested his lips away. She struggled to pull him back as urgently as he tried to push her away. He stilled her hands and held them, his own hands shaking with tension. "Leslie," he said with a sternness that surprised him—a sternness he did not intend. "Leslie," he repeated, trying to sound gentle and mostly succeeding. "Look at me."

She let out a little humming moan and moved into him again, trying to lean against him even as he restrained her hands. "No. No. Hold me. I need to be held." Her words were frenzied.

In desperation, he grabbed her wrists and held them firmly. This time he wasn't gentle when he shook her. His voice was harsh. "No. Leslie. Stop!" He sighed, and his tone quieted. "Open your eyes, honey, and look at me."

Slowly her eyes opened, and Ben watched as, in a breath, passion was replaced first by embarrassment and then by contrition. Her face turned red and then paled. She cringed and closed her eyes tightly. She tried to pull away from him, but he continued to hold her wrists.

"Please let me go." She whispered, "Brian. Brian, I'm so sorry. I didn't mean..." Her voice trailed off, and she started sobbing and fiercely trying to pull away from Ben's grip.

Fearing he would hurt her, he was forced to let go.

She fled from the kitchen.

PUSHING HER WAY into her bedroom and leaning against the far wall, Leslie felt panicked. She had disgraced herself. But what tore through the core of her heart was that suddenly she could not picture her husband. She tried, but all she could see was Ben.

Brian and Emma had been a constant part of her subconsciousness, and she could always recall memories with ease. Now, without warning, she had lost Brian's face. Anxious to regain the mental image of her cherished husband, she remembered that she had put his photograph between the pages of a book to make sure it would not get damaged. Wildly she tore through the books on the bedside table, dropping them to the floor as she quickly flipped through the pages until she found the photograph.

AT FIRST BEN was determined not to follow Leslie into the bedroom. He thought it best to leave her alone until he was in better control. The sound of multiple thuds alarmed him, though. Resigned, he went to investigate and paused at the doorway where he saw her sitting on the end of the small bed. Her head was bowed, and tears were dropping onto her lap.

He had to step over several books to reach her. Not knowing what else to do, he sat down beside her, carefully avoiding touching her. He looked at her hands and saw that she held a portrait of a young man. The man in the picture had dark blond hair and light blue eyes, and Ben was pounded by another wave of jealousy. But as he stared at the picture, the jealousy simply vanished, replaced by pity. Indeed, he was intensely sorry for the young man who had experienced so little time to be with this fantastic woman who so obviously adored him. He could not think of anything to say that wouldn't sound trite, so he closed his eyes and waited.

After a time, Leslie's tears were spent. She wiped her cheeks with one hand and looked down at the picture again. How could she have forgotten what Brian looked like? She knew his face as well as she knew her own. She smiled sadly at the portrait and smoothed it gently.

With reddened eyes, she turned to Ben and found that he was not watching her. Rather, he was leaning forward with his head resting in his hands and, as far as she could tell, his eyes were closed. He was so still, she wasn't certain if he was awake.

Delicately, she reached out to him and touched his forearm. At once he looked up and searched her face. In her expression he saw sorrow, fatigue and something else—perhaps resignation.

Her throat was dry, and she had to swallow before she could talk. "I'm sorry. Ben, I'm sorry I threw myself at you like that. I just… I'm so sorry…."

Ben placed his hands on her shoulders and, leaning forward, gently kissed her on the forehead. With a voice that was deeper than usual he said, "Sweetheart, that's the most uncalled-for apology I've ever received." He managed a self-deprecating grin. "Contrary to prevailing rumors, it's not every day I have a beautiful woman wanting me to hold her and kiss her. I can hardly complain." He sat back and dropped his hands.

She blinked with embarrassment and looked away. "Leslie, don't be ashamed. I can't even begin to conceive of the pain you've experienced." He took both of her hands in his. "But, Les, I do know a great deal about loneliness. I understand the ache of wanting to talk to someone, to be with someone, to hold someone. I was glad to be here with you tonight."

She saw the sadness in his eyes and heard the honesty in his words. "Ben, thank you. You have helped so much. It was just because it's the anniversary of..." She swallowed and blinked, trying to keep from crying again.

"Leslie, I truly do understand. There's no need to explain." He reached out and smoothed her hair. "Look, I'd really better be going. If you're all right, that is." He stood and watched her as he waited for an answer.

Leslie got to her feet. Biting her bottom lip, she stammered, "P-please, if you can stay a while longer. We can talk some more, or you can read. Anything." She swallowed hard. "Ben, please. I don't want to be alone tonight. I know it's asking a lot, but..."

Ben regarded her with compassion, this time working hard to hide the depth of his love. Finally, he caught her small hand in his and brought it to his lips. "Look, you're exhausted. Why don't you go to bed? If you want me to stay, I can drag one of the exam cots onto the porch and sleep there."

He gave her a lopsided grin. "But if you wake

up before me in the morning, just don't mistake me for a patient...."

She managed a little smile. "Thank you, Ben. That would be perfect." They stood in silence for a few seconds. It took all of the self-control Ben had left to refrain from taking her in his arms again. Finally, he turned to leave. At the door he paused and looked back at her. Her face was red, and her eyes were swollen. Her hair was mussed and her clothing askew. She had never looked more beautiful to him.

He smiled and whispered, "Good night." The door closed quietly behind him.

LESLIE WOKE EARLY the next morning feeling surprisingly refreshed. She dressed, washed her face and braided her hair quickly, then went to the front of the house to wake Ben. She thought she would make breakfast for him to show her appreciation. But when she made her way through the clinic and saw that all the cots were in their normal places, she knew her plan would not happen. He had already gone.

CHAPTER TWELVE

TITUS TURNED THE clinic's ancient Jeep through the compound's open gate and drove a hundred feet or so to Ben's house. It was fortunate that he'd been there before, for although the house was fairly close to the airstrip, the road was isolated and difficult to find.

From the passenger seat, Leslie studied the small buildings. Ben's house was built of rough boards painted tan, blending effectively with the surrounding savanna. There was no porch and little exterior adornment. Another small house, about the same size, was set to one side. Leslie assumed it was Simon's place when he stayed with Ben. Two additional outbuildings were located behind the dwellings. Like the clinic, an eight-foot cinder-block wall with a heavy wrought-iron gate surrounded the compound. Unlike the clinic, razor wire was attached to the top of the fence, effectively keeping out thieves and miscreants.

It had been five days since Ben slipped out of the clinic in the early hours of the morning. Since then, Leslie had often found herself looking out the windows, hoping to see his Jeep. She spent considerable time each day recalling fragments of their conversations and trying to analyze his words and actions. And, when she was alone in bed at night and allowed her thoughts to drift, she remembered the feel of his arms as he held her. She remembered the strength and compassion it had taken him to back away. In the depth of the night, she was willing to admit that she wanted to see him again. She longed for more soft words, another embrace, another kiss.

Her musings left her confused and conflicted. She was unsure of his actions, emotions and motives—just as she was unsure of her own. She was certain that he found her attractive. But his reputation with women made her skeptical that his response was exclusively directed at her. What surprised her was that he had been the one to halt their passionate encounter.

In any regard, Leslie was puzzled and distressed when he didn't come by. After the fourth day, she determined that she would go see him. In mental self-defense, she reminded herself that she did not want a relationship—she just wanted to thank him. But she knew that was self-delusion.

As an excuse, she decided to take him a small gift. With Judy's help, she gathered the ingredients needed to make chocolate-chip cookies and baked them early in the morning, before the first patients arrived. To justify the timing of her visit, she decided to see an elderly woman she was treating. The woman lived in a tiny village several miles past the turnoff to the airfield and was not able to walk the distance to the clinic. Titus could drive her to see the patient and then stop by Ben's compound on their way home. Leslie had carefully wrapped the plate of cookies in a towel and placed them in the backseat of the Jeep along with her supplies.

The house call lasted only an hour, and Titus drove into Ben's small compound around four. Although the gate was open, Ben's Jeep was missing and there was no sign of him or Simon. There were, however, two large brown dogs of no identifiable breed resting in the meager shade of a baobab tree. The dogs barked loudly at first, but they apparently recognized Titus and quickly quieted, returning to lie placidly in the shade.

"It looks like no one is home," Leslie murmured. She tried to tamp down her disappointment. "But I'll check to make sure."

It was Titus's habit to wait in the covered vehicle while Leslie made her house calls, so he remained seated as she climbed out of the Jeep, carefully balancing the cookies. Feeling foolish at the quivering in her stomach, she crossed the dirt path and knocked on the door.

BEN WAS WASHING at an aged porcelain sink when he heard a vehicle. He had just returned from several points along the coast and was in the process of removing the sweat and grime incurred during the three-day trip. Since the dogs had stopped barking and he was expecting Simon, he was surprised when someone knocked.

Hastily, he toweled his face and upper body and thrust his arms into a clean shirt. As he crossed to the door, he glanced out the window to see if he needed to arm himself—and was further surprised to see Titus sitting in Mama Joe's rickety Jeep. His heart rate rose as he opened the door to find Leslie holding a plate covered by a lightweight towel.

The aroma of sugar and butter was lovely, as was the appearance of the young nurse. She was neatly dressed in her normal attire: a khaki skirt and carefully pressed chambray shirt. As usual, her wavy brown hair was pulled back in a ponytail from which small wisps had escaped. His heart skipped a beat when her blue eyes found his and she smiled.

A little shyly, she held out the covered plate. “I wanted to pay you back for the ice-cream sundaes, so I made cookies.”

Ben stepped aside to allow her to enter. As she did, he leaned out to catch Titus’s eye and waved to the older man. After closing the door, he turned back to Leslie and found her studying her surroundings with interest.

“I’m sorry. I wasn’t expecting company,” he said.

The interior of Ben’s home contrasted markedly with the dusty, sparse exterior. The front room was a combination living room and bedroom. The furnishings consisted of a long cushioned bench and a comfortable wooden rocker. A wooden table and matching chairs stood in one corner, and in the corner farthest from the door was a small bed—really only a cot—neatly covered with a thin cotton blanket and draped with mosquito netting. A tall chest was located nearby. The small but well-appointed kitchen could be viewed through a door next to the cot, and there was a bathroom beyond that.

Although the main room was simply furnished, it was surprisingly homey and comfortable. The walls were painted the same beige as the outside of the house, and muslin curtains hung at the windows. Two oscillating fans sat on the floor next to open windows and helped cool the room. A laptop computer sat open on the table; several stacks of paper rested on either side of it. The most surprising feature of the room, however, was the shelves of books that lined much of one wall.

Ben watched Leslie as she looked around, and he was relieved when he saw approval in her expression. He held out his hand to take the plate. "Thanks for the cookies. It was very nice of you to go to all the trouble to bring them out here...."

His words trailed off. He felt disadvantaged, not really certain how she would respond to him after their last encounter. Awkwardly, he just stood in the center of the room holding the plate of cookies and trying to think of something to say. He chided himself for his inane inability to carry on a simple conversation with her.

To break the silence, Leslie said, "The other

morning you left without giving me the opportunity to thank you again." She moved past him to the shelves; her back was to him. Scanning the titles of books, she continued, "Ben, we both know that twice now you could have…um… well, taken advantage of me. And you didn't." She turned to face him. His stance suggested that he was highly alert. "Ben, I…"

She stopped, suddenly distracted. For once he didn't have his usual disheveled look about him, and he had obviously just shaved. Also, this was the first time she had seen him when his hair was not tied back. Down, his gold-streaked hair just skimmed his shoulders and was very thick. She found herself wanting to run her fingers through it, and she was alarmed by the intensity of her reaction. She felt her face redden, and her heart was thumping so hard she was afraid it was audible. Self-consciously, Leslie focused on his lips, idly wondering why she had never noticed how full and expressive they were.

"I really…don't know what I was going to say," was all she could manage.

He replied with exaggerated gallantry. "It was my pleasure, ma'am. I always try to keep ice cream handy in order to aid damsels in distress."

She gave a slight laugh but wasn't ready to

abandon her quest. Deciding to be blunt, she looked down at her hands and asked, "Ben, why did you leave like that and not come back? Was it something I did?"

He set the cookies on a small table and took her hand. He led her to the cushioned bench and when she was seated, he pulled the rocker forward and sat facing her.

"Les," he began. "I'm sorry if you were upset by my leaving early the other morning. And no, it wasn't anything you did or anything you didn't do." His expression was earnest. "Honestly, I wasn't sure what time people start coming to the clinic, and I wanted to leave while it was still dark, before anyone showed up and saw my Jeep." He shrugged. "I didn't want to start any rumors."

Ben's concern for her reputation surprised Leslie, causing her to chew her lip and blink rapidly to hold back tears. When she didn't respond, Ben continued. "I had to fly out unexpectedly that morning, and I just got back or I would've already come by to check on you." He flashed the half grin that she had first characterized as obnoxious but was now beginning to think of as charming. "Actually, you caught me getting ready. I was planning to drop by this evening." He stood and walked toward the kitchen, talking as he went. "I even had a mission."

He returned carrying a small cardboard box tied with a red ribbon, which he handed to her. The box was heavy. She placed it on her lap and looked up at him with her expression slightly wary. "What's in it?"

"Open it."

She untied the ribbon, lifted the lid and gave a cry of surprise. Inside were six jars of peanut butter of various brands and sizes.

"While I was in Nairobi, I stopped at one of the better grocery stores. I didn't know what kind of peanut butter you like, so I bought a jar of each brand they had. Most were imported from the U.S., but there is one from Germany and one from England. I've eaten some of the English peanut butter before and wouldn't recommend it though."

Leslie stared at the box on her lap, struggling again to keep her tears in check. She looked up and saw an expression of sweetness she would have previously thought him incapable of displaying. Her heart missed a beat, and she fumbled out a quiet "Thank you."

Ben was uncomfortable with tears. Trying

to lighten the mood, he headed for the kitchen. "You know, I haven't eaten since this morning, and I'm starved. How about some cookies? I have some milk in my refrigerator and several fairly cold cans of Coke. What can I get you?"

Relieved that he'd changed the subject, she followed his lead. "Yes, cookies sound great. I think I'll take a Coke. I still can't drink the milk."

He chuckled. "I understand. Believe it or not, I prefer the boiled, raw milk here to the processed stuff back in the States."

While he was retrieving the drinks, Leslie examined Ben's amazing collection of books. From the titles she discerned that he had a passion for history, particularly military history and anything related to aircraft and flying.

"You have a really eclectic book collection. Where did you get them all?" She pitched her voice so that the words would carry into the kitchen.

"Oh, here and there," he called back. "I brought quite a few with me when I came here, but most I've just picked up over the years."

She moved to the computer and saw that the papers were some sort of writing project. "What are you working on?"

He had returned from the kitchen carrying two glasses and small cloth napkins.

"Oh, that… Well… Here." He handed her a glass of cola and picked up the plate of cookies. Uncovering it, he passed it to her, then snagged one for himself and took a bite. "Well, wow. Great cookie! I haven't had one of these in ages. Here, sit down." He pointed to a chair and, after she was seated, he plopped down on the edge of the cot and sipped milk.

Not willing to be distracted, she persisted. "Are you writing something?"

She got the impression that he would've preferred to hide the papers and shut the laptop. "Uh, yeah." He took another bite of cookie.

"Okay…what?" Her tone suggested that she wasn't going to let the subject drop.

He fidgeted with his cookie. "Hmm…well, you see…"

"Tell me!" she insisted, grinning at his discomfiture.

He sighed and rolled his eyes. "Okay. But you have to promise not to tell anyone."

"I promise. Cross my heart." She continued to grin.

He sighed again and said under his breath, "It's my doctoral dissertation."

She blinked and leaned forward. "Your *dissertation?*" She could not have possibly heard correctly.

He rubbed his forehead and nodded. "Yeah."

"Your dissertation?" she repeated. "You're getting a *PhD?*" Her tone was incredulous.

"Yeah, I am," he huffed. "And you promised not to tell anyone."

She responded with a puzzled frown. "You're kidding, right?"

He sighed a third time and reached across to the table to pick up a stack of papers. The pages had been lying facedown, and when he turned them over, he took the top one and handed it to her. She read,

"Development and Application of
Aerial Reconnaissance and Surveillance
Throughout the Twentieth Century"

A Dissertation
By
H. Bennett Murphy

Submitted in Partial Fulfillment of the Requirements for the Degree of Doctor of Philosophy

Department of History
Graduate School of Arts and Sciences
Georgetown University, Washington, D.C.

Leslie read the title page again. She blinked and looked up at Ben, who was watching her with an odd expression. A hundred questions and comments popped into her mind. She went with the most pedantic. *"Bennett?* I assumed your name was Benjamin."

He shrugged. "Yeah, most people do. Bennett's a family name."

"Oh." She read the page a third time and then looked back at him. "So what does the *H* stand for?"

His lips quavered as he struggled to keep from smiling. He shook his head. "Nope. Not telling."

"What? Come on. You've gone this far."

He actually grinned before removing all expression from his face. He gave an exaggerated sigh and answered, "Okay—Herman. And if you *ever* tell *anyone,* I *will* find you."

She bit her lip to keep from giggling, but the effort failed. "*Herman?* Your parents actually named you *Herman?*"

Feigning vexation, he repeated, "It's a family name." He chuckled then; his green eyes were shining.

She gave up trying to control her reaction and burst out laughing. Ben's stomach clenched at the sound, and his own smile vanished. The room seemed to close around them, and he sat mesmerized. He absorbed her laughter and watched the mirth in her beautiful eyes—he couldn't imagine ever growing tired of it. He ached with the need to make her smile, to make her laugh, to keep her happy.

The sudden seriousness in Ben's expression confused Leslie, and she sobered. "Oh, Ben, I'm really sorry. I shouldn't have teased you. It's just that…well…" Guiltily, she tried to stifle her mirth. She shook her head in disbelief. "You just don't look like a Herman."

"Honey, for the record, I've never forgiven my parents."

Leslie took a sip of her Coke. "So tell me about the PhD."

He shrugged and finished off his second cookie before explaining. "I think I mentioned that I started graduate school when my wife and I moved to Washington. I had pretty much finished my coursework when we divorced." He picked up his glass and swallowed the remains. He hesitated a bit, then added, "Then there were some problems with my commission. The air force and I parted company, and I ended up here. By that time, I was starting the dissertation. It's pretty much complete now. I'm just doing final edits."

"Well, wow. I'm impressed. So you'll be Dr. Murphy… Dr. Herman Murphy." She smiled. "I'm sorry. I couldn't resist."

He was compelled to touch her then, but he settled for just taking her hand. His heart quickened when her fingers laced with his. They sat for a few minutes without saying anything, and then Ben broke the silence. "Les, I was serious. I need you to keep this a secret. I know my request sounds odd, but it's important."

"Why? I think it's fun and interesting." She smiled at him again. "For goodness' sake, Ben, it's impressive!"

Not wanting to spoil the mood, he attempted to joke his way through the issue. "Hey, if word got out, it would ruin my street cred."

"Your *street cred?*" She looked puzzled.

"You know—my credibility. How I'm perceived."

"This is about your *reputation?*" Her smile vanished.

He felt another twisting in his gut when he realized she was disappointed in him. His enjoyment of the discussion vanished, deflating like a burst balloon. A muscle in his jaw twitched as he clenched his teeth. Once again, he buried the emotions that were threatening to erupt with increasing regularity. His voice carried an edge when he answered, "Yes. It's important that I maintain my reputation."

Leslie looked at their joined hands and nodded. "Okay. I understand." Her eyes rose to meet his. "It's no problem, Ben. I can keep your secret." She gently squeezed his hand and then let go. She rose and walked to the bookcases, appearing to study the titles. "Do you have any fiction?"

He managed to cover his own disappointment and gestured to one of the bookcases. "That's the fiction. You're welcome to borrow anything."

She went to the spot he had indicated and discovered an eclectic collection. Charles Dickens, Herman Melville and Mark Twain were interspersed with books by Tom Clancy, Michael Crichton and Stephen King. "Where's the romance section?" she inquired, trying to recover the light mood.

He reached past her and pulled out a copy of Jane Austen's *Pride and Prejudice.* "This is it… the whole romance section." He grinned. "And for the record, I have read it."

She chuckled softly and took the book from him, laying it aside after caressing the spine for a moment. She pulled out what appeared to be a very early edition of *The Great Gatsby* and flipped through it before replacing it on the shelf. "I think I'll take you up on that offer. About all I have to read at the clinic are an excellent collection of medical and nursing books and some of Mama Joe's books on missiology. They're nice for reference, but not particularly entertaining." She indicated the books with her hand. "Other than *Pride and Prejudice,* do you have recommendations?"

With that prompting, Ben proceeded to pull out several books and place them on the table in front of Leslie. He briefly explained the plots of a couple she was not familiar with and teasingly chastised her for not having read some of the classics.

Leslie glanced outside and noticed the position of the afternoon sun. "I should get back to the clinic in case anyone comes in later." She picked up the selection of books, and Ben followed her to the door carrying the peanut butter. The pair stood looking at each other for a heartbeat before Leslie put her free hand on his shoulder. Standing on tiptoe, she kissed him lightly on the cheek. "Thank you for a lovely visit. It was one of my most enjoyable since I came to Kenya… And Ben," she said, continuing to look at him steadily, "thank you again for being there for me during the hard times."

Although he tried to refrain from reaching out to her, he could not keep his hand from caressing her hair. "Leslie…"

Instead of verbalizing his thoughts, he leaned down to gently touch her lips with his. It was not a passionate or demanding kiss, but its simplicity, coupled with the longing in his eyes, was devastatingly effective in melting her final resistance. She had been attracted to him for a long while—probably from the very beginning—and finally acknowledged that the attraction had grown to something warm and enticing. But, in the recesses of her mind, she feared giving in to the feelings. She was afraid to love, and she was even more fearful of loving Ben.

He pulled back and grinned at her. "Next time I'll expect peanut-butter cookies."

His teasing words allowed her to put aside her pensive musings, and she managed an easy smile. “You’ve got a deal.”

CHAPTER THIRTEEN

DURING THE NEXT few weeks, Ben and Leslie saw each other fairly regularly. Sometimes Ben would stop at the clinic in the early evening and stay for supper. One day they went to the Merdians' for dinner, enjoying time with the active family.

Another day, they took an afternoon and drove through the great Tsavo wildlife park, spending hours watching the herds of elephant, Cape buffalo and zebra. Ben spotted a small pride of lions in the tall grass, and the great cats did not stir even though he drove within twenty feet of them. For a long while, they watched rambunctious cubs rolling over tolerant mothers who lounged in the tall grass, completely ignoring the pair in the Jeep.

On the third Sunday in May, as was her habit, Leslie went to church. She sat near the front and, trying not to be obvious, she occasionally turned her head to look through the sea of faces, hoping to spot Ben. She'd learned that he always came to the service when he was in town, but he routinely arrived late and left early, standing at the rear of the structure to avoid attracting attention. That Sunday she didn't spot him so she was surprised to find him waiting for her.

He caught her arm as she walked out of the tent into the bright sunshine. His gaze swept over her as he pulled her to one side. She was wearing a simple, pale blue cotton dress that buttoned in the front from the conservative neckline nearly to her ankles. At the sides were thin ribbons that tied in the back, accentuating the smallness of her waist. A large tortoiseshell clip held her wavy brown hair on top of her head. She looked softly radiant.

"Hi," she said, smiling up at him. "I looked for you inside."

He smiled back. "I was in the far corner—trying to keep a low profile."

Her smile faded at his quip, and she said, "Oh. I see." The more involved Leslie became with Ben, the more troubled shc grew. His persistence in maintaining his hard-drinking, womanizing, ne'er-do-well persona goaded her—and because of it, she couldn't completely trust him.

A brief look of something that appeared to be pain flickered across his face, and she saw his jaw twitch. The moment passed, and he reached out to touch her hand. “Look, Leslie, I have an errand to run in Mombasa. If you’re not busy, I was wondering if you would come with me.”

She looked at his hand lightly holding hers. Despite her concerns, she was drawn to him by a force that was becoming impossible to resist. Her cautious nature—coupled with her ongoing worry about his activities—warred with her desire to be with him. She sighed inwardly as her better judgment lost the battle. “I’ve not been to Mombasa yet. I can’t be gone long, though.”

“It’s just for the afternoon. The flight is only about an hour and a half. We can have a late lunch at one of the nice hotels, and I’ll have you back by dusk, I promise.”

There was nothing Leslie needed to do at the clinic, and she’d been dreading being alone. Flying to the coastal city for a few hours would be a fun way to spend the afternoon. Besides, she reluctantly acknowledged, she could spend the rest of the day with Ben.

She nodded and smiled again. “Actually, I’d love to go. Let me tell Titus and Naomi.”

ON THE WAY to the airstrip Ben stopped briefly at his compound, explaining that he only needed a moment to change and suggesting that Leslie wait in the car. In less than five minutes he returned, fashionably dressed in black slacks and a blue dress shirt and wearing a beige linen sport coat. Leslie stared as he climbed into the vehicle. Only once before had she seen him wearing anything but khaki slacks and tan or white shirts.

"Goodness!" she exclaimed teasingly. "You do clean up well!"

He grinned. "The occasion warrants it. I'm having lunch with the most beautiful nurse in all of Africa." On impulse, he leaned over to kiss her lightly on the lips before starting the Jeep. Because he had turned away to put the vehicle into gear, he missed the blush and look of pleasure that crossed her face.

During the short flight, Ben explained the purpose of some of the dials and gauges on the instrument panel. He showed her how to monitor the altitude, attitude and pitch of the small plane, and she quickly became enthused with the idea of learning to fly.

As they neared the city, Ben radioed ahead and requested the control tower's permission to land at the busy airport; soon they were on the ground. Outside the bustling terminal, Ben found a reputable-looking taxi and told the driver to take them to Mombasa Island.

Ben cracked the taxi's window to let in fresh air. "I thought we could go to the Imperial Hotel. It's one of the venerable hotels built when the British were constructing the railroad. It's truly a landmark. Plus, they have a terrific chef."

"That sounds perfect," Leslie replied as she gazed out her window. As they drove toward the harbor, Ben explained the rest of his plans. "My meeting is scheduled for four o'clock. That will give us a couple of hours to eat. I don't want you to have to sit through it, so I was planning on dropping you off with the Gustafsons. They're another missionary couple who knew my parents. The meeting will only be an hour or so, and then I'll pick you up and head back to the airport."

She nodded and continued to stare out the window. "That will be fine," she replied, more interested in the sights of Mombasa than Ben's plan. Old mosques, Hindu temples, and churches were interspersed with modern buildings of glass and steel. Colorful, bustling bazaars dotted the narrow streets, and people of all races and cultures moved through them at a leisurely pace. The South Asian influence was evident, and she was captivated by the Moorish architecture. Domed buildings were beset with wide arches. Many of the window eaves were heavily decorated with plaster filigree, and colorful tiles adorned doorways. In odd contrast, the attire of the people seemed somber. Indeed, many of the women were modestly dressed in traditional Islamic black veils, which covered them from head to toe.

The Imperial Hotel was a huge white stucco structure on a palm-lined beach. The grounds were gorgeously landscaped with deep green lawns and huge shrubs laden with pink, red or white flowers. Two beautifully marked peacocks and several peahens wandered around, adding a perfect finishing touch to the exotic setting.

They dined on a shaded veranda overlooking the gardens on one side and the blue waters of the harbor on the other. Despite the heat and humidity, large overhead fans comfortably cooled the air. The table was covered with white linen and set with silver utensils. Fragrant pink and red flowers rested in a crystal vase in the center of the table. They arrived a little before two o'clock, after the normal lunchtime and before afternoon tea, so the dining area was almost deserted.

Throughout lunch Ben entertained her, sharing more tales of his African exploits. At his suggestion, Leslie chose an entrée of curried fish over rice, which was spicy and delicious. Over a dessert of custard with a light cream sauce and dark coffee, the conversation slowed. Leslie felt drowsy and slightly detached, thoroughly enjoying the beauty of her surroundings and the company of the man across from her.

Ben watched Leslie as she dreamily stared past the manicured lawns toward the sea. Moving slowly, he reached across the table to catch her hand, which was resting beside her china cup. Without moving her gaze, she turned her hand over to hold his.

The warmth of his fingers sent tiny tingles up her arm, which spread until her entire body felt flushed. Finally, she focused on their intertwined hands and then lifted her eyes to his face. His expression was unguarded, and she saw what she could only interpret as longing in his pale green eyes. She was certain she recognized deep affection, but she was reluctant to probe further into his emotions because she was unwilling to fully examine her own.

Suddenly anxious to break the mood, she removed her hand from his. As an excuse for the retreat, she picked up the dainty cup that contained the remainder of her coffee and finished its contents. Sensing her withdrawal, Ben looked away. He gestured to the waiter and presented cash to the man. After the waiter departed, Ben took a final sip of coffee and glanced at his watch. "We'd better get you to the Gustafsons, so I'll be in time for my meeting."

Ben gently placed his hand on the small of her back as they walked in silence through the cool lobby of the hotel. He was encouraged when she leaned toward him, tacitly welcoming his touch. A uniformed doorman requisitioned a taxi, and, inside the car, Ben consulted a piece of paper before giving the address to the driver.

"Sam and Charlotte Gustafson are Bible translators who worked with my parents. They have two sons, one on either side of me in boarding school. Their oldest son, Greg, returned a few years ago and runs an HIV program in Tanzania. You'd like him."

"Are you sure they won't mind us just dropping in?"

"Yes. I promise they'll relish the visit, and Charlotte will talk your ear off."

Less than ten minutes later, the taxi pulled up next to a dainty, peach-colored house surrounded by a walled garden. Ben asked the driver to wait and helped Leslie exit the car.

"Excuse me." A man's voice stopped them as they were mounting the front steps. "Whom are you seeking?"

The couple turned in response to see a small, thin man of indeterminate age on the porch of the house next door. He was dressed in white, loose-fitting pants and shirt and had swarthy skin and straight black hair.

Ben nodded slightly to address the older man with the formality befitting South Asian culture. "Your pardon, sir. I am Ben Murphy. My companion and I are in Mombasa for the day, and we wished for a brief visit with Mr. and Mrs. Gustafson."

The man nodded politely and answered, "I regret to inform you, Mr. Murphy, but Mr. and Mrs. Gustafson are not home at this time. They have gone to a conference in Switzerland. I do not expect them back for another week."

"Oh, I see," replied Ben. He digested this revelation then nodded to the man in white. "Thank you for your time, sir." He turned back to the waiting taxi and gestured for Leslie to precede him inside. Both Leslie and the driver waited in silence as Ben considered their options. Finally, he glanced at the driver and gave him the address of an office building in the Old Town.

Once en route, he turned to Leslie. He stared at her for a moment, then abruptly said, "Take down your hair."

It was more of an order than a request. She frowned. "What?"

He motioned to her head. "Your hair. Take the clip out of your hair and leave it loose."

Bewildered, Leslie nonetheless complied. In silence, she removed the tortoiseshell clip and combed her fingers through her wavy hair until it fell in a heavy mass well past her shoulders.

Ben nodded, pleased with the effect, but a scowl marked his brow and the corners of his mouth. He studied her for a moment and then reached across to touch the neckline of her bodice. Leslie recoiled in surprise and quickly put a hand up to hold the dress against her chest. Exasperated, she asked, "What *are* you doing?"

He gestured toward her dress. "Unbutton the top two buttons."

She gaped at him. *"What?"*

With growing impatience, he explained, "Look, Leslie. It really isn't safe or acceptable to leave you alone anywhere, so I'll have to take you with me. But you don't look right." Seeing her injured frown, he quickly added, "I mean, you look great, but you don't look right for this meeting."

She shook her head again. Her expression indicated a lack of comprehension.

"We don't have time to go into it now, but you know I have something of a reputation. You're different from the women I'm usually seen with."

Leslie understood that part, but his explanation had not helped his cause. Sarcastically, she replied, "Look, Ben, I'm sorry if my appearance doesn't exactly fit your precious reputation—"

Ben stopped her. "Leslie, this is serious." He gripped both of her arms above the elbow and explained in quiet tones he was certain the driver could not overhear. "It's not my reputation that concerns me. I don't want anyone we meet today to connect *you* to a certain visiting nurse. Honey, there's probably nothing to worry about, but it's best that nothing be out of the ordinary." Abandoning the serious demeanor, he gave her his lopsided grin. "Look, I would not bring a gorgeous missionary nurse with me… So you need to turn into a gorgeous something else."

She was flattered by the offhand compliment. Willing to hear him out, she looked at him skeptically. "What exactly do you want me to do?"

He answered immediately. "First, we need to alter your appearance." At his instruction, she unbuttoned the top two buttons of her bodice and several of the buttons at the bottom of her skirt. He contemplated her face again. "Do you have any darker lipstick?"

She shook her head and pulled a small silver tube containing pale coral-colored balm out of her pocket. "No. I just have this."

He nodded. "Okay. It'll have to do. Apply it fairly heavily." After she had finished with the lipstick, he eyed her critically. "That's better. But you need to do something more to your hair. Can you poof it a little?"

"Poof it?" she practically squeaked.

"You know. Make it bigger."

Sighing, Leslie leaned her head down and brushed her hair forward with her fingers to add fullness. She then threw her head back and smoothed her hair slightly. He nodded approvingly.

"Oh, here, give me your watch." He held out

his hand, and she removed the chunky black Casio that was decidedly more functional than fashionable. Obediently, she handed him the watch. He perused her appearance again and then nodded with satisfaction.

"Okay. You look great. Now we need to work on your character. What's your middle name?"

Caught off guard again, she gave him another worried frown. "Ann."

"Hmm," he responded. "No, that won't work." He thought a moment. "Meredith Woodward."

"*Who* is Meredith Woodward?"

"Actually, Meredith Woodward was my ninth-grade English teacher. I had a ferocious crush on her. But, today, you're Meredith Woodward, and you're vacationing in Kenya with your family. Let me think." He contemplated possibilities. "Okay. You're from Birmingham, Alabama, and—"

"Birmingham?" she interrupted.

"Yes. The accent is similar, and it will take you farther from the nurse from Texas."

She threw up her hands in resignation. "Okay," she sighed. "I'm Meredith Woodward from Birmingham, vacationing with my family. Where are we staying, if I might ask?"

"You're staying at the Mara Serena. It's a

well-known lodge in the Masai Mara, and very expensive."

"Fine." She sighed again. "Anything else?"

He gave her a grin. "Act like you adore me."

"What?"

The driver reacted slightly to her exclamation, and Ben frowned at her, indicating that she needed to keep her voice down. In hushed tones, he expounded, "You know. Look at me longingly… Be kinda touchy-feely… Giggle a lot."

She stared at him in disbelief. *"Giggle?"*

"Sure. Act like a flighty, witless female. Pretend you're in a play. Look, it'll be fun."

She shook her head but then replied, "Okay, Ben. Whatever. You want adoring and witless, you'll get adoring and witless."

"Okay, good," he said of her declaration. But as Leslie watched his response, she caught something in his expression. Although he seemed relieved that she'd agreed to the charade, he could not completely hide a trace of worry.

CHAPTER FOURTEEN

BECAUSE IT WAS SUNDAY, the lobby of the office building was deserted except for a security guard sitting behind a high desk. Like many residents of Mombasa, he appeared to be of South Asian descent. Ben led Leslie to the desk and spoke to the guard in a language she didn't recognize. It was more abrasive and much less melodious than the local tongues. The guard made a call and, after apparently confirming their appointment, he hung up the receiver. He pointed to the elevators behind the security desk and gave Ben instructions. Ben responded politely.

As they turned toward the elevator bank, the guard smiled shyly at Leslie and said, "Welcome, miss. Have a nice visit."

Ben had warned Leslie to avoid speaking too candidly in the building, because there was a possibility microphones were scattered about, but she could not curb her curiosity. As they entered the elevator, she asked, "What language was that? It wasn't Swahili, and it didn't sound like the local dialects."

"Urdu," Ben answered. "It's one of the most common languages of Pakistan. But most of the Pakistani people who live here speak English, too."

"Oh" was the only response Leslie could make before the elevator stopped. A young man of about thirty was waiting as the door opened directly into a reception area. He was well dressed in a gray suit with a colorfully patterned silk tie.

The man smiled broadly. "Ah, Ben!" he said with exaggerated enthusiasm. "It's very good to see you again." He held out his hand. His black eyes were small and seemed somewhat disproportionate for his face. Despite that, he was a very good-looking man.

Ben clasped his hand warmly. "Kareem, my friend," he responded. "It is my distinct pleasure to visit with you and your esteemed uncle again."

Kareem turned to consider Leslie. "And who is the beautiful lady you have brought with you to brighten our dull afternoon?"

The intense stare the man turned upon Leslie was disquieting.

Ben answered smoothly. "This lovely lady is a new friend of mine, Miss Meredith Woodward. We met a few days ago, and she consented to keep me company on the long trip to Mombasa." He shrugged nonchalantly. "I warned her that I had a meeting this afternoon, but she informed me that she wouldn't mind waiting while we conduct business."

Kareem bowed slightly to Leslie. "How do you do, Miss Woodward? I am Kareem Rasheesh. It is my great pleasure to make your acquaintance." He held out his hand as he had with Ben, and his gaze seemed less formidable.

Leslie placed the fingers of her right hand in his, and when he lifted it to his lips, she affected a giggle. Trying to follow Ben's instructions, Leslie raised her hand to partially cover her exposed throat in a gesture of shy embarrassment and smiled sweetly. With a slightly exaggerated Southern accent, she answered, "And I'm pleased to make your acquaintance, Mr. Rasheesh."

Leslie continued in her soft drawl, "I sure do hope y'all don't mind me tagging along with Ben. I promise I'll just sit out here in the waiting room and not bother a single thing."

Kareem's eyes were riveted on the hand that

rested on her sternum, and it was a moment before he responded. "There is no problem at all, Miss Woodward. My uncle and I welcome you to wait here."

He reluctantly returned his attention to Ben, and while they exchanged a few more words of greeting, Leslie studied their surroundings. They were standing in a reception area that was sparsely but expensively furnished. In the center was a small desk made of some intricately carved dark wood, possibly ebony. The desk held a telephone, a closed laptop and a notepad and pencils. Leather chairs and low tables were grouped on both sides of the desk, resting on beautiful Oriental rugs.

With one hand, Kareem indicated the chair farthest away from the door to the inner offices. "Miss Woodward, please have a seat. I trust that our meeting will not take long."

Leslie sat down obediently, then crossed her legs. Ben felt a surge of irritation when Kareem watched intently as Leslie's dress parted where it had been unbuttoned, exposing one leg to midthigh before she discreetly pulled the skirt across it. Ben cleared his throat and said with excessive respect, "Kareem, we must not keep your uncle waiting."

Slightly reprimanded, Kareem nodded and led Ben to the door at the end of the reception area. Following a few steps back, Ben glanced at Leslie and gave a slight frown of consternation. She wrinkled her nose in response, and he winked before turning to accompany Kareem. The inner door closed behind the two men, and Leslie was left alone.

Time crawled. There were no books or magazines to look through, so she was forced to simply sit quietly. She could hear the men's voices through the closed door, but she wasn't able to discern what was said. Once, the discussion grew heated, with angry words being exchanged, but the voices quieted quickly. Since Leslie didn't have her watch, she was unsure how much time passed, but she surmised that nearly an hour had gone by when the door finally opened.

Kareem emerged first, followed closely by Ben. Both men were smiling while continuing a conversation that had apparently started inside the office. A third man was a few paces behind Ben—he seemed to be listening absently to the exchange. Happy to have an excuse to move, Leslie stood, drawing the attention of all three men.

Kareem abruptly stopped the discussion with Ben and spoke to the other man with considerable deference. “Uncle, please allow me to introduce our other guest.” He led the older man to where Leslie waited. “This is Mr. Murphy’s friend, Miss Meredith Woodward. Miss Woodward, this is my esteemed uncle, Shamir Rasheesh.”

The elder Mr. Rasheesh was about fifty. He had a thick mustache and black hair that was liberally peppered with gray. Like his nephew, his eyes were small and very dark. As Kareem had done earlier, the uncle delicately bowed his head to lightly kiss her hand, and Leslie felt a chill run up her spine. It was a work of supreme will not to wrench her hand away but to allow it to drop naturally to her side. Looking into his sharp, black eyes, she sensed an undercurrent of malevolence. Never before had she felt such a deep, intuitive fear.

“How do you do, Miss Woodward?” he said. “It’s truly a pleasure to meet you. I’m sorry you had to wait so long.” His voice was deep and beautiful, and his perfect English suggested an American education.

To hide her aversion, she concentrated on maintaining Meredith’s affectations. With the hand that had just been kissed, she pushed her hair away from her face and said with only a touch of nervousness, "It's nice to meet you, too, Mr. Rasheesh. And my goodness gracious, there was no problem waiting for you men to finish with your important business." She shrugged daintily, drawing all three men's attention to her open bodice.

"Have you enjoyed your visit to our lovely country, Miss Woodward?" the elder Rasheesh inquired.

"Oh my, yes!" she exclaimed. "Why, we went on a safari for three days and saw just all sorts of animals." She giggled and looked at the two men through widened eyes. "Why, I have to admit I was scared out of my wits when we saw the lions in the Mossy Mara." She deliberately mispronounced the name of the renowned animal park. "They looked big and mean… I felt like they wanted me for dinner!"

Kareem joined the conversation. "Will you be staying much longer, Miss Woodward?"

"Just a few more days, I'm afraid. My daddy has to get back home to his medical practice in Alabama. He's an anesthesiologist, you know, and very busy."

For the first time, Leslie looked directly at

Ben, who had moved to stand beside her. His expression was casually detached, but she saw faint signs of strain behind his eyes and at the corners of his mouth. Anxious to leave, she turned to the pilot and said with a pout, “Ben, honey, I’m hungry. You promised we could eat at a lovely restaurant and then go dancing when you got through with your business. Besides, we’ve kept that nice little taxi driver waiting for a long time.”

Ben was standing on her right side, and as she was speaking, she moved toward him. In keeping with her Meredith persona, she placed her left hand on his left biceps and slid her right hand between his upper arm and chest, intending to take his arm in what she hoped would be interpreted as a clingy, possessive embrace. But as she slipped her right arm through his, the back of her hand brushed against something large, hard and unmoving under his jacket. It took only a heartbeat to register that the object she had touched was a gun.

Ben felt the slight movement of the leather shoulder holster. Fearing that Leslie might jerk her hand away in response to contact with the weapon, he reacted instantaneously. He tensed his arm and pulled it to his side, discreetly pinning her hand between his arm and ribs. Simultaneously, he turned toward her and clasped both of her hands with his right one, patting them reassuringly. There was a smile on his lips but a glimmer of warning in his eyes as he responded in a carefree tone, "I know you're anxious, gorgeous. I'm starving, too. But mostly I need a drink."

Inadvertently touching the gun had startled Leslie. In all of her travels with Ben, she had never known him to carry a handgun. She was aware that he had a shotgun in the airplane, and she had seen a rifle in his cabin, but that was normal for rural Kenya. Even the Merdians and Mama Joe kept shotguns handy.

Confused and alarmed, she grew more impatient by the second—she wanted to be removed from whatever "business" was being conducted at this place and she wanted to get away from the men. *All* of the men. Her attention was drawn to the warning look in Ben's eyes, however. She understood; she would have to play the scene through.

Dropping his right hand but holding her firmly at his side with his left arm, he turned back to address the two men. He nodded and smiled graciously. It occurred to Leslie, as she witnessed the exchange, that Ben's smile held a peculiar combination of deference and threat. She sensed a stark ruthlessness in him that she'd only glimpsed before.

When she focused back on the room, she heard the elder Rasheesh addressing Ben. "And I am certain there will be no problems with the shipment. I look forward to your visit in ten days."

With that, the man turned back to Leslie. "Miss Woodward, if you are ever again in Mombasa, you must come to see me and my nephew. It would be our distinct pleasure to show you more of the city." His tone was not quite sincere.

She licked her lips and tried to give a little giggle, but it sounded flat to her own ears. "Why, thank you, Mr. Rasheesh. I'm not sure if we'll get to come back. I really want to go to England on our next vacation. The food is not very good, but the shopping is simply to die for."

The elder Mr. Rasheesh idly nodded his head in a gesture of fluid dismissal and motioned for the couple to precede him and his nephew to the elevator. In contrast, Kareem looked at her with poorly disguised lust as Ben stood aside for Leslie to enter the elevator. Ben gave a final nod and said, "I will be in touch," as the door closed. Finally removed from the penetrating stares, Leslie stepped away from Ben and closed her eyes. He watched her from the slight distance and whispered, "Not yet, honey. Don't lose focus yet."

She glanced back at him and nodded. The door opened, and Ben put his arm around her. Playfully, he said in a rather loud voice, "Come on, baby, I'll show you the town." He led her through the front door and onto the steps leading to the street. The taxi driver, who'd been waiting nearby, had obviously spotted them and was waiting at the curb.

Ben tightened his arm around the young woman and said in a serious voice, "There's one more scene we need to play." With that, he took her in a hard embrace and kissed her deeply.

Eager to do virtually anything to expedite their departure, Leslie allowed herself to be pulled into his arms and didn't resist when his lips closed upon hers. For the benefit of anyone watching, she responded with the passion she believed the flighty Meredith would exhibit.

Ben had intended the kiss to be a ruse to further delude any of Rasheesh's men into thinking he was a womanizing rake, more interested in his conquest than business. He'd been confident throughout the afternoon that he was in total control. But Leslie's response took him by surprise, and in seconds he became lost in her warmth.

Leslie felt the change in Ben and recognized what had occurred. Given their current circumstances, his response was serious. Deftly, Leslie pulled out of the embrace and placed both hands on Ben's chest in what she hoped would appear to be a caress. Under her breath, she said, "Get me out of here *now!* I've learned more than I want to know about the people you work with. Take me back to Namanga."

In a manner she hoped would be construed as teasing, she patted his cheek, then turned toward the taxi and climbed in.

Leslie's words worked like a bucket of cold water thrown in Ben's face. Effortlessly reverting to the role of alcoholic playboy, he responded by laughing heartily as he got into the taxi. Without looking at Leslie, he told the driver to take them to the Hotel Splendid.

Leslie was about to protest when he silenced her with a raised hand. Looking straight ahead rather than at her, he quietly explained, "We'll go to the bar and stay for a few minutes. Then we'll take another cab to the airport."

She nodded, then turned to stare out the window, sitting as far away from Ben as she could. She was no longer interested in the colorfully charming city. She had heard snippets of rumors about Ben's "activities" but had not wanted to believe them. Now she had seen firsthand the type of men he worked with. She wasn't exactly sure what had been discussed at the meeting, but she recognized evil. She didn't believe Ben was evil, but there could no longer be any doubt that he was motivated by greed and dealt with truly bad men. So what did that make him?

A single tear slipped out of her eye and down her cheek unhindered.

BEN AND LESLIE spoke very little during the next several hours. As planned, they spent a few minutes at the bar in the Hotel Splendid, both choosing to drink coffee. After a taxi ride to the airport, they were ready to take off before six o'clock. The timing had been close, however. It would be dusk before they landed at Namanga.

While they waited at the end of the runway, Ben took a moment to remove his jacket and the shoulder holster. These he carefully laid on the rear seat. From the corner of her eye, Leslie noted that the gun was the sort of large, black, semiautomatic weapon that seemed to be preferred by police on television and in movies. Involuntarily, she shuddered and turned to stare out the window.

For the most part, Leslie refused to look at Ben. In stark contrast to the lovely afternoon, the events of the past two hours had confused and frightened her. It wasn't just the uneasiness she had experienced in the presence of Rasheesh and his nephew, or the realization that Ben had felt the need to carry a handgun. It was the validation of things she had been trying to ignore.

She understood that Ben's occupations ranged beyond charter air-service operator and occasional tour guide. Rumors were infrequent, but smuggling had been mentioned several times in her presence. It was logical. In her heart she had known it, but she had chosen to disregard the rumors. Without really considering it, she had vaguely imagined that he traded liquor, animal skins, rhino horns, ivory or even diamonds, all of which were very serious and held severe consequences if he was caught. But today's meeting did not exactly fit her preconceived notion of how ivory smugglers operated. It had to be something more serious, more deadly. Drugs, maybe, or, even worse, it might be weapons. Facing the likely criminal nature of his work left her disillusioned and disheartened.

And yet, she was beset by confusion. What she had learned today didn't correspond with other things she knew of Ben. With the Merdians, with Simon, and with others—but mostly with her—he had been genuine, honest and caring. He was intelligent, funny and surprisingly humble.

The thing she was most fearful of considering, but which was becoming increasingly unavoidable, was what she felt for him. She had known for some time that he was very attracted to her, perhaps even in love with her. It was in his eyes and in his touch. He no longer tried to hide the longing. Reluctantly, she admitted to herself that she was very attracted to him, too—probably in love.

After the loss of Brian, she had sometimes considered that she might fall in love again. But she had assumed it would be with someone like her husband, not an itinerant pilot who was engaged in something criminal. She leaned her head against the window of the Cessna and tried to fight back the tears.

Ben was likewise deep in thought as he flew

home. The incident on the steps of the building had shaken him. For more than three years he had maintained his safety by remaining in constant control of his thoughts and actions. There had never been even a momentary lapse in his focus as he worked to accomplish his objectives. Inwardly he cursed himself as he realized he'd made more mental and procedural errors in this single day than he had during the past three years combined. Fortunately, they had pulled off the meeting, but he shuddered with the realization Leslie's life may have been in danger because of him.

He stole a glance at Leslie and saw that she was leaning against the passenger door. Her eyes were closed, but he doubted she was sleeping. Painful introspection made him realize that he was completely and totally distracted by her. He'd been neglectful of his work in the past months. More than once he had shortened trips and even failed to fly out when he should. His love for her simultaneously left him warm and expectant and cold and fearful.

He still had work to complete. There was a real possibility this could be his last dealing with Rasheesh and those like him. He'd had enough of the lifestyle, as well as the pervasive need to be alert and on guard. If he completed this deal as planned, he would be done. But he knew one thing for certain—to preserve his life, and possibly even Leslie's, he *had* to regain focus.

IT WAS DARK when they arrived back at the clinic. Titus had been watching for their approach, and he opened the gate and waved to them as the Jeep passed. In silence, Ben walked Leslie to the door and stood aside for her to precede him into the dark, deserted waiting area.

Just inside the door, Leslie groped to find the light switch and flipped it on. That accomplished, she faced the pilot. After an awkward moment, Leslie looked down at her hands and murmured, "Ben, I'm rather tired…I…uh…"

Ben's eyes never left her face as she struggled to find polite words to dismiss him. The wariness and withdrawal had returned. She didn't want him around. He nodded and retraced the short distance to the door. Rather than going through, however, he paused. With a deep sigh, he placed one forearm on the jamb and leaned into it, resting his head on his hand.

Leslie could think of nothing to say, so she waited until he turned back to face her. His expression held such intense longing that she had to look away.

He thrust his hands in his pockets and stepped toward her. "Leslie, I'm sorry about today. I should never have involved you in my… uh—" he paused to search for a word "—activities." He reached forward to touch her, but she stepped back, and he dropped his hand. "I'm sure you're wondering—"

"Ben, I really don't want to know," she interrupted. She walked a few paces, pausing near the center of the room. She turned toward him, and her pent-up emotions rushed forth. "You confuse me! I don't understand you!" Her voice broke a little. "I don't understand what you do, and I'm very afraid for you. And what's worse, I'm afraid of what I feel for you."

He saw her shoulders shake. She was crying. He led her to a section of chairs that lined the wall of the waiting room. He gently pushed her into one and moved another so that he could face her. Taking her hands in his, he said quietly, "For the past couple of months, I've been thinking it's time for me to go home."

Expecting some sort of confession or explanation, Leslie glanced up to watch his face.

Ben studied their joined hands. "Leslie, I want

to tell you what I dream about." He looked up and held her dark blue eyes with his. "I want a family. I want a house on the edge of some town in the South or the Midwest." Her expression showed bewilderment. Tears continued down her cheeks.

He looked away and continued. "I want to teach history.… I want to watch my children grow—to show them how to ride bicycles and throw footballs. And when they're old enough—you know, like seven or eight—I want to teach them how to fly." As he spoke, tears formed in his eyes, and they slid freely down his cheeks.

Despite her disillusionment and frustration, Leslie responded with a brief smile. "You'd make a wonderful father."

He smiled, too, then became serious once more. "Leslie, I'm going to be finished here soon." He ignored the tightness that formed around her mouth. "When I'm done, I'm going home. I just have to finish."

Leslie jerked her hands away and stood abruptly. "No!" She paced across the room. "Stop *now! Please!*" Her angry words echoed the disappointment in her expression as she turned back to face him. "If you want money, I have it. I have a lot of it." Her voice rose with each word, and she used her hands for emphasis. "Money's nothing. It's not important! *You can have it!*" Then, with a sobbing breath, she added quietly, "Take it, but please stop. Don't do any more..."

He shook his head. Objectively, he wondered if she realized the implication of what she had said. More than anything else, he wanted to go to her and hold her and reassure her, but he forced himself to refrain. He remained seated and leaned forward, resting his forearms on his knees and staring at the floor. "No, Les. I don't want money."

She moved forward then to kneel in front of him, looking intently into his eyes. She could see conflict, coupled with pain and worry. Suddenly needing to touch him, she grasped his hands and pleaded, "Why, then? Tell me why."

Staring at their hands, he whispered, "I have to. That's all I can say right now. Leslie, I have to finish."

Frustrated, she stood and backed away. She was suddenly exhausted. "It really is getting late, Ben. There will be twenty or thirty people here by seven in the morning."

At her prompting, he stood and walked slowly to the door. His movements were deliberate, signifying he was still reluctant to go. As before, he turned abruptly. They were standing very close. Gently, he pulled her into his arms. "I can't leave like this."

She was stiff initially but, despite her desire to remain detached, she found she was unable to resist him. Little by little, Leslie gave in to the embrace. She felt him kiss her hair and, with her eyes closed, she raised her face to welcome his lips. The kiss was deep and loving. His arms tightened, and his hands moved across her back to grasp her dress in a gesture akin to desperation. Ben removed his lips from hers and touched them to her temple. She was incapable of letting him go. She held her arms around his neck tightly and buried her face in his shoulder.

Finally, Ben sighed deeply and pushed her until she was standing at arm's length. He searched her eyes and found both love and emotional turmoil. "Think about what I said. I know I'm asking a lot, but I want...no, I *need* you to trust me."

She chewed her bottom lip and nodded in reply, then kissed his throat gently before dropping her hands and stepping back to let him leave.

This time, he made it through the door before

he turned again to face her. His demeanor had lightened a little, and his expression now held a hint of his usual impertinence. “You have to tell me something.”

Leslie pushed away a trailing tear and gave him a puzzled look. “What?”

“Is your ‘daddy’ really an anesthesiologist?”

For the first time in several hours, she actually laughed. Through a watery giggle she answered, “Hardly. *Dad* is a mailman, but I didn’t think that would fit Meredith’s profile.”

Heartened, he grinned at her. Shaking his head, he said with wonder, “You were terrific, you know. I had to bite my cheek to keep a straight face or else I would have blown the entire thing. Shoot, you almost had me convinced that you were afraid of ‘those mean ol’ lions.’” He was still smiling as he climbed into the Jeep.

CHAPTER FIFTEEN

LESLIE'S OBLIGATION to the clinic in Kenya was nearing an end. Mama Joe was due back in just three weeks, and then she would go home. When she considered the rapidly approaching time for her departure, her emotions were mixed. She was anxious to see her family and experience the wonderful conveniences of American life, which she vowed to never again take for granted. But at the same time, she dreaded the thought of leaving Namanga and saying goodbye to the people who had come to respect and rely on her—and those she had come to care for, too. And at night when she was alone, she conceded that what she dreaded most was the possibility of never seeing Ben again.

The days following the eventful trip to Mombasa were busy, first with routine clinic patients and then with the pervasive crises that were faced almost daily. Wednesday afternoon, Paul stopped by to invite Leslie to dinner. She readily agreed, but, as he was leaving, Paul mentioned that Ben was coming, too. That bit of news gave her pause as she was both reluctant and eager to see him. She sighed in resignation, knowing it was too late to back out.

It was after six that evening when Titus dropped Leslie off at the Merdians' house. Ben's Jeep was parked next to Paul's Land Rover, and Leslie steadied her emotions for the meeting, telling herself she would be friendly but detached. As soon as she saw him, though, she knew that following her plan would be impossible. Where Ben Murphy was concerned, she would never be detached.

Beth opened the door before Leslie had a chance to knock, and the little girl welcomed her excitedly. Ben and Paul stood to greet the new arrival, and Leslie walked forward to give Paul a quick hug. "I'm sorry I'm late. As we were about to leave, Mrs. Ngundu brought in her youngest son. Evidently he'd found a broken bottle he was trying to use to store trinkets." She laughed and shook her head. "He just needed a few stitches."

Paul chuckled. "I know that little guy. He's a walking accident."

Leslie finally turned her attention to Ben and

was struck by the undisguised yearning in his expression. Her reaction was involuntarily physical. She felt herself flush deeply, and her heartbeat rose to an uncomfortably rapid rhythm.

He grasped her shoulders lightly before kissing her on the cheek. "Evening, Leslie."

Her mouth was suddenly dry, and she swallowed with some difficulty before replying, "Hi, Ben. It's good to see you."

Both waited for the other to speak again, and when neither did, Paul announced, "Uh…Judy's in the kitchen. I'll go tell her you're here."

As he turned away, Leslie stopped him. With lightness in her tone that she did not feel, she said, "No, let me. I'll see what I can do to help." She did not glance back as she escaped to the kitchen.

After the initial awkwardness, an ease settled on the group as they gathered around the dinner table. The meal was delightful, full of laughter. After dinner, the men entertained the children while Leslie helped Judy with the dishes. Initially, their conversation centered on Leslie's work and Judy's school, but midway through the cleanup, Judy asked, "Did you and Ben have some kind of argument? You're both acting like something is wrong."

Keeping her attention on the plate she was washing, Leslie answered, "It wasn't an argument. It was really more like..." Struggling for an explanation, she bit her lip and glanced at her friend. "Judy, do you know anything about what Ben does? I mean, other than the charter service?"

Judy paused in the process of drying a glass. "Honestly, Leslie, I'm not sure. Ben never discusses it. I think Paul may know more, but he hasn't shared it with me." She sighed and set the glass on the counter. She placed one hand on Leslie's arm to gain her full attention. "Leslie, it's clear that in many ways Ben is not what he seems. I can't tell you what he does or why. But I do know this—" she looked squarely at her friend "—he loves you."

Tears threatened, and Leslie nodded. "I just don't know what to do about it," she whispered.

A short time later the women joined the men and children in the living room. Despite the serious discussion in the kitchen, the conversation was unforced and natural, and soon they were all laughing companionably. Titus arrived at the appointed time, and Leslie rose to leave as the Jeep pulled into the driveway. She hugged each member of the Merdian family. She knew that she'd have only a few more opportunities to be with them, and the realization saddened her deeply.

Impulsively she took Ben's hand and pulled him toward the door. Paul and Judy glanced at each other and in unspoken agreement allowed the pair to leave the room unaccompanied. Judy closed the door and distracted the children by telling them to get ready for bed.

Alone on the covered porch, Leslie and Ben studied each other with uncertainty and expectation. Leslie broke the awkward silence. "I've been thinking about what you said."

His expression did not change, so she continued. "You know, about what you want." There was still no reaction. She took a deep breath. "I need to tell you what I want…but, Ben…"

When she did not immediately continue, he put his hands on her shoulders. She looked away from his eyes and stared at the top button of his shirt. The tears that had threatened earlier formed now, and she blinked hard to hold them back. "I want to tell you, but I…" Shaking her head, she whispered, "I want you. But I'm afraid…I'm afraid for you…and what I feel for you." She bit her lip. "I can't lose someone again."

Finally, he pulled her into his arms. His voice was a little hoarse when he said, "Leslie, it's all right. It'll be all right." He closed his eyes and stroked her hair. "I'd do anything—*anything*—to keep from hurting you."

"I know," she whispered. She rested in the embrace for a minute more before she raised her face to him. His kiss was gentle and loving, and she gave up trying to fight her emotions. Her hands clasped his neck, and she stood on her toes trying to get closer.

It was Ben who finally ended the embrace. He lightly touched her forehead with his lips before stepping back. Leslie blinked, then wiped her damp eyes with one hand and said with a reticent smile, "Titus is going to wonder what's going on."

He grinned. "Honey, Titus already knows what's going on."

He walked her to the Jeep and opened the door. After she had settled into the seat, he leaned down and said quietly, "I'm leaving tomorrow and will be gone for a few days. I'll stop by the clinic as soon as I can. Okay?"

She responded with a sweet half smile and a nod as he closed the door, and Titus backed out. As they drove through the compound gate, she turned back. Ben stood watching the Jeep depart. During the drive home, Leslie recognized an expectancy she hadn't known in ages. On reflection, she realized the feeling was hope. She was beginning to consider possibilities for the future—and, unexpectedly, the future appeared full of promise.

FIVE DAYS PASSED before Leslie saw Ben again. Early Tuesday morning the following week, she was packing supplies with Titus and Naomi to take into the countryside for a two-day trip holding immunization clinics. They would leave shortly, visiting three villages in the next day and a half. They planned to return Wednesday evening.

As the trio loaded the Jeep, they observed a vehicle driving up the dirt road. Leslie recognized it as Ben's, and she grew nervous in anticipation of seeing him again. But it quickly became evident that it was Simon, and he was going much too fast on the pothole-filled road.

The Masai pulled through the gate and skidded to a stop, sending dirt and pebbles flying. Leslie's nervousness turned to alarm when she saw his face and heard his words as he addressed Titus, all the while looking at her. Trying to understand, she caught enough of the dialogue to know something had happened to Ben. He spoke the English words "rifle" and "airplane," and she recognized the Swahili words for "wound" and "blood." She was overcome by a feeling of dread as she waited for Titus to translate.

"Miss Leslie," Titus said while Simon was still speaking, "Ben was shot by bandits when he landed this morning. Simon was on his way to the airport and heard the gunfire. Ben killed the bandits, but he was badly injured. Simon left him at his house because the ride from the airport made him bleed badly."

Leslie had heard enough. Acting quickly, she addressed Titus. "Take me and Naomi to Ben's." Fortunately, the supplies she would need were already in the car, as they always carried a full stock when they traveled in order to manage emergencies. She knew, however, they would need a better vehicle if they had to drive to Nairobi. "Tell Simon to go get Paul, and have him bring his Land Rover for transport." In less than a minute, the two Jeeps sped off in opposite directions.

Despite driving at a speed that threatened to disable the vehicle, the trip took a nerve-racking fifteen minutes. Leslie jumped out of the Jeep before it came to a complete stop, her bag of emergency supplies and equipment in hand. She ran across the short path and through the door but stopped short when she saw Ben lying on the cot against the far wall. His face was deathly pale, his eyes were closed, and his shirt and pants were covered with dark blood.

"Oh, dear God!" she cried as she rushed to kneel by the bed. Trying not to panic, she touched his chest and waited for movement, then said a quick prayer when she felt it rise and fall. With that small reassurance, she began assessing the extent of his injuries. Within moments, fear threatened to overwhelm her as she realized how inadequately equipped she was to save his life.

CHAPTER SIXTEEN

BEN WAS BLEEDING to death. Leslie's initial assessment revealed his breathing was rapid but not labored. She found one wound in his upper chest and one in his abdomen. The most urgent problem, however, was the damage to his right thigh. Evidently a bullet had entered anteriorly, then exited, leaving a gaping hole in the back of his leg. Fortunately it had missed his femur, but he was bleeding heavily. The cot below him was wet with blood, and an alarming amount had soaked through the canvas fabric and dripped onto the floor.

With Naomi's assistance, she cut away his pant leg. Acting quickly, she ripped the packaging off two large dressing pads and pressed them firmly over the wounds. "Hold these here—*tight,*" she directed Naomi. She opened two more pads and hurriedly rolled a bandage around his thigh to keep the cotton dressing securely in place, putting pressure on the wounds.

She tore at the buttons holding his shirt, completely exposing his chest. The wound was high on his left side and was bleeding very little externally, which gave her a small measure of relief. With her stethoscope, she determined the breath sounds over his left side were diminished but present. Although this was reassuring, she knew there could be significant internal bleeding, and the lack of an exit wound meant the bullet was lodged in his chest. She hardly noticed that her hands and the front of her blouse were covered in blood, eerily reminiscent of the incident in Nairobi. She hurriedly placed a sterile dressing over the wound and directed Naomi to tape it into place.

She next moved to examine the abdominal wound. There appeared to be minimal internal bleeding. The bowel, however, was sure to be involved, and if he did not have surgery to repair any nicks or holes, peritonitis would occur within a few hours. She had to get him to Nairobi.

Titus stood by the door, unwilling to leave but not wanting to come closer. Anxiety covered his expressive face. Leslie shouted to him, "Go watch for Simon and Paul! Let me know when you see them!"

She turned to Naomi and said, "Take his blood pressure." As Naomi complied, Leslie grabbed infusion tubing and a liter bag of fluid from her supplies to start an intravenous line.

"Eighty-four over forty-four." Concern was clear in Naomi's voice.

"Damn…damn…" Leslie muttered as she turned the IV to run wide open, knowing that he needed fluid to avoid circulatory collapse. His pulse was rapid, and he was simultaneously sweating and shivering—all signs of hemorrhagic shock. The IV saline would help, but he needed blood. She lamented that she didn't have a store of whole blood or plasma. If his transfer was delayed, she would have to devise a way to give him a person-to-person transfusion. She rummaged in her bag to locate her precious store of injectable antibiotics and added medication into the IV bag to try to forestall infection.

Leslie looked around the room for something to raise Ben's legs. She dragged a crate over, and she and Naomi were able to lift the foot of the cot to rest on it. Ben moaned in response to the movement of the small bed; it was the first sound she had heard him make.

Leslie paused to wash the blood from her hands and dampen a towel, and then she cleaned

Ben's face, which was spotted with dirt. His eyes were still closed, and there were no other signs he was regaining consciousness.

"Ben...Ben..." She managed to keep her voice calm. "Ben, can you hear me?" She talked to him quietly as they worked. "We're here with you. You're going to be okay."

He remained motionless. Frustrated and desperate to overcome her own sense of panic, Leslie was hugely relieved when Titus called her to the door and she saw a cloud of dust on the road. "Thank God," she said out loud. She motioned for Naomi to join her. "Stay here and wait with Titus," she insisted. "See if you can help them."

She returned to Ben. His normally sun-darkened face was ashen. She took his blood pressure again and was relieved it had not dropped. She checked the IV bag; half of the liter had been infused. She gave a small sigh—at least the volume of fluid circulating through his veins was better.

She knelt beside him again and gently touched his brow and cheek. "Ben...Ben, can you hear me?"

This time, he blinked and then opened his eyes. He frowned, and for a second he didn't seem to recognize her. Then he blinked again.

"Les? Leslie, what?..." His voice was low and hoarse. He licked his lips and tried to swallow.

Weakly, he reached out for her, and she clasped his hand tightly with both of hers. Her voice cracked. "S-Simon told us that someone, uh...ambushed you this morning at the airfield. He, uh...he said that you killed the attackers. He brought you here and came to get me." She struggled to blink back tears. "I sent Simon to get Paul. They're nearly here." She squeezed his hand. "We're going to come up with a way to get you to Nairobi."

He nodded slightly and then tried to swallow again. The green eyes did not leave her face. He whispered, "I'm thirsty. Can I have something to drink?"

"Okay, but just a couple of swallows. You have an abdominal wound, and you need surgery. Drinking a lot could make it worse." She poured a small amount of sterile water into a clean cup and held it to his lips. She stroked his hair while he sipped. "That'll help a little."

He nodded his head and she removed the cup. "How do you feel?"

"It hurts," he answered. Pain etched his face.

"Okay." She nodded. "I have some morphine. I'll get my bag."

He stopped her as she started to move away. "No, not yet. I need to talk to Paul." He closed his eyes tightly and winced as a wave of pain speared through him. She clasped his hand, holding it until the spasm passed. A moment later he looked back at her. "I need to be able to think… I have to stay awake…."

Leslie shook her head, hating to see him in pain. "I can give you a little. Just enough to take the edge off."

He swallowed again. "Not now…later. I need to talk to Paul."

She nodded in acquiescence. "Okay…but let me know when you want anything." She watched him closely, still holding his hand, desperately wishing there was more she could do.

Despite his pain, he pulled their clasped hands forward and kissed her fingers. Although his eyes were clear and steady as they held hers, his words were barely audible. "I love you."

Tears streamed down her face, but she managed a weak smile. She leaned forward and gently touched his lips with hers. "I know," she whispered. "I love you, too." She kissed his forehead before she sat back.

His eyes caught hers again. "Leslie, I need to tell you—" His words were cut off by another wave of pain arising from his abdomen. He clenched his teeth and grimaced. The spasm left him breathless.

She held his hand until it passed. In a tone that was meant to convince them both, she said, "We'll have plenty of time to talk later. Right now, just rest."

From her spot at the door, Naomi motioned to her, indicating that the men were near.

"Thank God!" she whispered as she heard the sound of gravel flying and a door slam.

Only seconds later Paul entered. He was alarmed when he saw Ben, but he managed to disguise it. "How're you doing, Ben?" His voice was almost casual as he knelt beside the cot, much as Leslie had done.

Ben tried to smile, but it became a grimace. He gripped the preacher's hand. "I'm glad to see you!"

Paul's eyes sought out Leslie. He asked, "How does it look?"

"I think the wound in his chest will be all right, but he needs surgery on his abdomen—soon! The leg wound will give us problems if it keeps bleeding. We've got to get him to Nairobi *now!*"

As Paul was nodding in response, Ben interrupted. His words were choppy and weak, and he was panting heavily. "Paul…there's a phone…" He motioned toward the kitchen and cringed again; the waves of pain seemed to be increasing in both frequency and intensity. "Under the fridge…"

Paul gestured to Titus and Simon, who were standing near the door, and instructed them in rapid Swahili to move the refrigerator. Leslie remained beside the cot and watched as the three men examined the floor. The aged linoleum had been cut in a semicircle. Titus pulled it back, and they discovered a two-foot-square piece of plywood. Paul moved the plywood, revealing a fairly deep hole out of which he removed a cell phone with some type of sophisticated antenna, a laptop, Ben's passport and a medium-size canvas bag, all wrapped in heavy, clear plastic.

Ben had managed to partially turn on his side and watch from the cot. "The phone." His words seemed a little more strained. "I need…"

Paul covered the distance from the kitchen in three steps and handed the phone to the injured man. With shaking fingers, Ben flipped two switches, then tried to press a button but didn't have the coordination. Paul pushed it for him, and they were rewarded by faint static.

Ben struggled to depress several buttons and finally hit Send.

Taking a deep breath, Ben said, "Charlie, Foxtrot, Quebec…" but was gripped by another stab of pain. Paul looked at Leslie in alarm, but she simply shook her head. Over his shoulder, she glanced at the IV fluid and noted that it was more than three-quarters empty. She would need to hang another bag soon and hoped that Ben would let her give him some pain medication then.

He tried the sequence again, this time with more success. "Yes, Center, this is Falcon Station. Fifty twenty-seven, thirty-thirty. Do you copy?"

Ben closed his eyes and gave a small sigh of relief. Only Ben could hear the reply, but each of the others in the room was reassured when they realized his call had been answered.

Ben tried to lick his lips before continuing but was unable. Leslie poured a little water into the cup and held it to his mouth. He wet his lips before he said, "Center, I have been shot. Repeat, I have been shot. I was ambushed this morning. It's critical." He paused for a few seconds, evidently listening, then replied, "There were five—three were Bantu and two South Asians… probably Pashto…Rasheesh's men."

Leslie felt her stomach clench when she heard Ben mention the name of the man from Mombasa. There was another pause, and Ben frowned before he replied, "Dead. Charles Endebbi was killed, too."

Paul and Leslie looked at each other upon hearing about the death of the man who took care of the airfield. Paul shook his head, and they returned their attention to Ben. They saw him nod, apparently responding to something. He closed his eyes and listened for a few more seconds. With his eyes still closed, he said, "Yes, Center. Rendezvous, Site Two. Sixty minutes. Stand by, and I'll check the timing." He opened his eyes and zeroed in on Paul. "Can you get me to Ngulia Lake within the hour?"

Paul answered, "That's only forty or fifty miles…but the condition of the road is abominable, where it exists at all." Paul's fear for his friend was evident. "Yeah, Ben. I think the truck can make it. But I'm worried…"

Paul turned to Leslie, and she gave him a dubious look while shrugging slightly. Turning her attention to Ben, she said, "Ben, we need to take you to Nairobi." Looking toward Paul again, she pleaded, "Nairobi is by far the best place to take him. He needs surgery!" She looked confused. "Isn't Ngulia Lake the other direction?"

Ben ignored the exchange. Into the phone he said, "We'll be in a white Land Rover." His breath caught, and he clutched his abdomen. Precious seconds passed before he was able to continue. "Roger, we'll make Site Two at eight forty-five." He listened again for a span and said with considerably less strength, "Roger that, Center, Falcon Station out." He switched off the phone and lay back on the cot in exhaustion.

The small group looked at one another. Finally, resigned to the decision that had evidently been made, Leslie said, "Ben, who is going to meet us at Ngulia Lake?"

Without opening his eyes, he answered tiredly, "The people I work for."

She was stunned. She had known Ben for six months, and he'd never given any indication that he worked for anyone other than himself. Not comprehending, Leslie asked, "Will they take you to Nairobi?"

Ben looked up at her and said, "I don't know."

He seemed to regain a measure of strength, and before she could protest, he motioned to Simon, "Get the Land Rover ready for the trip, then come back for me." He turned to Leslie and Paul and said, "Look in the large coffee cans... also bring the laptop and drives." He closed his eyes, and Leslie jumped to look in the coffee cans, finding rolls of American bills as well as substantial amounts of Kenyan and Tanzanian currency; these she stuffed into her medical bag. In the meantime Paul picked up Ben's backpack and shoved the laptop, money, passport and satellite phone into a compartment, while Simon and Titus returned for the injured pilot and carried him, cot and all, to the Land Rover.

Simon opened the rear of the vehicle, and, with Leslie directing, the trio carefully used the bloody sheet to lift Ben. As he rushed into the driver's seat, Paul instructed Titus to take Naomi back to the clinic, and then he started the vehicle.

Simon rode in the front with Paul, while Leslie crawled into the back to be with Ben. He was awake but glassy-eyed and obviously in pain as they departed. She held his hand and gave a faint smile. "We'll be there before you know it." She tried to sound encouraging. "They'll get you to the hospital and take care of your injuries. In a few days, you'll get a shower in clean water, and before you know it you'll be good as new."

He responded with a weak smile and then closed his eyes. Shortly thereafter, they hit the first pothole. Ben grimaced, gritting his teeth. Less than a minute later, there was another jolt. Ben groaned and gripped Leslie's hand.

Leslie let go of his hand and hastily dug through her bag. Finding the vial and a syringe, she drew up the pain medication. She leaned over him and saw that he was even more ashen than before. "Ben…Ben, I'm going to give you morphine now. We're on our way, and there's nothing more you can do. You need to rest."

His nod was almost imperceptible, and she slowly injected the medication into the IV line. As she put the syringe back into her bag, she saw the money. Quickly, she slipped the rolls of bills into the canvas bag that held Ben's phone. As she did so, she noticed that it also contained three smallish devices—made of black plastic. Each device was a little larger than a deck of cards and had a short cable that obviously connected it to a computer. She closed the bag with a puzzled frown before returning her attention to Ben.

She was relieved to see the bleeding from his

leg appeared to have stopped. His pulse was still too fast and his blood pressure too low, but they were stable, and there was nothing more she could do except pray. So for the next fifty minutes, she did just that. "Please, God. Please God. Please," she whispered over and over. "Don't take him from me...please."

CHAPTER SEVENTEEN

THE LAND ROVER STOPPED. Leslie glanced out the window and saw that they were parked on one of the dry lake beds that dotted the arid regions of southern Kenya. The ground was thick, dried, broken mud, and, other than widespread clumps of knee-high golden grass, very little vegetation was visible in any direction. Nervously, she looked around for wildlife; lions were known to inhabit these grassy areas. The two men got out of the vehicle and moved to the front to watch for the promised transport. She was relieved to see Paul was holding a shotgun.

She looked at her watch—eight-forty. Amazing. They had made the trip in only fifty-five minutes, a tribute to Paul's aggressive driving and the durability of the Land Rover.

Ben appeared to be sleeping. "Ben," she whispered, "please, please stay with me. I need you. I love you." She kissed him on the forehead, and he opened his eyes.

"Are we there?" His voice was gravelly.

She nodded. "Yes. Paul and Simon are watching for a plane." She tried to smile. "I hope this guy is as good a pilot as you, because this looks like a really impossible place to land."

His lips curved slightly. "Maybe he'll let me help…." His voice trailed off, and he was asleep again.

Only a few minutes passed before Leslie became aware of a low hum. She scrambled out of the SUV and searched the sky for the source of the sound. In the distance she saw a silver speck, and as she watched, the speck grew larger and louder. Paul and Simon waved frantically, and as the plane neared the Land Rover, the pilot dipped its wings to each side.

As she observed the plane, Leslie concluded that it was strange, somehow different from any she had seen before. She was surprised by the route the pilot was taking. He approached them at an alarmingly fast speed until he was almost directly overhead. The plane slowed but flew a little past them. While still at an altitude of several hundred feet, the pilot made a quick, banking turn and headed back.

Just before the plane reached them, it appeared to stall. The trio on the ground stared as the twin propellers moved from being positioned in front of the plane to being above it, like rotors on a helicopter. Then, like a helicopter, the aircraft continued its descent as it moved slowly toward them. Within a minute, it landed less than sixty feet away. The aircraft was marked with a U.S. flag, an identification number, and, in bold black letters, "USMC."

The small group was still staring at the odd plane when three men wearing olive coveralls climbed out and jogged toward them. There were no markings or insignias on their clothing, and they were all hatless. Two pilots remained on the aircraft and could be seen waiting in the cockpit.

One of the men carried a large canvas bag; another held what appeared to be a collapsible stretcher. As the three reached them, the one in the lead spoke to Paul. "We're here for Ben Murphy." He had to raise his voice to be heard over the roar of the rotors.

Paul nodded and pointed to the Land Rover. "In there."

The men moved to the vehicle, and the one carrying the bag crawled into the back. Leslie started to follow but was detained by the nearest man. He said, "Stay here, ma'am. He's going to check the patient."

Leslie pushed his hand aside. "Excuse me, but Mr. Murphy is *my* patient." The guard scanned her bloody shirt and skirt, registered the determined look in her eyes and wisely stepped aside.

Inside the Land Rover, she briefly studied the man who was bent over Ben. He looked to be in his early twenties and had black hair, dark brown eyes, and an olive complexion. She watched him pull a stethoscope out of his bag and take Ben's blood pressure. After he got the reading, she informed him, "It's been running about eighty over fifty. His pulse has ranged between one hundred and one-ten."

The man nodded. He pointed to the bag of fluid hanging from a coat hanger above Ben. "Is this the first liter?"

She shook her head. "No, it's the second. I ran in 1000 cc with one gram of cephalosporin. He's also had ten milligrams of morphine."

He nodded as he listened to Ben's chest. "Any problems breathing?"

She shook her head a second time. "No. I'm less concerned about the chest wound than the abdominal wound. He lost a lot of blood from the leg, but that's stopped for now."

The man pulled an insulated container from his backpack and removed a large syringe filled with yellow fluid. He handed it to Leslie and said, "Plasma. Push it."

Although not as good as a blood transfusion, the plasma was considerably superior to the IV fluid Ben had been receiving, and she quickly complied. While she was injecting the plasma into the IV tubing, the young man hurriedly assessed the bandaged wounds. Apparently determining there was little else that could be done in the rear of the SUV, he balled his stethoscope and shoved his equipment into his backpack. Leaning toward the door, he shouted, "Sid! Marty! Open out the stretcher. Let's get this guy out of here!"

The pair hurried to comply. The man in the truck turned back to Ben and said, "Sir, I'm Corpsman Enrique Garcia. Our team is going to lift you out of here. You should be fine."

Leslie saw Ben open his eyes and nod. He made a brief, waving gesture with one hand and said in a tired voice, "The bag… Get the bag… hard drives. Need to destroy the phone…" He closed his eyes again.

Garcia replied with a sharp "Yes, sir," then squatted at the back of the truck to help the other two with the little stretcher. In a few movements they slid the stretcher into the vehicle beside Ben, and Garcia rolled him carefully on his side to place the apparatus under him and then let him roll back on top of it. When Ben was in position, they pulled the stretcher from the truck.

Without a word to Paul, Leslie or Simon, Garcia and the man called Sid carried Ben to the waiting plane. As they passed the third man—evidently Marty—Garcia said something and jerked his head toward the SUV. Marty then jumped into the truck to retrieve the canvas bag. He checked the contents and, apparently satisfied, exited the vehicle. He paused momentarily to address the little group. "Thank you for your assistance."

With that, he turned and jogged to the plane, climbed aboard and shut the door. In only seconds the rotors were turning faster, and moments later the aircraft was aloft. When it had risen a few hundred feet, the three on the ground watched in amazement as the aircraft started moving forward. Steadily the rotors shifted downward to become propellers once more. All the while, the plane was moving away with increasing speed. Within a minute it was only a speck in the eastern sky. Then it disappeared.

Leslie looked at her watch and was astonished to find that the entire process had taken less than ten minutes. They'd been so focused on the bone-jarring drive through the savanna that she hadn't really stopped to contemplate what would happen when they arrived. She had been terrified for Ben, and the relief she felt that he was evidently being flown somewhere for emergency care was beset with concurrent uneasiness about the events that had just transpired. She turned to Paul. His eyes were closed, and she suspected he was praying. *Good,* she thought with gratitude. *Ben needs all the help he can get.*

As she watched Paul, she finally paused to analyze the events of the past hour. She'd been so caught up in her concern for Ben and doing what she could to save his life that she hadn't thought to consider what was going on. Why had Ben been shot? What was the deal with the hidden laptop? The black computer devices? The phone? Obviously there had been a known threat, and certainly the possibility of injury had been anticipated—there'd been a contingency plan for just this sort of occurrence! And he'd asked for Paul because the preacher would know what to do. Paul hadn't even questioned driving to the middle of nowhere rather than trying to take Ben to Nairobi. Suddenly, it became clear that Paul knew more than he was letting on.

The cautious drive home took longer than the rush to the rendezvous site, and Leslie spent most of the time musing on the events of the morning and trying to avoid dwelling on Ben's condition.

Paul dropped Leslie by the clinic first, planning on taking Simon back to his own house to retrieve Ben's Jeep. She asked Paul to accompany her to the door, where she paused to ask, "What happened?"

He hesitated a breath before answering, "Leslie, it might have been bandits trying to rob him, or maybe steal the plane…"

She frowned. "Paul, you know that's not what I mean. What was the deal with the phone and the funny-looking airplane and the three men and all? Obviously, they were military. And Ben said something about Rasheesh…and he asked for you. I know you know… What is Ben involved in?"

Paul sighed and looked her in the eye. "Leslie, I promised I wouldn't tell. He only told me in case something like this happened. He needed someone to know where the hard drives were—"

"Hard drives?" she interrupted.

Paul rolled his eyes in exasperation, "Oh, good grief. I can't believe I said that. I am really rattled… I'm usually better at keeping confidences than this."

"Paul, I'm not asking you to break a confidence. I just want to understand. I have no intention of doing anything that would harm Ben. You know that."

He took her hand. "I know, Leslie. And I know that he's in love with you. He's been afraid to say anything. He wasn't sure what you felt—well, because of his lifestyle and all…"

He closed his eyes and rubbed them with his fingers before looking back at her. "Leslie, I can't tell you everything, mostly because I don't know everything. But I will say this. Since he's been here, Ben has been doing some work for the CIA and the Defense Department."

Leslie stared at him. "The CIA? The Defense Department?" She recalled the title of his dissertation—*Aerial Reconnaissance and Surveillance*. She experienced a moment of disjointed confusion that suddenly cleared, as if puzzle pieces had jumbled and some fell into place.

She absorbed the new revelation. Her voice was slightly tremulous when she asked, "Is…he a spy?"

"I don't think so—not exactly, at any rate," Paul answered. "While he's gone, for the most part he looks for evidence of terrorist activities and plans by groups like the pirates who are working off the east coast of Africa. He talks to people, observes movements and plots his findings on maps and in databases, which he gets to analysts somewhere via satellite." Paul's attempt to look blank failed miserably, and he was noticeably uncomfortable as he paused.

Finally, he sighed and said, "He also acts like an arms broker of sorts. He tries to learn who is buying and selling guns and other weaponry. They're particularly worried about short-range missiles—you know, SAMs, or surface-to-air missiles—the kind that can be used to shoot down airplanes. I'm not sure what else is involved, but Ben's been at it for almost three years now. The drinking, the smuggling, the women—that's all a ruse."

Leslie nodded and smiled slightly, but the smile was rueful. "I figured out that part." She looked puzzled then. "But I thought he was kicked out of the air force. Was that real?"

"I don't know. It wasn't part of what he shared."

Neither of them spoke for a while. Finally, Leslie asked, "So do you think those guys were marines?"

"That would be my guess. Either that or CIA…or maybe both. I'm not sure."

Leslie frowned. Concern and fear were interspersed with a growing sense of relief that Ben's activities were honorable. As she considered all that Paul told her, her emotion grew into pride and even awe. Regret quickly followed. She had doubted him. She wished she could tell him she was sorry. "I wonder where they took him."

Paul shook his head. "Leslie, I have no idea. Why don't we wait a day or two, and then we can go to Nairobi to try to find out where he is."

Leslie nodded, grateful for the suggestion. She was anxious to find out news about Ben, but she didn't want to be alone in case the news was bad. Besides, she knew Paul would probably be more successful in getting information from reluctant bureaucrats, military officials or intelligence agencies. "Okay. Day after tomorrow, we go to Nairobi."

CHAPTER EIGHTEEN

PAUL AND LESLIE'S quest was initially met with interest and concern. But concern turned to skepticism when they told officials at the American embassy about the tilt-rotor aircraft and the three U.S. military servicemen who had picked up the seriously injured man they were seeking.

The ambassador's assistant they spoke with first referred them to the marine master sergeant in charge of security for the embassy. He simply stared at the pair with his eyebrow raised and in essence dismissed them. They were informed that the aircraft they described was only a prototype. He was certain it was not currently being used by the marines in the Indian Ocean. He sent them back to the ambassador's assistant.

In desperation, Paul asked the assistant whom they might speak with about American military or CIA operations in the region. They were politely but firmly told that if there were any such activities in the area—which there weren't—

they would not be privy to the details. Anything covert was classified.

After leaving the embassy, Paul and Leslie checked the hospitals. They were not surprised to find that no Americans had been brought in with gunshot wounds in more than six months. They returned home discouraged.

The following week, they drove back to Nairobi. It had been nine days since Ben's assault, and Leslie was extremely anxious for news. But they met with similar results on the second visit. Once again, the embassy officials insisted they'd heard of no U.S. military activity in the area and they assured Leslie and Paul they knew nothing about a pilot named Ben Murphy.

Frustrated, Paul suggested visiting a man named Kenneth Day. Mr. Day was a retired diplomat who'd worked in East Africa for more than thirty years and knew virtually all of the expatriates. He had a reputation for having contacts outside of routine channels, which most likely included American intelligence officials.

Mr. Day saw them at once, and they talked with him for more than an hour. Leslie was impressed by the elderly man, who in some ways reminded her of Mama Joe. He was in his eighties, slight and apparently frail, but his eyes and demeanor retained a youthful exuberance that inspired confidence. After listening to the entire story, he told Paul and Leslie he'd make a few calls and see if he could help. He told them to come back in the afternoon for tea.

When they returned at the appointed time, Mr. Day regretfully told them that he'd been unable to learn any news about Ben. He admitted that he was surprised about the brick wall he had encountered. "Frankly," he mused, "either my contacts really don't know anything about Ben, or this is so top secret that no one is talking."

Seeing their discouragement, he took Leslie's hand in his. "I'm sorry I wasn't any help. I hope you find your young man." His words were heartfelt.

Paul and Leslie thanked Mr. Day and left to make the long drive back to Namanga. It was after dark when they arrived at the clinic. As Paul walked Leslie to the door he saw that tears of fear and disappointment clouded her eyes.

"Paul, what can we do now? I need to know if he's all right."

He shook his head in frustration. "The only other avenue I can think of is his parents." He thought for a moment then asked, "Have you made arrangements to pick up Mama Joe next week?"

Leslie wiped her eyes. "Yes. I had Elizabeth contact Andy Singleton, and it's all scheduled. I'll be going along to meet her."

"When you're there, stop by the East Africa Mission office and get Ben's parents' address in Florida. When you get back to the States, you can either call them or go by. Surely they'll have been informed about his injuries." Both of them thought, but neither said out loud, that his parents would certainly have been informed if Ben had died.

It wasn't much, but it was a plan. Leslie tried to control her voice. "Yes, that sounds like a good idea." She wiped her eyes and managed a soggy smile. "It's hard to believe that Mama Joe will be back in a week and I'll be going home."

He gave her a smile, and she kissed him on the cheek. "Thanks, Paul, for trying. You've been a terrific friend."

IN A REVERSAL of the scene almost six months before, Leslie was waiting at the airport in Nairobi when Mama Joe returned. Because of the pervasive worry over Ben, the last days had been among the most challenging since Leslie had arrived in Kenya, and she was eager to see her friend. She never allowed herself to dwell on the possibility that Ben was dead—it was too painful. She recalled the long, hopeless days that had followed Brian and Emma's deaths, and she resolutely battled sinking into that type of depression again.

Happy tears filled Leslie's eyes when she spied Mama Joe hurrying toward her, dragging her large suitcase. After an enthusiastic embrace, Leslie stepped back and studied her friend. She touched the gray hair that had been shortened significantly. "You look terrific! I love your new hairdo. It makes you look like a teenager!"

Mama Joe laughed and self-consciously smoothed her new bob. "My daughter and daughter-in-law gave me a spa day for my birthday. This was part of it."

"You also gained a little weight—which you needed to do! I'm guessing American food agreed with you. And hopefully you got a little rest."

Mama Joe studied Leslie in return and was both pleased and alarmed by what she saw. The emotional fragility and sorrow that had been so evident were almost gone. Leslie seemed confident and content. But there was an unmistakable air of worry in her eyes that bordered on fear, and Mama Joe was aware of its cause. Through a series of emails and other contacts between Leslie and the home EAM office, Mama Joe had learned of Ben's injuries and knew that he'd disappeared. "Is there any news about Ben?" she inquired.

"No." Leslie's smile vanished. She bit her lip and blinked several times to try to hold back the tears that threatened all too frequently. "I don't know what to think. I'm afraid..." She shook her head and tried to smile.

Mama Joe hugged her again. "I've been praying since I heard." She patted Leslie's hand. "Leslie, it will be okay."

Leslie looked at the warm brown eyes. "Mama Joe, I'm in love with him."

"I know, dear. I can tell by your expression. And I'm certain he feels the same."

TWO DAYS LATER, the nurses were seeing the last of the day's patients. Leslie was tired and her back ached, but she was grateful the work kept her busy.

She was at the reception area charting her findings from her final patient when she heard the sound of a vehicle. She peered through a window expecting Paul or one of the tour guides who occasionally brought patients to the clinic. Instead she saw two unfamiliar men driving a covered Jeep.

Somewhat apprehensive, she ventured onto the porch to meet them. The men were identically dressed, wearing plain khaki shirts and pants. As they approached her, almost in unison they removed their canvas hats. Both were rather lean and of average height. One appeared to be in his early thirties and had dark red hair and a smattering of freckles scattered across the bridge of his nose. The other man was a few years younger, with black hair and dark brown eyes.

A powerful sense of déjà vu accosted Leslie as the men approached. Her heart rate soared and she stood motionless in the clinic's doorway as she recalled being notified of Brian and Emma's deaths.

The redheaded man climbed the steps and stopped in front of her. "Good afternoon, ma'am. I'm Major Bradley Littlejohn from the U.S. Air Force." He presented her with an official-looking picture identification card. He gestured toward the younger man. "This is Lieutenant Josh Smith."

Leslie's vision blurred, and she grew lightheaded. *Oh God,* she prayed silently. *Not again. Please, God, not again.* Her hand was unsteady when she took the card. She nodded slightly and said, "Yes?"

"Are you Leslie Carpenter?" Major Littlejohn questioned.

She nodded again. "Yes" was all she could manage. Her mouth was dry, and her peripheral vision darkened. She desperately needed to sit down.

Apparently alarmed by her sudden pallor, the major stepped toward her and clasped her arm. "Ma'am, are you okay?" He studied her carefully.

His touch steadied her, and she answered, "Yes, I'm sorry. I'm just a little dizzy." She nervously rubbed her forehead and glanced from one man to the other, trying to read their expressions. They were not foreboding; rather, they seemed intent. Leslie's heart was still racing, but she managed to say, "Is there something I can do for you?"

Littlejohn reached into his shirt pocket and

pulled out a plain white envelope. "I've been instructed to give this to you."

Leslie's hand trembled as she took the envelope. She fortified herself with deep breaths then looked down to discover that her name was printed neatly in black ink on the back. Her fingers were shaking so badly she had trouble tearing open the envelope. She pulled out a plain sheet of paper and had to blink a couple of times to read the words:

"Thanks for saving my life. Will you marry me? Ben."

He was alive. Tears stung her eyes, and she turned her back on the air force officers. Despite the blurring caused by the tears, she reread the short note. In a heartbeat, her fear was replaced by elation. Hastily, she wiped her eyes and turned to face the two men. With a voice much calmer than she felt, she asked, "Where is he?"

"He's at a hospital in Europe," the major replied.

She swallowed and asked the question that was foremost on her mind, "How is he?"

"Recovering very well, from all accounts. He had a couple of surgeries, but that's all I'm at liberty to discuss." Major Littlejohn watched her closely as he added, "We've also been instructed to take you to meet him."

Relief made tears threaten again, but Leslie did not waver in her reply. "When?"

Lieutenant Smith spoke for the first time. "If we leave within the hour, we can fly to one of our bases tonight. Then tomorrow morning, you'll take a transport to Germany. If we wait much later, it will be tomorrow morning before we can leave."

Leslie was unwilling to consider waiting even one more moment than necessary to see Ben. "Please come in. I need to pack a few things." She hesitated. "I'd like to make one quick stop on the way."

THE NEXT HOUR was a blur. Leslie introduced the men to Mama Joe and showed her Ben's note. Tears of joy clouded the older woman's eyes as she hugged Leslie. "I knew it would all work out! I am so happy for both of you! I was there at the beginning." She laughed and rubbed the wetness from her eyes with the back of her hand. "Well, get going. Naomi and I can finish up here. You need to pack!"

Hurriedly, Leslie packed her nicest clothes, toiletries, money and her passport. Everything else would be left, either to be picked up when she returned or shipped to her at home. She paused to hug Naomi, Titus, Elizabeth and Agnes and to kiss them all goodbye. "I'll email you as soon as I can and let you know what happens."

Leslie looked lovingly and longingly at her mentor and friends and at the little clinic. She would have liked more time to say goodbye, but that couldn't be helped. She blew kisses and waved to everyone as they drove off.

Before they left Namanga, she directed the air force officers to the Merdians' house. Fortunately, Paul and Judy were both home, and upon hearing the sound of the vehicle, they met the trio at the door.

They were clearly surprised to see the two men dressed in neat khaki, and Paul was even more surprised to see Leslie with them. But Leslie was beaming, and she greeted them with a smile that left no doubt the news was good. Quickly she showed her friends Ben's note. In the few moments she could spare, she kissed each of the children goodbye. She hugged Judy and then Paul. "Thank you both for everything! I'm not sure when we'll be back…"

Judy laughed through her tears and said, "I

can't wait to learn what happens. I just wish we could see the wedding!"

Major Littlejohn cleared his throat, and Leslie pulled away and climbed into the Jeep. She waved at the family as they drove down the dusty road.

It was nearly dusk when they arrived at the airfield. As they approached, Leslie blinked at the unusual sight of the relatively small silver twin-engine plane sitting at the edge of the grass strip. Two uniformed men armed with automatic weapons were standing watch, and two more came from the small hangar when they heard the Jeep approach.

Hastily, the group loaded Leslie and her bag into the plane. On board, she was introduced to Captain David Wilson, who, along with Lieutenant Smith, piloted the plane. She was shown where to sit, and within minutes, the small jet had taxied to one end of the field and was airborne.

About an hour into the flight, one of the young airmen who'd been guarding the plane left his seat and rifled through an ice chest that was anchored at the rear of the compartment. He handed Leslie a soda and smiled shyly; he couldn't be much older than twenty. "Here, ma'am. I'm about all we have in the way of a flight attendant."

"Thank you very much. I think I could use the sugar and caffeine." He started to make his way back to the rear of the plane, but Leslie stopped him. "Excuse me, please. Can you tell me where we're going?"

"Oh, yes, ma'am. Didn't the major tell you? We're going to Incirlik."

Leslie blinked. *"Incirlik?"* The word was unfamiliar. It sounded like something one might find at a dentist's office or hear in a sci-fi movie.

"Yes, ma'am. Incirlik Air Base." Evidently Leslie still looked confused, because he added, "Turkey, ma'am." He smiled again, nodded and returned to his seat.

THE FLIGHT TO southern Turkey took nearly five hours, so it was long after dark when they landed at the massive American installation. Despite the lateness of the hour, the landing area of the giant air base was brightly lit, allowing Leslie the opportunity to observe the bustling activity. Servicemen and -women were moving with varying purposes across the lit taxiways and among the hangars and other buildings that bordered the runways. A large collection of trucks, containers and military equipment appeared to be in various stages of being loaded or unloaded from transport planes and service helicopters in an impressively choreographed manner.

Major Littlejohn was giving a report to one of the ground mechanics as Leslie was exiting the plane. He paused when he saw her and motioned her forward.

She held out her hand. "Thank you so much for coming for me."

"You're welcome," he replied. "But you're not done with me yet. I didn't realize I hadn't made myself clear. I fly the cargo plane you'll be taking to Germany in the morning. We'll be leaving at precisely 0700 hours. I'll make sure that someone wakes you by six."

She nodded and smiled with considerable relief. "Oh, that will be great. I'm glad to have a familiar face… I'll see you in the morning, then."

A young woman with short brown hair and a lively disposition met the plane. Identifying herself as Sergeant Connolly, she explained to Leslie that she would take her to the visiting officers' quarters for the night. The women made their way through a maze of buildings before the sergeant deposited her in a two-story structure that appeared to be a small apartment building. "It's not the Hilton, but it's quiet," she said. Smiling companionably, she rapped her fist on the thick cinder-block wall. "You'll appreciate the quiet when you're trying to sleep a quarter mile from a runway!"

As she showed Leslie inside she said, "Lieutenant Smith said you haven't eaten anything. It's past mess, but I can go to the kitchen and find you something."

Leslie dined on a ham sandwich, an apple and a Snickers bar before taking a long shower. Finally she lay down on the bed with her hair still wrapped in a towel, doubting she would be able to sleep. In only seconds, however, she succumbed.

At precisely 6:00 a.m., there was a loud knock. Leslie awoke immediately as a man called through the heavy door, "Miss Carpenter, I have a breakfast tray for you. I'll leave it here. Also, there will be a Jeep here in fifty minutes to take you to the plane."

Quickly Leslie prepared herself for the day ahead. She showered again and, wanting to look her best, she put on her nicest dark blue skirt and lightweight blue sweater. She used the hair dryer provided in the room to brush her hair almost straight before leaving it down.

The Jeep was already waiting, and the driver escorted her to the plane that would take her on the second leg of the journey. Dawn was breaking as an airman met her on the runway, took her bag and led her up to the small passenger compartment of the massive cargo plane. Major Littlejohn greeted her from his seat in the cockpit and introduced her to his copilot, Captain Phil Stallwood.

Although the men did not say anything directly about Leslie's appearance, their double takes and appreciative expressions gratified her.

"As soon as all the checklists are complete and we get clearance, we'll be ready to take off," Major Littlejohn informed her.

Captain Stallwood appeared to be a few years younger than the major, and he seemed eager to put her at ease. "It looks like we're going to have great weather, miss." His eyes were intelligent, and his smile was friendly. "That's a good thing because these transports can get kind of bumpy in turbulence."

"Okay…that's good, I guess." She fidgeted with her purse. "How long is the flight?"

"Just a little over four hours," Littlejohn answered. He angled his head toward his copilot and added, "We'll do everything we can to make your first trip on a transport a smooth one!"

FOR THE NEXT FEW HOURS, Leslie tried to keep her mind focused on a book she had brought. She chuckled as she realized it was the slightly worn copy of *Pride and Prejudice* she'd borrowed from Ben's library, but she found it difficult to concentrate. She managed to doze for a while to pass the time, and finally Captain Stallwood informed her that they were beginning their descent.

Suddenly, Leslie felt almost overwhelmed by nerves. Within twenty minutes of Stallwood's pronouncement the aircraft came to a halt near a row of huge, immaculately maintained hangars. Peering out one of the plane's few small windows, Leslie saw military aircraft of all types, shapes and sizes—helicopters, fighter jets and cargo planes among others. Two crewmen came into the forward cabin to open the doors and secure the movable stairs to allow Leslie and the pilots to disembark. Leslie gathered her belongings and quickly moved toward the door of the craft. She paused a minute to thank the officers once more for coming all the way to Kenya for her.

"You're very welcome," Brad Littlejohn said, shaking her hand. He turned to the copilot. "Phil, when you go to the office to drop off the flight manifest, take a few minutes to assist Ms. Carpenter to find her ride. I'm sure someone has been dispatched to pick her up." Stallwood nodded, and, taking her bag, he gallantly led the way down the stairway.

CHAPTER NINETEEN

LESLIE PAUSED AT the door of the cargo plane and blinked several times. It was nearly noon, and, in stark contrast to the interior of the aircraft, it was brilliantly bright outside. The air smelled of jet fuel and smoke, but compared with Kenya it was cool and dry. She paused to look around the massive base, noting the hangars and buildings to one side and huge runways and taxiways to the other. Off in the distance, she could see a small city nestled among foothills, eclipsed by the peaks of low mountains. *Well,* she told herself, *you're not in Kenya anymore....*

Refocusing her thoughts, she looked down to where Captain Stallwood had paused in front of two uniformed officers. As she watched, he saluted and said something to them. He turned and glanced upward, gesturing in her direction. She studied the two. One was very tall and lanky; the other was fairly short and stocky. They were both dressed in full air-force blues, complete with customary billed hats pulled down to shade their eyes. Stallwood handed her bag to the shorter man and turned to wave at her before saluting the men again and heading toward the nearest hangar.

Leslie waved back before starting down the stairs. Near the bottom, she returned her attention to the two men who were now only about thirty feet away. For the first time, she noticed the taller man was leaning on a crutch, which was tucked under his right arm. As she descended the last step, he removed his hat, and Leslie stopped abruptly.

She wasn't prepared. She felt her face go pale and then red. Her heart rate soared, and the nerves were back in her stomach, this time with a vengeance.

He was almost unrecognizable, but there was no doubt—*Ben*. Much of his perpetual tan had faded, attributable to more than two weeks of hospitalization. He had lost weight, perhaps as much as ten pounds. Years of living in Kenya had made Ben lean; now he was bordering on thin.

She studied his face, trying to merge what she had known with what she was seeing. There was a marked disconnect. Gone was the incessant two-day growth of beard she could only remember being absent a few times. The most amazing change, however, was that his pony-tail was gone. In its place, Ben's hair had been neatly barbered into a standard military cut. The difference it made to his appearance was astonishing, and Leslie could not keep from staring. Before, he had been very good-looking in a way that snubbed conventional society, with his strong features, expressive mouth and long hair. Now, neatly combed and shaved and wearing a freshly pressed uniform, he was unbelievably handsome—and disconcertingly different.

Leslie blinked and swallowed hard.

Leaning lightly on his crutch, Ben moved forward several steps until he stood only a few feet away from her. His heart had been thundering in his chest as he watched her descend from the plane. He'd rarely seen her wearing anything other than her standard uniform of white or light blue shirt and khaki skirt, with her hair pulled into a long ponytail or held on top of her head with a large clip. She was always pretty, always appealing—now she was gorgeous. He wanted desperately to gather her into an embrace and carry her away. But he could see the surprise and confusion in her eyes. To combat the overwhelming desire to whisk her into his arms, he gripped the crutch tightly with one hand and his hat with the other. Although he tried to smile, he was uncharacteristically tense as he watched her search his face and wondered—*What if she doesn't find what she's looking for?*

For a few moments they stared at each other, oblivious to the activity all around. Finally, looking deeply into the pale green eyes, Leslie found what she needed—assurance. He looked different. Probably he *was* different. But she had found Ben. Leslie also recognized his hesitation and understood it was her move. Tentatively, she closed the small space between them and reached up with one hand to touch his hair.

His eyes never left her face as she studied him. The feel of her hand as she lightly caressed his hair sent shivers through his arms and legs. Finally, after what seemed an eternity, she smiled. It was a lovely, joyfully welcoming smile.

"Well, wow." Her words were soft. "I didn't think you could surprise me again.... I was wrong." Then with a glad cry, she threw her arms around his neck.

The crutch made a soft *thunk* as it hit the ground when Ben let go to catch her in his arms.

He gently kissed her cheek and then her hair as they held each other tightly. Finally, she loosened her grip enough for him to pull away to stare into her eyes again. He lowered his lips and lightly kissed her. It was a soft kiss, but one that bore a mountain of promise.

Reluctantly, they pulled apart. She spoke first as they searched each other's faces. Her words came pouring out. "I was so frightened. We tried and tried to learn where you had been taken. I didn't know if…" She stopped in midsentence, unable to continue. Tears suddenly threatened.

He pulled her into another embrace. "I know, sweetheart. I'm sorry. There was no way to tell you. The brass insisted on secrecy with the airlift, and I had to wait until I'd recovered enough to commission a request for a team to go after you. But it all worked out. You're here now. I'm just sorry you were worried."

Not completely letting go, she stepped back a pace to study him. "You really do look terrific—much better than I expected! You need to put on some weight, but I guess that after all you've been through, that's understandable." With that, her clinician's concern emerged. She bent to retrieve the crutch and asked, "Your leg—is it all right?"

He glanced down at the crutch and then back at her. "It'll be as good as new in a few weeks. The orthopedist had to do some reconstruction to my quadriceps and hamstring, which explains the immobilizer. But I'll only need it for about ten more days. I have physical therapy twice a day with guys named Randy and Guenther." He grinned. "Guess which is the sadist?"

She giggled, and he continued, "The PT will continue for another few weeks, but that's not too bad."

"What about your abdominal wound? Your chest?" Her worried expression returned.

He laughed at her directness. "I'll show you the scars later, and answer any and all questions you will no doubt have. Suffice it to say that all bullets have been removed, and holes patched. I am healing nicely and will be a hundred percent very soon." He took her hand and turned her toward the man who had been standing with him. "But now, you need to meet someone."

Ben replaced his hat and managed to keep his free arm around Leslie as he limped toward the stocky man. "Leslie, this is one of my best friends, Major Charlie Neatherlin. Charlie, this is Leslie."

Leslie reached out to shake the major's hand. "It's nice to meet you, Charlie."

The officer quickly removed his billed hat, revealing a close-cropped head of ash-blond hair. His blue-green eyes seemed to sparkle with good humor. "Me, too, Leslie. Ben has told me a lot about you. I was certain he'd exaggerated," He laughed heartily. "Now I'm not so sure."

Leslie glanced at Ben. He shrugged and smiled innocently. Looking at Charlie, she asked, "Just what did he tell you?"

Charlie chuckled. "Well…that your Swahili is atrocious. That you are beloved by the people of southern Kenya. That you do a great impersonation of a spoiled Southern belle. And that you would make an excellent bush pilot." He paused in his recitation, then added a little more soberly, "And that you saved his life."

She blushed and smiled. Inwardly, she was touched. To keep the mood light, she squinted her eyes and frowned at Ben. "My Swahili isn't *that* bad. *You* try to pronounce all of those syllables with a Texas accent and see what *you* come up with!"

Both men laughed as her drawl thickened

with every word. She wrinkled her nose at them. Ben could not restrain his crutch-free hand as he reached up to lightly stroke her cheek. "Honey, it wasn't the purest pronunciation of the language I've heard, but it was certainly the most interesting. And you did get much better."

She liked the feel of his hand, and she smiled into his eyes. The deafening sound of a jet taking off only a few hundred feet away reminded them of where they were and Charlie grabbed her bag and headed toward the waiting Jeep. "Why don't we get you back to the officers' quarters? And I don't know about you two, but I'm ready for lunch."

Ben dropped his hand and motioned for Leslie to follow his friend. Loudly enough for the other man to hear, he explained, "Les, I fear we have to bring this walking commentator with us everywhere we go. I can't drive because of the brace, and, unfortunately, the air force won't let civilians operate the equipment. So we're stuck with Charlie."

"Hey, it could be worse," Charlie called back as he climbed into the driver's seat. "You could have some crass, nosy driver, prone to voyeurism and gossip—someone you'd have to pay to keep quiet. Me, I'm a quiet, unassuming guy who's just happy the stick here is going to make it."

Ben was chuckling as he gallantly assisted Leslie into the passenger side of the Jeep. Then with surprising ease, he deftly stepped up into the rear of the vehicle, angling into the corner and propping his immobilized leg on the seat beside him. When they were all situated, Charlie took off toward a gap among the rows of planes, hangars and assorted buildings.

As they drove between the buildings and onto paved streets, Leslie witnessed the bustle on the large base. She saw military personnel in all manner of activities. They passed an open field on which a group of at least sixty or seventy men and women were marching in formation. As they made their way down a busy street, she observed service personnel, sometimes alone but often in pairs or small groups, walking from one site to another. Some people were dressed in regular street clothes, and it was impossible to tell whether they were family members or civilian employees. Those in uniform appeared to be mostly U.S. Air Force, but she recognized uniforms of the U.S. Army and Marines as well as occasional soldiers from other countries.

Charlie paused at a corner and yielded to a large truck towing a flatbed trailer with an Apache helicopter—minus its rotors—perched on it. Leslie blinked in astonishment as Charlie waved at the driver, who gave him a casual salute as they passed. He then turned right and said, "It's a pity you missed yesterday's ceremony, Leslie. It was impressive."

"Charlie," Ben growled. "Don't get—"

"What?" Charlie interrupted with feigned innocence. "What's the big secret?"

Ben's reply sounded exasperated. "It's not… well…" He did not continue but fidgeted a little as if trying to get comfortable.

Leslie could see both men from where she sat in the front of the vehicle, and she looked from one to the other. Finally, she addressed Ben. "What ceremony?"

She was stunned yet again as it appeared that Ben actually blushed. He gave a dismissive wave and shrugged. "Just an awards thing."

"Jeez, man," Charlie commented. "Not any old 'awards thing.'" He glanced at Leslie and then back to the road. "In addition to a promotion, Ben received a Bronze Star, a Distinguished Flying Cross, the Distinguished Service Medal *and* a Purple Heart. *Major* Ben Murphy had a very good day, finally being recognized for what he's been doing for three years. It was too bad that I was the only close friend to share the occasion with him."

"Okay, that's enough, Charlie." Ben frowned at his friend.

Leslie blinked a couple of times and watched him carefully. "Ben, you know that I'm really at a loss here."

Ben sighed. "Look, about the medals and all—I was just doing my job."

"*Hell,* no, man! Sorry, Leslie," Charlie countered. "Just doing your job? Give me a break!"

Ben gave a quiet guffaw and then acquiesced a little. Addressing Charlie, he said, "Well, okay, I did earn the promotion. At least I caught up with you!" He glanced over at Leslie and then back down at his injured leg. "And the Purple Heart, well..." He fingered the crutch. "That's a no-brainer. But about the others, *I was just doing my job.*" The last was spoken with considerable annoyance.

"There's no telling how many lives you've saved." There was an edge in Charlie's tone and he looked over his shoulder at Ben before returning his eyes to the street. "Obviously, the brass agreed with me. About the Flying Cross, man, if they hadn't caught it on the satellite feed and radar, no one would have believed it. Like anyone has *ever* taken out a couple of fighter jets while flying a single-engine Cessna."

"Charlie, that's classified," Ben growled through clenched teeth.

"Good God, Ben! Who's *she* going to tell?"

Ben rolled his eyes, then looked a little sheepish. He sighed. "Okay, that was a pretty good—er—encounter. But those guys were absolute *idiots*...and the jets were Cold War era Yugoslavian POCs. So I kind of feel bad about getting the medal."

"Yeah, but hell, man. A *Cessna?*"

"It was a pretty nice Cessna." Ben spoke matter-of-factly as if trying to credit the plane. "It was me or them. I was mostly just trying to stay alive."

Charlie growled, "Harrumph," but did not comment further. Leslie also kept silent. She just glanced from one man to the other as she witnessed the exchange. She was becoming more enthralled by the minute with the man sitting behind her. He was more—much more—than she had recognized or been led to believe. Furtively, she took in some of the details she had missed previously. Although both Ben and

Charlie bore the same rank and wore similar insignia, probably indicating their status as pilots, Ben had nearly twice as many ribbons. Not only was he an officer, evidently he was now a decorated one. She had just become privy to the fact that he was still an air force officer, and the more she learned, the more she realized that she didn't know. Suddenly she was awash with a new concern—did she really know him at all?

A short time later, Charlie stopped the Jeep in front of an attractive three-story redbrick building. Ben swung his legs over the side and stood on his good leg as he pulled his crutch from the rear seat. Once steady, he reached up to help her out of the Jeep. She tried to stifle a giggle, recalling the times she had crawled in and out of his plane or Jeep with only a rare offer of assistance.

He watched the amusement flicker in her eyes and questioned, "What's so funny?"

She smiled. "I was just thinking there's more different about you than just your missing ponytail."

"Ponytail?" Charlie interrupted. He'd retrieved Leslie's bag from the rear of the Jeep and made his way to stand beside the couple.

Leslie looked at Ben. She grinned teasingly and would have sworn that he blushed again.

"Who had a ponytail?" Charlie insisted. His attention zeroed in on Leslie.

She chuckled. "Ben. You mean you didn't see him when they brought him in?"

"You've *got* to be kidding!" Charlie responded. "Mr. Clean-Cut, All-American Ben Murphy had a ponytail? Wait'll they hear about this back at Edwards." He started laughing.

Ben groaned audibly. "Now, wait a minute. There are some things that are classified—"

"And I'm sure that's not one of them!" Charlie interrupted. "Do you have pictures?"

"I've got one." She laughed, and conspiringly whispered, "I'll show you later."

Trying to change the subject, Ben turned to precede the laughing pair into an apartment building. "Leslie, this is the temporary officers' quarters. It's for visiting officers and their families. Since there are no elevators, I was given a two-bedroom flat on the first floor. Charlie the Comic here is staying on the third floor. I thought you might want to freshen up before lunch, and then we can talk about..." He hesitated as he unlocked a door midway on the right-hand side of the hall and turned to her.

His expression sobered as he searched her face. Quietly, he repeated, "Then we can talk."

He stood aside to allow her to enter.

Charlie set her bag down just inside the door and said affably, "I have a couple of things I need to take care of upstairs. Why don't I come back by in a half hour or so?" Not really waiting for a response he closed the door, chuckling to himself as he headed toward the stairs that led to his room.

CHAPTER TWENTY

ALONE WITH BEN, Leslie's nervousness returned. To cover, she took a few moments to wander around the small room. The furnishings were fairly new and very clean. There was a kitchen area at the back and doors on either side of the room, obviously leading to bedrooms. She paused to gaze out the open window, watching several children on a small playground.

She was still struggling to reconcile the faultlessly uniformed man with the irreverent, disreputable character she had known and, surprisingly, fallen in love with. The differences were more than physical, although the physical changes were striking. His demeanor and mannerisms were also different. He'd been playing a role in Kenya. Now she was meeting the real man—someone she'd only glimpsed traces of over the past few months. What was he really like?

Silently, she chided herself. *What's wrong*

with you? Ben isn't a stranger. You're crazy in love with him! She took a couple of deep breaths to try to slow her pounding heart and control her trembling hands.

BEN WATCHED HER pace the small apartment. His heart had literally leaped when he'd first seen her. He ached with the need to pull her into his arms, hold her, keep her near him, love her. The exchange in the Jeep, however, had made him self-conscious, and her noticeable withdrawal suddenly left him doubting the strength of her feelings for him.

He was certain Leslie had been overjoyed when she embraced him at the plane. But he could tell that his altered appearance and the subsequent revelations had been a significant shock. Plus, he had a niggling concern that perhaps she preferred his other persona after all. He shook his head at the thought that Leslie had fallen in love with the act and not him. No, he refused to believe that.

The room seemed overly warm, so he doffed his coat and loosened his tie.

To occupy himself, he headed toward the kitchen area, leaning lightly on the crutch. "Would you like something to drink?" he asked.

"They do a good job of keeping these apartments stocked with the essentials—you know, milk, bread, peanut butter and soft drinks."

"Yes, that would be great," she answered.

She walked to where Ben was standing in the kitchen area removing glasses from a cabinet. "What can I do to help?" she inquired.

He brushed her offer aside. "Nothing. Just have a seat. I know that air force transports don't generally leave at what most people consider reasonable hours, and you're probably tired."

Agreeably, Leslie sat down on the sofa and watched as Ben placed glasses and two cans of ginger ale on a large plate and deftly carried the drinks into the living area.

Leslie took the plate from him and placed it on the coffee table. Setting his crutch aside, he sat down on the sofa near her. Leslie opened a can, filled both glasses and handed one to him. As she did, their hands brushed, and her heart raced. She averted her eyes, picked up her glass and took a sip, willing her hand not to shake. She was not completely successful. Attempting to hide her unease, she set the glass down and, with growing desperation, looked around the apartment, hoping to find something to discuss.

Leslie's shyness oddly helped dispel much of Ben's tension. Following her example, he set his glass back on the plate and reached for her hands. "What's wrong?"

He was watching her face, but she was watching their hands. To direct her attention to him, he slowly brought both of her hands up and then kissed her fingers. "Leslie, talk to me. Please."

Hesitantly, her eyes moved from his lips to his eyes and her heart quickened at the look of love she saw there. "I know it's silly." She shifted nervously and reached up to tentatively skim her hand across his cheek and then his hair. "It's just that you're so different from before.... In some ways, you're almost a stranger." She bit her lip and said quietly, "Could you...would you just hold me for a minute?"

Placing her arms around his neck, she buried her face in the light blue cotton fabric of his shirt.

"That would be my pleasure, ma'am." Responding to her touch, he pulled her even closer, adjusting their positions until she was sitting on his lap. When she started to protest, he shushed her. "Don't worry. My leg is fine." His voice was soft.

She settled against him, her head resting

on his chest, and slowly relaxed as he gently stroked her back and arms. Her words were slightly breathless. "This helps. I know how you feel. This feels familiar."

"Well, all right then." She felt the smile when his lips brushed her hair. "I guess I'll just have to keep on holding you." He pulled away a little and gazed down at her. Then, carefully gauging her reaction, he touched her lips with his. He was rewarded with complete surrender as she answered his kiss.

After a moment, he placed his hands on her arms and gently eased away. Tears threatened again when she looked back at him, and his heart melted anew.

"Ben… I was so scared!" Her voice was hoarse with emotion, and a single tear slid down her cheek. She whispered, "I love you."

He pulled her head down onto his shoulder and stroked her hair. "Leslie, I love you more than I can express… I want more than anything right now to be with you. But…" He repositioned her, placing her on the sofa beside him, facing him. She looked away, and he put his hand on her chin to draw her eyes back to his. "Leslie, I understand how you feel. I want you to feel that way about me. I want you to want me. I want you to let me love you, and we will—I hope really soon. But right now, we need to talk." He sighed deeply. "And besides, Charlie will be back in about fifteen minutes."

The frustration evident in his last declaration startled a giggle from Leslie, and Ben could tell that his confession had comforted her. The adoration in her eyes produced an abrupt change in the plans he'd been formulating since his extraction from Kenya. Intently watching her, he said, "Um…Leslie, you haven't answered my question."

She gave him a puzzled look. "What question?"

"The letter…"

Her lips rolled inward before they broke into a huge smile. Her arms clung to his neck again, and she blessed him with multiple kisses on his cheeks and lips. Words were absent as she pulled back to take in his face.

"Okay. Well, I'll take that as a yes." Ben's voice was hoarse. "Then, I have something that's yours." He reached into the breast pocket of his shirt and picked up her left hand. "Leslie, please marry me," he said as he slid a ring onto her finger.

Her gaze moved from his face to their joined

hands, and she gasped. "Where did you…? How did you…?" She gulped and stared at the stunning oval sapphire.

His hand slipped from her chin to gently touch her cheek. It was a moment before she could answer. "Today, Ben. Can we get married today?"

He kissed her tenderly. With a brief laugh he said, "*Today?* Honey, are you sure that's what you want?" He studied her face. "Are you certain you don't want a real wedding with family and flowers?"

Needing to touch him, her hands caught his. She saw joy in his sea-colored eyes. "Ben, I don't care about *getting* married. I just want to *be* married to you."

He cleared his throat and answered, "All right then. I'm not *real* sure we can manage today, but we can try." He laughed and kissed her again. "I was afraid you might want to wait until we got back home, but I'm *really* glad you feel like I do."

She looked back at the ring and shook her head. "Ben, it's absolutely beautiful." Her eyes were shining, and all traces of shyness were gone. She gave him a wry smile. "But what if I hadn't come? Or I might have said no."

"Leslie, I didn't let myself even consider the

possibility that you wouldn't come. As to your saying no…" He shrugged. "I'm very patient. I would have persisted until you gave in." His expression became more serious as he continued. "You've become the most important thing in my life." He waited a heartbeat, then grinned again. "Besides, I have another ring that goes with that one. You can have it, too, just as soon as you marry me."

Leslie smiled as she said teasingly, "You know, I had plans of my own."

At his questioning look, she continued. "I was going to find you, no matter what it took. I would have gone to Florida to see your parents—I got their address from the mission—and I would've bribed, begged or pleaded with them to help me find you."

He was smiling when he interrupted. "What were you going to do when you found me?"

"Well. I hadn't exactly thought that far ahead." She looked pensive for a moment and then smiled. "Probably bribed, begged and pleaded until you agreed to marry me."

There was laughter in his voice as he said, "Not that I needed convincing, but I'd like to know what you would've said."

Leslie was playfully pensive. "Hmm, let's

see…I'm a really good cook when I have a stove that always works and a supermarket around the corner…. I know all the rules of football—I was a Cowboys fan from way back." She gazed at the ceiling and then back at him. "What else? I'd like for you to teach me how to fly." She suddenly grew serious. "And I love you so much I ache. I want to take care of you…and, I want you to be the father of my children." Her voice had been light and carefree, but near the end of her recitation, it cracked with emotion.

He gently reached up to push her hair away from her brow. "So, how many children do you want?"

It took a moment for her to answer. Frowning slightly in a hushed voice, she said, "Ben, I really don't know…. Until now I haven't thought about it."

Suddenly dealing with a flood of new and different emotions, she pulled away. She rose and walked a couple of paces toward the kitchen. "I want more children…not to replace Emma. I can't replace her. I don't know how to describe it, but it's like—well—how I feel about you compared with how I felt about Brian. I'm not replacing Brian…. What I feel for you is something different."

She faced him again and saw the animation

was gone from his expression. He seemed to have withdrawn, and he appeared hurt or even a little angry. "Ben, no. Please listen. I want to explain. I need you to understand that I loved Brian with all of my heart. But my love for you is somehow more and somehow beyond how I loved him. Because of the loss, I'm different. Because I loved him, I know how precious love is, and how tenuous life is."

She bit her lip and looked at Ben, imploring him to understand. "I'm afraid, desperately afraid of losing you the way I lost him. But much more desperately, I want to be with you. When I didn't know what had happened to you, the urgency grew stronger. I needed you—I needed to be with you all the more." She took a breath and finished. "And Ben, I feel the same about more children. I am terrified about the possibility of loss, but I'm much, *much* more frightened by the thought of never having those feelings again."

Ben's eyes were dark with emotion. He had been trying to keep the conversation light and carefree, but somehow it had taken a serious turn. He instinctively recognized that he was facing another of what might be many instances when patience and love would be required to help her past the lingering shadows.

He stood and limped toward her. He reached out a hand to lightly caress her cheek and said in a quiet voice, "Leslie, I love you. You are the one, the only woman for me, and I've been searching for you my whole life." He let his hand skim down her arm and then lightly clasp her hand. "I'm here. I'm yours. Love me, and let me love you." Then he grinned. "And please, *please,* use me to make as many babies as you want!"

She blessed him with a watery smile. "Okay, but I have one condition that you must absolutely and positively agree to."

He looked skeptical. "A condition? What kind of condition?"

By clenching her jaw, Leslie was able to keep a straight face. "If someday we are fortunate enough to have a baby boy…" She paused and looked at him seriously. "Under *no* circumstance will we name him Herman."

The smile that crossed his face made her heart jump. He pulled her into yet another embrace. He was laughing when he answered. "You've got a deal."

THE NEXT SEVERAL hours were a blur of activity. Immediately, Ben and Leslie went in search of Charlie. He agreed to help as much as possible but insisted on first taking the newly engaged couple to lunch.

The two men were enormously entertaining throughout the meal at the Officers' Club. Their banter, along with Ben's obvious infatuation, helped alleviate Leslie's nervousness. It also gave her time to observe him without his facade, and she desperately needed to reconcile what she thought she knew with reality.

As she nibbled her salad, she managed to turn the men's conversation from the major league baseball season to Ben's activities in Kenya. During a break in the conversation she said, "Okay, Ben. You have some explaining to do." She pointed to his uniform and shook her head. "I had no idea…"

He nodded and leaned forward slightly, his demeanor less casual than before.

"I know… You're right," he agreed. He took a deep breath. "Okay. As I told you, I was stationed in D.C. when it became clear that my marriage was over. I considered trying to get back into training for the B-1, but I'd been out of it for nearly two years, and that didn't seem to be a viable option. Then an air force liaison approached me with an assignment. The CIA wanted to embed an agent in East Africa.

They needed someone on the ground who could gather and evaluate data on potential threats to our assets in the region.

"I was a good fit because I was already assigned to the Pentagon and had high security clearance. I'd been raised in the area, was familiar with the cultures, and spoke several of the languages and dialects. So I could easily mix with the various groups and factions." He took a sip of beer. "I was fairly well-known in the region, so it was necessary for us to manufacture a falling-out with the air force—to give legitimacy to my return. So we concocted a story about my being dishonorably discharged The persona just kind of took off from there. I quickly became known that I drank too much would do pretty much anything to make a buck and—" he studied Leslie "—that I...er...pursued women."

She glanced at Charlie, who simply shrugged She frowned then said, "Well, go on."

"At first I was mostly involved in reconnaissance. After a while, I let it be known that was interested in smuggling. Initially, it was supposed to be alcohol and animal skins— wouldn't even pretend to smuggle drugs." He gave her a wry look. "Quickly, though, I made the transition to getting involved with arms dealers, which was our objective from the beginning."

Charlie interrupted Ben by asking, "When did you start working the Pakistan connections?"

Ben glanced around the room, then leaned forward. Dropping his voice he answered, "Only about a year ago. Up until then, I was focusing on small runners who sold to local chiefs. In that capacity, I was able to help stop some of the arms going to Somali thugs who pass themselves off as pirates." He shook his head in disgust. "It was a joy to shut them down.

"Anyway, about a year ago, I learned of a Pakistani broker who was selling a variety of weapons through Mombasa and Mogadishu—SAMs and rocket-propelled grenades, along with other small missiles manufactured in China and North Korea. These were being traded and sold into Libya, Syria and Iran to insurgents and terrorist groups. Rasheesh didn't care who he sold to, he just cared about his bottom line."

"Rasheesh?" Leslie paled and swallowed hard. "He's the one who tried to kill you?" It was both a question and a statement.

Ben looked grim. Taking her hand, he said, "Yes, Les. I am truly sorry. I should never have involved you in that sordid mess." He addressed Charlie, "You see, I…well, accidentally took Leslie on my last meeting with Rasheesh."

"Accidentally?" Charlie repeated.

"I didn't intend to; it just worked out that way." He turned back to Leslie. "Ironically, your being there probably served to seal the deal. You see, despite my reputation, they didn't trust me. They suspected I was a spy. But my bringing you along that day helped dispel their doubts. As far as they were concerned, only a sold-out bottom-dweller with no scruples would bring a woman with him to a meeting of that sort."

He shook his head. "Leslie, the truth is, had I not taken you with me, they probably would've turned me away, or maybe even killed me. As it was, I cut a deal that gave me access to vital information regarding arms shipments." He paused, hesitating to tell her more.

Seeing that his friend had stopped, Charlie huffed, casting a significant glance at Leslie. "The rest of the story—what Mr. Oh-Shucks-It-Was-No-Bother isn't telling you—is that he was able to give the location of and details about the shipments to his CIA and DOD contacts.

In turn, they sent teams of SEALs to board the vessels. After confirmation…well…" He grinned. "The ships met with unfortunate accidents at sea, and the SAMs, missile launchers, and other assorted implements of destruction are now at the bottom of the Indian Ocean."

Ben gave a slight nod and then picked the story back up. "Not surprisingly, when Rasheesh found out his ships were lost, he knew what had happened. So I was targeted for—uh—removal."

Leslie looked grim. "So they were waiting for you that day?"

Ben put up his hand, requesting silence, as the waitress returned. The trio ordered coffee, and after she'd left, Ben answered. "That morning, I radioed Charles Endebbi to let him know I was about thirty minutes out, and I asked him to contact Simon. As I approached the field, things didn't seem quite right, so I did a slow circle of the area and spotted a couple of poorly camouflaged jeeps about a kilometer away."

The waitress returned, and he paused while she placed a steaming mug in front of each of them. When they were alone again, he continued. "As I lined up my final approach, I pulled out the M-4 I kept hidden in a compartment under the rear seat. When I taxied toward the hut after landing, Charles didn't meet me as he normally does. I took my time pulling in, letting the prop continue to spin. Sure enough, three men came out of the hut with automatic weapons blazing. I gunned the plane toward them, and they scattered. When they hit the dirt, I took out all three with the M-4. After that, I taxied the plane around a little trying to spot any others."

When he paused for a sip of coffee, Leslie asked, "What's an M-4?"

Charlie replied, "An M-4 carbine. It's an assault rifle. They're very useful in certain situations."

Ben shrugged. "I wanted to take the Cessna back up, but I smelled gasoline, so I swung the plane back around and jumped out. As I did, another guy popped up from under that old Piper Cub and fired." He looked grim then. "He hit me in the chest and stomach before I was able to tag him with the carbine."

His gaze dropped to the coffee cup. "I fell and was trying to get up when the fifth guy approached me. I saw him coming, but couldn't react quickly enough."

His hand was shaking a little as he took another sip of coffee. "Fortunately, he was a bad shot and only caught my thigh before I heard the sound of another automatic weapon." Ben grinned. "And then, miracle of miracles, I saw my guardian angel take the form of a giant Masai warrior jogging toward us, shooting."

Leslie gaped at him. "*What? Simon* killed the last guy?"

"Yep. I can't describe how I felt when I saw him. At that point, I was lying in the dirt trying to stop the blood flow from my leg. I didn't have the strength or coordination to get on my knees, much less pick up my gun. And there was Simon. He'd heard the gunfire and quickly figured out what was happening. Simon can stalk anything, and he was able to approach unnoticed."

She shook her head in confusion. "But…I just can't picture Simon with a gun."

Ben grinned again. "Although he loves to carry around that spear—and believe me, he knows how to use it—his weapon of choice in a gunfight is an Uzi. He took the guy out in one burst. The rest is pretty much a blur until I woke up in my cabin with you taking care of me. And you know what happened from there." He sat back, his tale complete.

"No! Not a chance, Ben Murphy!" Leslie leaned toward him, flummoxed. "You can't stop there. What about the funny-looking plane-helicopter and the guys in the coveralls? Then Paul and I looked all over Nairobi trying to find out where you had been taken. You fell off the face of the earth!"

Ben looked askance at Charlie, who gave a slight shrug. Looking pensive, he turned back to Leslie. His hand captured hers on the table, and he rubbed her fingers with his thumb. "I can't give you all the details, but the Navy usually has a carrier group patrolling the western part of the Indian Ocean. They work to ensure that the shipping lanes remain open into the Red Sea and help thwart pirate attacks.

"The plane was a V-22—called an Osprey. They've only been in regular use for a few years. Well, the Osprey transported me to the carrier and I was taken into surgery. Fortunately for me, those guys are used to working on people with gunshot wounds, and they did a great job of patching me up. I was on the carrier for a couple of days before being evacuated to a military hospital in Kuwait. After a few more days a transport brought me here." He smiled at her. "That's pretty much where you came in this morning."

Leslie shook her head at his nonchalance. "Ben, you're amazing. It's like you're describing a ball game, not a life-and-death situation." She leaned over to kiss his cheek. "This is going to take a lot of getting used to." Ben kissed her in return and then gestured for the waitress.

Charlie said, "Given Ben's—uh—abilities and who he knows, we're all glad he's one of the good guys."

Ben frowned at his best friend. "Hey, man, don't scare her. She could still change her mind." He said the words jokingly, but there was an edge to the statement. He stood and looked at Leslie. His expression was compelling when he said, "Let's go see about a wedding. I want to give you as little time as possible to reconsider."

Leslie took his hand and rose. "Ben, you *are* one of the good guys, and you're the one I can't live without." She stood on her toes to kiss him on the cheek. "It's too late anyway. You're not getting rid of me now."

CHAPTER TWENTY-ONE

BEN AND LESLIE WERE relieved to find that getting married on a military base in Germany was relatively simple. They were able to collect the required documents courtesy of an efficient air force administrative assistant and the seven-hour time difference with Texas. With the paperwork in hand, they sought and received approval from the base commandant. Finally, the chaplain was contacted; he agreed to meet them at the base's church at eight.

Leslie and Ben had only a short time to prepare for the ceremony, and they retired to their separate rooms to get ready. Forty-five minutes later, Leslie emerged to find Ben waiting for her in the main room of the borrowed apartment. Her breath caught. He was wearing his dark blue dress uniform, complete with brass buttons, gold braid, and an impressive array of medals.

Oh my Lord, she thought, and then her mind

went blank. Once again she had a feeling of being with a stranger—an unbelievably handsome stranger. And then he smiled, and her heart soared.

Leslie was wearing a simple, pale blue linen dress that she'd purchased earlier that afternoon at a small boutique on the base. It was midcalf in length, with cap sleeves and white lace adorning a scoop neckline. She had allowed her hair to curl naturally, and it flowed to the middle of her back. As he stared, she felt her cheeks grow pink, and she stopped in the doorway, unwilling or unable to cross the room to him. He crossed to her, took her hands and kissed her softly. "You're incredibly beautiful," he said quietly. "I can't believe how fortunate I am to have you."

She reached up and tentatively touched his hair, much as she had that morning. She tried to speak and had to swallow before she managed to whisper, "You're so amazing that you scare me." She stared at him for a moment. Finally she stood on her toes and threw her arms around his neck. "Let's go find Charlie," she whispered.

CHARLIE HAD CONSPIRED with the officers' mess to have "room service" delivered at eight o'clock the next morning. Fortunately, he had warned the newlyweds, and Ben was dressed and ready when a young private delivered their hearty breakfast.

Leslie had neglected to pack any sleeping clothes, so she was clad in one of Ben's T-shirts when she sat down to eat.

"This has been the most wonderful two days," she declared as she dined on German pastries and a boiled egg. She reached over to touch Ben's cheek in a loving caress. "I woke up yesterday morning somewhere in Turkey—I'm still not sure where—and now I'm somewhere in Germany—I'm still not sure where—and we're married…"

Ben had never seen her more lovely, with her curly hair mussed and her eyes shining. All vestiges of the shadows were gone. He knew there would be times when they'd return, but for now he gloried in seeing her happy.

Following breakfast, Ben added more coffee to their cups and said, "Let's go sit on the couch. There are some things we need to talk about." Seeing her concerned expression he leaned over and kissed her nose. "No, it's nothing bad. We just haven't really talked about what's next, and it's time we did."

"Oh." She smiled. "Yes, things started moving a little fast, and we missed a few steps." She picked up the cups and led the way toward the living area of the small apartment.

Ben stopped by the bedroom to snag a blanket. He draped it around her as they sat on the sofa. "I have to cover you up. We need to talk, and looking at you is a serious distraction."

She rewarded him with a quick kiss. Chuckling a little, she crossed her bare legs and dutifully covered them before turning to face him. She picked up her coffee and took a sip, then looked up at him adoringly.

He groaned. "Stop it, will you? We need to talk, and you're killing me." He took her coffee cup and set it on the low table where he'd propped his leg. Taking her hand, he said, "You married me on incredibly short notice, and you haven't even asked about the future. About what's next."

She sat back and frowned slightly. "Ah, well. I guess it didn't occur to me to ask, because I really don't care. No, that's not right. Of course I care. What I mean is it doesn't matter where we go or what you do. The only thing that matters is that we're together."

Humbled, he pulled her to him and kissed

her hair. "That's what's most important to me, too." He set her back onto her side of the couch. "Okay, but we do need to talk."

His tone became serious. "The brass wanted to send me stateside for the remainder of my therapy, but I insisted on waiting here for you. If you're game, we can head to D.C. either today or tomorrow. I'll finish my therapy in a few weeks and, well… I've completed the dissertation, and Georgetown's graduation is coming up." He sighed and looked a little self-conscious. "I kind of need to go to the ceremony."

"Ben, that's wonderful! For goodness' sake, that is a *huge* deal. It needs to be celebrated. Of course we'll go!"

He shrugged. "I don't like big fusses, I guess. Well, my parents will probably come up from Florida for the graduation, which is great. That'll give them a chance to meet you. After that, I thought we could go to Dallas to visit your family…"

"That's perfect!" she exclaimed. "Even though Mom and Dad said they were happy for us, they need to meet you to be reassured."

"Then maybe we can pick a place for a semi-delayed honeymoon. And after that… Okay, here it comes." He paused, considering how to proceed. "You know I can't go back to Africa for a while. My cover was blown, and there will be quite a few—em—bad guys after me if I show up anytime soon. So the air force brass came up with an assignment. It's not exactly optional, but they give you the impression that you have a choice..." He watched for Leslie's reaction.

"Ben, what is it?" When he didn't answer immediately, she said, "I meant it. I really don't care if it's here in Germany, or Washington, or even Incer...Incerlin, Turkey, or somewhere else. But *please* tell me I can go with you. I *have* to be with you!"

He smiled. "Don't worry—it's okay. How about Colorado?"

"Colorado?" She blinked and sat back. "I love Colorado."

"I've been given a joint assignment teaching part-time at the Air Force Academy in Colorado Springs and serving as an intelligence analyst for the Department of Defense at the Cheyenne Mountain Facility. I'll be helping monitor terrorist activities in East Africa and the western part of the Indian Ocean. Basically, in addition to teaching military history to cadets, I'll be part of the team intercepting and interpreting communications among the various groups and factions in that part of the world. They need my language abilities and experience with the different cultures." He shrugged and added absently, "My Arabic will need to improve, and I may have to learn Farsi, but that's in the same language group as Urdu…"

Leslie shook her head. "Ben, you amaze me." She rewarded him with an eager smile. "That sounds absolutely perfect. Colorado Springs is beautiful, and it would be a wonderful place to raise a family."

"Speaking of raising a family…" he interrupted. He tugged the blanket away from her. "It's been nearly two hours since we made love."

SOMETIME LATER, THEY LAY in bed intertwined. Leslie's head rested on Ben's shoulder, and he lightly caressed her back. Finally, she sighed. "Ben, it's my turn. I, um… I need to talk to you about something."

She raised up on her elbow and gazed at him, running her hand across his chest and abdomen to stroke the reddened, puckered scars. "This is kind of serious."

He caught her hand and kissed her fingers. His eyes held hers. "Okay. What is it? You look worried. Honey, whatever it is, we'll work it out…"

She sensed that her apprehension had spread to him, and she tried to dispel it. "It's nothing scary." She sat up and pulled the sheet to cover herself. "Ben…" She took a deep breath. "Whew, this is awkward."

He sat up, too. "Leslie, what is it?" He looked more curious than concerned.

She glanced down at her lap and bunched the sheet with her fingers. "Hmm… Well, when Emma was born, Brian insisted on taking out a life insurance policy. Since he was a young doctor with high income potential it was a very generous policy."

Sensing where the discussion would go, Ben became visibly uneasy. His voice was low, nearly a growl. "Leslie, I don't want your money." The playful mood had evaporated.

"Just listen, please." She raised her eyes to his.

He took a breath and nodded. "Yes, okay. I'm sorry."

"Anyway, there was an accidental-death attachment, which tripled the amount." She took Ben's hands as he seemed to have retreated. "Ben, that's not all…the truck…" She bit her lip and paused for a moment. "The truck that hit them was from a soft-drink distributor. The driver was speeding, and he ran a red light. He was probably under the influence."

Ben scowled as he stared down at their joined hands. Leslie continued. "I wasn't in any shape to pursue it, but my father took over on my behalf. There were negotiations…the company was eager to settle the claim." Teardrops dotted the sheet and her voice was pleading. "Ben, I didn't care. I wanted to be left alone. I just signed the papers. I didn't want the money… *I don't want the money.* It's about their deaths… That's what it represents to me." She sighed and whispered, "Ben, it's millions."

He surged out of bed. As hastily as he could, given his injured leg, he pulled on his undershorts and slacks. He paced the room with an awkward limp, barefoot and bare-chested, before turning back to her. "Leslie, damn it…" She saw his jaw tense as he moved away again to stare out the window.

She slid out of bed and, following his example, slipped on his discarded shirt. She sat down to wait. Finally she broke the silence. "Ben, I'm sorry. I didn't want to make you angry. I thought you needed to know, and I wasn't sure when or how to tell you."

HE GLANCED BACK at her and said to himself, *You idiot!* She looked small and sad, where only a few minutes before she'd been carefree and joyful. He wanted to beat his head against the wall. Instead he gave a deep sigh and scrubbed his face with his hands. Limping back to the bed, he sat beside her. He took her hand and kissed it.

"Leslie, I'm sorry I reacted so poorly. I just… it's a weird sort of jealous, macho thing. That's all. It's just pride and stupidity on my part." He continued to frown and gently massaged her fingers. "But that said, I need you to understand that I can't take another man's money. I'm sorry, I just can't." His eyes were eloquent as he pleaded with her, praying she would understand.

"Ben, I…"

"No, wait." He touched her lips gently with his fingers. "Let me finish. It may be stupid, self-centered and even outdated, but I have this need to support us, to support my family… I can't take the money. But Leslie, I know it would be unreasonable to prohibit you from doing whatever you wish with it. I want you to have whatever you need..."

Leslie kissed his cheek. "Ben, I meant it. *I don't want it.* But I have an idea." Her words were emphatic, and her smile sweet. Suddenly she was childlike with enthusiasm. "It's something I've been considering for a couple of months, and if you'll hear me out, I think you'll approve."

Ben listened for the next several minutes as she explained her proposal. When she finished, he slid from the side of the bed to kneel before her. She started to protest, but he stopped her with a look, a shake of his head and a simple "No." On his knees, he laid his head in her lap and wrapped his arms around her waist. Stark emotion was in his voice when he said, "Dear God, you're beautiful."

Her tears were falling onto twin damp spots on the sheet, and he drew up a corner of it to dry her face. "I love you so much—and I have from the start. From the moment you walked into the Rift Valley Bar and turned those big blue eyes to me... You took my breath away." He caught her hand in his and sweetly kissed her fingers. His voice had calmed, and he smiled.

"I haven't been able to completely regain my balance since then."

After holding her for a few minutes, he rose to his feet and pulled her up to stand with him. He kissed her gently. "I hope," he finally said, "that I get to spend the next fifty or sixty years with you. It'll take that long to even begin to show you how much I love you."

EPILOGUE

Six years later...

THE TWIN-ENGINE PLANE slowed almost to a stop on Namanga's grassy airfield before turning to taxi toward a group of people waiting near the small building that now served as the office. Next to the new building were twin metal hangars, large enough to hold small aircraft. Other subtle improvements were also evident. Indeed, the field was more level and well tended. A series of floodlights were periodically spaced along the sides of the grassy area, making nighttime landings possible.

A huge smile crossed Leslie's face as she waved to Paul, Judy and the others. Paul's head was now almost completely bald and his beard mostly gray. Otherwise, he hadn't changed at all since she'd first seen him. Likewise, with crinkling, smiling eyes, petite build and short blond hair, Judy was much the same. Leslie barely recognized the three children, however, even though she had seen them only eighteen months before when the Merdian family had visited Colorado. Johnny was now almost fourteen, and Beth twelve. Both were gangly adolescents with bony knees and elbows and big smiles. Little Stephen—she still thought of him as little even though he was eight—was standing nearby, anxious to get a closer look at the plane and its occupants.

Naomi and Titus seemed ageless. Both had short gray hair and clear, lineless faces. And both were smiling broadly, eager to welcome the Murphy family.

The others, two men and a woman, were also waving enthusiastically. They stood a little removed to allow the old friends a few minutes to reunite first. Leslie had met each several times, both in the U.S. when they were first hired and here in Africa on a previous visit, and she was eager to learn how they were faring. Finally, standing slightly apart but impossible to miss, was Simon. In honor of the occasion, he was dressed as she had first seen him: draped in a bloodred tunic, complete with beaded collar, claw necklace and eight-foot spear.

As the plane rolled to a stop, the propellers ceased and the doors flew open. Ben hopped out of the cockpit, and a tall, lanky five-year-old boy with blond hair scrambled down after him, not needing or wanting help. Ben rounded the plane to assist the remaining occupants. First he lifted out four-year-old Anna Jo. Like her mother, Anna Jo had big blue eyes and a head full of curly brown hair that was loosely tied back in a messy ponytail. He set her on her feet where she stood close to her brother, more than a little shy as she gazed at the people nearby.

Ben reached back into the plane and took Gracie, the toddler, from her mother's arms. Like her sister, Gracie had curly brown hair, but to Leslie's delight, she had inherited her father's pale green eyes. Ben placed Gracie on her feet and then reached up to catch Leslie, who needed little help as she jumped down, eager to greet each member of the waiting group. Happy cries and welcoming hugs ensued as the Merdian family and Naomi and Titus reunited with the Murphy clan.

Through the initial gathering, Simon stayed removed, waiting. This was Ben's first return to Kenya since the assassination attempt, and he hadn't seen Simon since the day he was so severely injured. The rest of the group quieted and observed in silence as Ben put his hand on the shoulder of his young son and led him to the periphery of the field where the Masai giant stood. Ben and Simon faced each other without expression, and Leslie was reminded of the times when she had thought the two seemed to communicate telepathically. Ben finally said something and reached down to pat the boy's head and spoke again. The boy, in turn, lifted his small hand. To his credit, he did not flinch or look frightened, although, as Leslie was well aware, Simon's appearance was fearsome to anyone seeing him for the first time.

Simon took the boy's small hand with both of his huge ones and said something in reply. Not surprisingly, the child's voice was a little hesitant as he spoke to the man in Swahili. The trio stood for another long minute, simply looking at one another. And then, in unison, the two men grinned and gripped each other in a monstrous hug. They pulled the boy in with them. He was lifted into Simon's arms and held for a span before being let back down to the ground.

"Okay. What was that all about?" Jake Davies asked. Jake and his wife, Tiffany, had joined the foundation a few years before. Like Leslie, Tiffany was a nurse-practitioner, and she now worked with Naomi to operate the Namanga

Clinic. Jake was a paramedic and pilot, and in that capacity was able to act as a first responder and air ambulance operator.

"I've never seen a Masai that demonstrative," noted Will Schumann. Will was also a pilot and a mechanic. He had joined the foundation the year before to assist with coordinating supplies, ferrying patients to the clinics or practitioners to the patients as needed.

Paul, Judy and Leslie looked at each other. "That was a ceremony of sorts," Paul explained. "You see, years ago, Simon saved Ben's life, making Ben obligated to him. It also makes Simon part of Ben's family. So, following a local tradition, Ben's first son is also Simon's 'son' or 'nephew'—the word and connotation are very similar. Simon was just introduced to his namesake. The boy is Simon *Paul* Murphy." He grinned then, emphasizing the middle name. "See, I'm kind of part of the family, too."

Over the next few minutes, the friends mingled. Eventually, they separated along gender lines, with the women grouping together on one part of the field and the men together nearby. Simon Paul and Anna Jo accompanied Beth, Johnny and Stephen as they explored the office and hangars along the airfield.

"How is Mama Joe's health?" asked Naomi, who had joined Leslie, Judy and Tiffany.

"She's completely recovered from the stroke that sent her home four years ago," said Leslie. "I think that was actually a positive thing, in that she wanted to be near her family. Plus, it's given the foundation the perfect spokesperson. I know she misses the field, but she's a terrific public speaker. That, coupled with her aptitude for effectively badgering wealthy donors, has helped us more than double our original endowment."

The Carpenter-MacDonald East African Health Foundation was now six years old and was becoming well-known in the region for providing high-quality health care to the people in rural villages. After the first couple of years, the foundation had expanded from Kenya into neighboring Tanzania, and they were in the process of starting two clinics in Sudan. Altogether, ten clinics were in operation, with plans for three more in the next few years.

Initially Leslie had headed the foundation, but as their family grew, she turned the day-to-day administration over to others. Her primary responsibility now involved working with medical schools and nursing schools in several states to recruit students and faculty willing to donate a year of service in the clinics while having all of their expenses paid. Response from students and faculty had been tremendous, and now there were waiting lists of people eager to participate. Through the years, several of the students had chosen to stay past their committed time and, with the support of the Carpenter-MacDonald Foundation, had opened clinics of their own.

Leslie continued, “Mama Joe was sorry she couldn’t be with us for the first part of the trip, but she’ll be here next week. There was a big engagement she really couldn’t miss. Her goal is to raise another quarter-million this month!”

Tiffany glanced over to where the men had congregated around the plane Ben had ferried to Namanga. “Jake has been really anxious for you to get here. He’s been like a kid at Christmas waiting for that plane!”

Leslie laughed. “Ben and I have both been really eager to come back—together, finally!” Although this was Leslie’s third trip back to Kenya, it was the first time the Pentagon had approved Ben’s return. They believed that pretty much everyone who’d had contact with Ben years ago had been removed, so it was finally safe for him. "Bringing the new plane gave him an excuse," Leslie said.

Judy tugged at Leslie's hand, and her attention moved to her old friend. "Here, let me hold Gracie." Judy took the toddler from her mother and kissed the baby's hair. "She was only a couple of months old when we visited you last year. And I can't believe how much Simon Paul has grown—and how much he resembles his father!"

Leslie nodded and looked across the field to where Simon Paul was running around the hangar with Stephen. "Except that he has my eyes, he could be a Ben replay. It's almost eerie." She shook her head in mock frustration. "And there's no doubt he has Ben's language gene! His Swahili is much better than mine. Of course, Ben has taught him phrases since before he could walk. And did I tell you he speaks Spanish to the lady who cleans for me every week?"

"But Anna Jo is like you, isn't she?"

"Not really. She looks like me, but she's the one who won't let Ben fly without wanting to go along. She just turned four and can already name the instruments on the flight panel. Most kids that age can't tie their shoes, and she can set an altimeter. That's how she learned numbers."

Naomi laughed. "What about Gracie?"

"Maybe that one is mine." Leslie smiled at the toddler in Judy's arms. "She loves to play with her dolls—she calls them her babies—and she always wants to take care of them. She's a natural-born nurse!"

On the other side of the field, the men were talking animatedly. Jake ran his hand admiringly across the fuselage of the new plane and said to Ben, "It's great to finally meet you. You're kind of a legend around here, and I'm looking forward to getting twin-engine instruction from you." He gestured toward one of the planes housed in the new hangar. "I've been flying the Piper Cherokee that we'll be taking to the clinic in Tanzania. This baby will be a perfect replacement to use as an air ambulance and to ferry people and supplies among all of the clinics."

Will joined in the conversation. "I mostly fly the Skylane, but like Jake, I'd love to fly with you and get some twin-engine time. I've never had a chance to fly a Cessna 340. Perhaps we can take her over toward Tsavo while you're here?"

"That'll be great," Ben answered. "We'll be here a couple of weeks. That should give you both plenty of twin-engine time."

"Anytime, sir, anytime," Jake replied, looking a little self-conscious. "Just let us know when you can go up, and we'll be available." Clearing his throat, he asked, "Um, by the way, what should we call you? Doctor, or Colonel?"

Ben chuckled and slapped the young man companionably across the shoulders. "Neither," he replied. "Call me Ben."

LATE THAT AFTERNOON, Ben and Leslie finally found themselves alone, sitting in a swing on the screened porch of the clinic building. Naomi and Titus had taken Gracie to their home for a nap, and Anna Jo had gone home with Paul and Judy to be watched over by Beth. They would pick her up later that evening when they drove to the Merdians' for dinner.

At the far side of the large, walled yard, Simon Paul was receiving his first lesson on how to throw a spear from his surrogate uncle. It was fascinating to Ben and Leslie to watch the small boy interact so easily with the tall man. After his initial caution, Simon Paul was remarkably at ease with the Masai warrior, and as Leslie had explained to Judy, he was able to communicate surprisingly well in Swahili.

Beside her on the swing, Ben chuckled. She intertwined her fingers with his, laid her head on his shoulder and glanced up at him. “What’s funny?”

“Watching Simon with that spear reminded me of something.” His turned to look at her. “Do you remember that night here in the kitchen when we ate chocolate sundaes?”

She nodded. “Of course.”

“Do you recall the story I told you about hunting for the rock python and Simon’s brother killing it?”

“Sure, I remember.” Leslie grinned. “You told me you were disappointed because when you cut it open, there was no gold.”

“Yeah, that’s the story.” He searched the depths of her blue eyes and saw only joy. There were no more shadows, and he realized there hadn’t been in a long time. “It just occurred to me that I was wrong—about the gold, I mean.” His eyes were eloquent as he kissed her tenderly. “I did find gold here—it just had nothing to do with that gigantic snake.” He paused a bit, and when he continued, his voice was rough with emotion. “In truth, I didn’t just find gold—I found the mother lode.”

Leslie wrapped her arms around his neck and whispered, “I love you, Ben Murphy.”

“I know,” he answered. He buried his face in her hair and said, “That’s what I’m talking about.”

* * * * *